CRAZY LITTLE TOWN CALLED LOVE

BOOK 2:
THE TO-HELL-AND-BACK CLUB SERIES

By
Jill Hannah Anderson

www.pandamoonpublishing.com

Jacket design and illustrations © Pandamoon Publishing
Art Direction by Don Kramer: Pandamoon Publishing
Editing by Zara Kramer, Rachel Schoenbauer, Forrest Driskel, and Jessica Reino, Pandamoon Publishing

Library of Congress Cataloging-in-Publication Data is on file at the Library of Congress, Washington, DC

Edition: 1, version 1.00

ISBN-13: 978-1-945502-90-3

Reviews

The To-Hell-And-Back-Club: Book Two

"Fun, witty, and engaging, Anderson crafted a wonderful story of friendship, renewal and second-chances that fans of women's fiction and her debut novel will quickly devour. Crazy Little Town Called Love is a fast read that I truly enjoyed." — **Kerry Lonsdale, Amazon Charts and Wall Street Journal bestselling author**

"With her latest novel, Jill Hannah Anderson has created a warm and inviting town full of secrets, and layers, and richly drawn characters that all feel so real. I had all the feels reading this one…right up to the heart-warming, tear-producing last page. I didn't want to leave that Crazy Little Town Called Love!" — **Amy Impellizzeri, Award-winning Author of *The Truth About Thea***

"In Crazy Little Town Called Love, Jill Hannah Anderson delivers characters you'll want to know, a quirky town you'll never forget, and the cold edge of suspense. Family secrets, the slow burn of romance, and a heroine to root for round out a heartfelt adventure you won't want to miss." — **Kathleen Long, USA Today bestselling author of *Broken Pieces***

"Book 2 of The To-Hell-And-Back Club series follows Molly O'Brien from Minneapolis to the small town of Love, Minnesota. Molly finds friendship, fulfillment, independence, and yes, love, in this heartrending story. A hint of danger keeps the tension up and a bit of heat makes the pages fly! A fun, uplifting read for summer!" — **Kate Moretti, New York Times bestselling author of *The Vanishing Year***

The To-Hell-And-Back Club: Book One

"In The To-Hell-And-Back Club, Jill Hannah Anderson shines light on a love that's rarely explored: the deep ties between friends. Her understanding of these extraordinary connections, and the soul twisting grief when we lose them, colors every page of this novel." — **Randy Susan Meyers, bestselling author of *Accidents of Marriage*, & *The Widow of Wall Street***

"The To-Hell-And-Back Club is a heartwarming story about navigating tragedy and secrets with a little acceptance, a little resilience, and a whole lot of friendship. A perfect book club pick!" **— Barbara Claypole White, bestselling author of *Echoes of Family*, & *The Perfect Son***

"Anderson's debut about a middle-aged woman surviving devastating loss and rebuilding her life with 'a little help from her friends,' is at turns heartbreaking, bittersweet, funny, and darn right inspiring. Don't miss it!" **— Lesley Kagen, NYT bestselling author of *The Mutual Admiraton Society*, & *Whistling In The Dark***

"Jill Hannah Anderson spins a bittersweet tale of loss and love, fear and forgiveness, reminding us of the brittle nature of life and its uncertainties. Tempered with brushstrokes of humor, The To-Hell-And-Back Club illustrates the resilience of the human spirit and the healing power of friendship. You'll want to hug your girlfriends a little closer after reading this novel." **— Lori Nelson Spielman, #1 international bestselling author, *The Life List*, & *Sweet Forgiveness***

"Set against the backdrop of Minnesota's 10,000 lakes, Anderson's debut follows the grief-stricken Peyton Brooks on her journey from despair, to hope, to wholeness in a story that reminds us of the jarring truth that life can change in an instant." **— Julie Lawson Timmer, author of *Five Days Left*, *Untethered*, & *Mrs. Saint and the Defectives*.**

"In The To-Hell-And-Back Club, Anderson takes on an interesting 'what-if' premise: What-if your three best friends all died in the same car that you were supposed to be in? This is an interesting frame which allows her to explore a different kind of empty-nest syndrome and how you might recover from that with pathos and humor. A heartfelt read." **— Catherine McKenzie, bestselling author of *Hidden*, & *Arranged*.**

Dedication

To my daughters, Jamie & Heidi ~

They put up with bats and other critters,
endless interrupted meals and not-so-fun store jobs…
yet came through their years in the store
with happy memories and a unique upbringing!

CRAZY LITTLE TOWN CALLED LOVE

Chapter 1
April 2009

The subtle aroma of lavender and jasmine created an aura of peaceful warmth as Macie worked her magic in my Molly-pampering day at Salon Nouveau. I was as relaxed as a dog curled on its master's lap gnawing on a thick steak bone. My blood pressure would rise soon enough.

I'd have to go home eventually.

"Four more foils and then we're done." Macie smiled at me via her salon mirror. Full body massage? Check. Pedicure for the finally-here Minnesota spring? Check. French-tip manicure? Check. Highlights? Almost done. Next? Dancing around Nick's weekly sour mood.

"Where are you and Nick wining and dining tonight?"

"I'm not sure. He had to get up early to catch his morning flight home and was too tired to talk before I left." Stress worked its way back inside my chest. Macie has done my hair since I graduated from college eight years ago. She's been here through Nick's and my six years of ups and downs in our dating…more "downs" and too few "ups" this past year or so.

I wanted to pick her brain but was smart enough to know that when your relationship is circling the drain the first person you should talk to is the one you're with in the cyclone.

When I'd called Nick Wednesday night to ask about the late notice we'd received in the mail from our mortgage insurance company he indicated it was somehow my fault. Me, the person who Mr. Money-bags-control-freak never let touch a single bill.

When I'd asked about the dinner with the 3M bigwigs, Nick was as vague as a dream. He used to count on me being his eye candy at business events in the Minneapolis area. I chose not to think about who may be my replacement at business meetings when he traveled. The events used to be fun. Now my companion at those dinners was a bottle of expensive wine.

I'd become just another business expense Nick could write off. Our mortgage insurance was a different matter. I've offered several times to take over our bill paying. He's met each offer with an eye-roll as if I wouldn't know what to do even though I minored in accounting. Nick makes the money. Nick spends the money. Nick keeps track of the money. His rules.

And Nick likes blondes. My real hair color is two shades past brown… That's where Macie comes in. Honey and caramel hues lighten my curls to Nick's specifications.

Nick had always been generous with his money, and for our first years together, his love. Now our fun times together are rare, and our communication, nonexistent.

The ties that bind us are nothing more than a heavy mortgage and a poor economy.

"When you were here last month, you said your sixth anniversary was the following week. Did you guys do anything fun?" Macie's freckled nose wrinkled up with her smile. I watched in the mirror as she fluffed the last of my foils. My silver halo would be followed by my last hour of peace for the day while I read gossip magazines.

The lie rolls off my tongue as I hide behind a People magazine. "Nothing too exciting. Nick was tired after a week-long business trip to California." Honestly, who celebrates sticking together for six years with no commitment other than a mortgage as inflated as a bloated fish left out in the sun? Neither of us had bothered to plan a night out. I'm pretty sure I went out that night with my best friend, Ella. As if on cue, "Pink Houses" by John Mellencamp plays on my cell phone, breaking off my thoughts. Ella's a realtor at Edina Realty where I work in marketing.

"Go ahead and answer. I'll be back to check your highlights in twenty minutes," Macie said before scurrying out of the room. I hopped up from the salon chair and grabbed my phone.

"You're interrupting my primping Saturday, remember?" I teased when I answered the call from my best friend. A chat with her would undo the knot in my stomach caused by thoughts of Nick.

"Get your ass home right now! Nick has a moving van in your driveway and some guys are helping him load your furniture!" Ella's words fired out.

"Are you freaking kidding me?" I shouted loud enough to disturb every peaceful massage in the serene salon. I hopped up and fumbled in my Coach purse for my keys.

"I wish I was, Mol. Seriously, you better get over here right now."

I jammed my phone in the overstuffed tiny purse and flew out the salon door. My foiled hair flapped like silver wings around my head, and Salon Nouveau's black plastic cape billowed out as I sailed across the parking lot to my car.

In the few miles from the salon to our house, my tires barely touched the road. I careened around the corner and spotted Ella on the side of our street flagging me down as if I wouldn't see her electric blue skirt and her bouncing red hair. Four doors down a yellow moving van was parked in our driveway as two of Nick's friends slid the metal ramp back up.

"What's going on?" I scrambled out of the car.

Ella rattled on about being in the area to put up a For Sale sign down the block. Her hazel eyes were electrified. "I'd say the snake is slithering away while you're gone."

I reached in and shut off my car. Hoping to catch Nick, my apparent ex-boyfriend, off guard, I ran through the meticulously mowed yards of our neighbors, the spike heels of my Vince Camuto sandals aerating the fresh grass as I hustled toward the moving van.

No way in hell was I letting him bail on me and our mortgage. The jackass was stacking boxes in the back of his brand-new pickup. If I wouldn't have just gotten my nails done, I'd have gouged his weasel-eyes out and tied his nuts up into an ugly, hairy bow.

Nick turned and caught me lurching his way. He hustled to the side of the moving van and shouted for his friends to pull away. He'd been within my grasp and I found myself falling forward, my target gone. I landed face first on our tarred driveway.

A strap broke on my sandal. As I pushed up my lanky body, still encompassed in the plastic cape, I wielded my shoe, spike-heel out, and resembled Quasimodo amped up on caffeine as I limped at lightning speed, waiving my Vince Camuto weapon at a cowering Nick.

His friends peeled away in the moving van, while Ella, not exactly a fitness queen, did her best to help me corral Nick. "Don't you even think about leaving, you spineless excuse for a man!" I screamed as I limped along. The melody of the old nursery rhyme, "Diddle, Diddle, Dumpling My Son John" played in my brain as I pointed my broken sandal at him.

Nick stopped, his hand resting on the pickup door. I took several deep breaths before turning and waving Ella back toward her car. "You sure?" She questioned the idea of leaving me alone with Nick, likely afraid she'd be visiting me in prison when it was all said and done.

"Yes." I bit down, determined to keep my chin from quivering. My five-inch-sling-back-sandal dangled from my fingers as I made my way to Nick, whose lanky frame was as stiff as his smile had been for months. "What the hell is going on?" Each syllable hit my clenched jaw.

The back of Nick's military short hair still faced me. I reached over and jerked him around by his favorite A.P.C. shirt. Who wears a designer shirt when they're moving? And why did I care?

information about that old store Mom was willed years ago. Didn't you say the elderly woman who owned it passed away recently?"

"Rosie? Yes, she died last spring. Why?"

"Isn't Love close to where we vacationed every summer? I liked that area and was thinking of checking out the store and town. I need a place to live, and a steady income. If it looks decent, I'd have a home, a business, no mortgage, and a chance to start over…unless you planned on selling it?" I didn't think my dad was in need financially, but even if he was, he'd likely never tell me.

"I could use my marketing and accounting degrees." I'd thought of nothing else ever since I remembered my conversation with my mom.

"Remember how I'd wanted you to major in math or science? You'd be able to support yourself now if you had a degree in one of those fields. Maybe you should go back to school."

I struggled with math and science in high school, let alone trying to major in college with either degree. Accounting was one thing. It was straight numbers. My head spun in calculus, physics, and beyond—which was no doubt a disappointment to my dad, a microbiologist.

"I don't have the money to go back to school, Dad. I need a non-commission job and a place to live." I needed stability.

"You won't like that hick town. I think the population is less than a few thousand."

It was obvious where I got my fine Irish-stubborn streak. I was talking to it.

Mom had done most of the parenting, never pushing Dad to contribute much in the way of guidance. Yes, he loved me, but I feared I walked a fine line with my father's approval and disappointment ever since I was in the fifth grade.

It was no better now with Mom gone.

"Well, it's an option I need to consider. Can you tell me more about the place? Do you know why the woman didn't change her will after Mom passed away?" My mother rarely spoke of her years growing up in the small town.

"Rosie is the woman your mother worked for when she was in high school. The will stated your mom would inherit Rosie's store when she passed away, and Rosie had filed a warranty deed putting the property in your mother's name 'and her survivors' with a life estate for Rosie. After your mom was diagnosed with leukemia, she contacted Rosie, pointing out she could easily go before Rosie did. Rosie said she wasn't changing anything. Don't ask me why."

"She was aware Mom died, right?"

"Yes. Rosie was at your mother's funeral. Didn't I introduce you two?"

"Was she tall with short gray hair? I remember her hands were calloused." I'd been too distraught to remember much of the day.

I locked up and we walked the two blocks to the café tucked in the middle of Main Street, Flap Jack Fever Café. The few customers inside all looked our way as we slid into a corner booth. I'd been warned about small-town life where everyone knew everyone, especially in winter with few tourists around. Locals tended to size up any 'outsiders.' We were it.

A young waitress made a beeline to our table providing us with plastic covered menus and a smile. "Welcome to Love." The blonde teen's long hair was pulled back in a neat ponytail, her pretty face freshly scrubbed. She wore a pink T-shirt with the café's logo.

After taking our orders, she asked if we were just passing through. I decided to jump in with both feet. "I'm here to look at possibly reopening Rosie's store."

"You're the one from Minneapolis who was dumped by her boyfriend? I figured you'd be younger. Are you really gonna open Rosie's again?" Her genuine smile offset her words.

"Possibly." Ella stifled a laugh. I'd be thirty-two in a few months—hardly "old"—unless you're a teenager. I'd stopped at the real estate office on my first trip to town. The chatty office staff must have twisted and spread my life story. I already regretted sharing anything with them.

As soon as the teen left to place our order, Ella chuckled. "Don't get your underwear all knotted up now. You've been warned about small towns. People are curious about you."

"I'm glad you think it's funny. I find it scary. What else has been said about me?" How had I worked into our conversation that I'd recently broken up with my long-term boyfriend?

"I hope I didn't confess I had to do a short sale on my home."

"You know how those pesky realtors are. They suck the personal information out of you like a leech." Ella winked. She wasn't pushy, which is why she did so well.

While we waited for our meals, I produced my notepad from my purse. "Here are some ideas I have for improvements." I'd have to cash in some of my 401k. "Next spring the outside will need a good soaking of paint. I'll stick with the gray, something a little lighter though, and trim everything in a deep barn red. I'll get some vinyl red and white checkered tablecloths for the tables on the deck. I'd like to replace the old card tables outside with wood tables that have a hole in the middle for big umbrellas." My mind ran off possibilities too quickly for me to write.

"You've put a lot of thought into this." Ella studied me.

"There isn't much left for me in Minneapolis—besides you, of course. My friends have either marched down the aisle, or will soon, and are having babies. It's time for me to do something different. I don't see a good marketing job for me in the Twin Cities anytime soon."

"Aw, Mol, you could wait it out at our house. What'll I do without you?"

"Thanks, but you two are planning a wedding. You don't need me in the way." I leaned my chin on my fist. "Do you know how it feels to apply for two dozen jobs and not get a single offer? It's demeaning, one more thing telling me I'm a loser. I need a confidence builder. The challenge of the store should do it…more than do it."

I sighed. "And in answer to your question, you'll come visit me. This will be like a mini-vacation place for you, especially in the summer." I imagined us relaxing with a drink on the deck after I closed the store. Or walking across the street and taking a swim late at night.

The waitress appeared with our chicken Caesar salads and retreated quickly as more customers came in. I got back to my list. "I need a lot of inventory since they sold all the perishables before closing. The thin window panes in the front of the store need to be replaced. And did you see the relic air conditioner? I hope it lasts the summer…"

Ella's interest was suddenly diverted. "Yummy!" Her fork was stopped in mid-air.

"The salad? I haven't tasted it."

She shook her head. "Not the food, although the salad is good. I'm talking about the eye candy that walked through the door." She pointed toward the front counter with her fork.

A man around our age had just settled himself at the counter next to an elderly man who'd been sitting there when we walked in. The younger guy looked like he'd slept in his clothes. "Are you talking about the wrinkled Paul Bunyan at the counter? You've got to be kidding. You need to get your eyes checked." I turned back around, uninterested.

Ella leaned over the table and hissed under her breath. "Are you crazy? Look at his rock-solid body. And when he walked in, he smiled at the old couple sitting at that table over there. His smile and dimples are better than dessert. And his wavy, messy hair looks like he just rolled out of bed. I'd like to run my hands through it!" She itched at her palms.

I rolled my eyes. "Do I need to remind you of the engagement ring you're wearing?"

"Aw, what happened to fun-Molly?"

I shook my head. "I don't know Ella. Fun-Molly has turned into a worrywart."

We turned our focus back to eating and my growing list of improvements. The jukebox was turned low, muting the other café conversations. Until I caught the name "Rosie" coming from a conversation at the counter. It was the guy Ella had been ogling, talking to the old man.

I reached over and stopped Ella's hand as she pierced her salad with her fork. "They're talking about Rosie over there." I nodded in the direction of the counter. We sat in silence.

"Well, I'll be surprised if she bothers with the place. Word over at Lakes Realty is that the only reason Celia's daughter might leave the fine life in the cities is to run from her broken heart. I can't imagine her actually surviving here without malls or cement under her high heels. She'll probably want to replace the bait section with a sushi bar." This came from Ella's so-called hunk.

His last comment brought a loud guffaw from the elderly man who chimed in. "If she's anything like her family, she'll be lucky to keep the store going through her first winter."

I froze, listening to them discuss me. It was hard enough to ignore my own inner voice questioning my capabilities without having others who had never met me pass judgment already. Steam bubbled inside me as Ella reached across the table to hold my hand.

"Easy girl, you're foaming at the mouth. Don't go making a scene here in the town you might soon call home. They don't know you. Prove them wrong."

Pride was as hard to swallow as the salad I could no longer taste. I gave up on my meal, folded my list and dug out my wallet. "Can we please leave?"

"Sure." Ella took a final bite. Curiosity nudged me to turn around. The waitress stood by the men. She must have told them the person they were talking about was sitting right here.

She caught my look and made her way to our table to offer some of their freshly baked pie. When we declined, she handed us our bill. "Don't pay attention to Jackson and Old Lloyd. They loved Rosie to pieces. Her store won't be the same for them."

I gave her a weak smile. "Thanks. You needn't apologize for them. As my friend Ella here pointed out, I'll have to prove them wrong if I decide to open the store." I looked over to where the men sat. The one Ella had been drooling over stared me right in the eye.

His face was covered in a day or two of stubble. With his blue flannel shirt and white T-shirt peeking out around his throat, he looked like a Brawny paper towels guy. Brown wavy hair grazed his collar, and I sensed his light-colored eyes challenging me. I decided then to prove everyone, including myself, wrong. I was going through with the store.

No man was going to make me feel I wasn't capable of doing something ever again.

"You ready?" I grumbled to Ella. In a louder voice, I said, "I've got a lot of things to do if I'm going to get my store up and running soon."

The waitress met us at the register and took our money and generous tip. "I heard you talking about some of the improvements you plan on doing at Rosie's.

They sound great." She spoke loudly enough for all the nosy customers to hear. I mouthed a silent thank-you to her.

The wind had picked up while we'd been inside the café. Huddled in our ski jackets, we made a beeline for the store. Nagging doubts of running a business followed me with a scoop of feeling unwelcome on top.

"Most small-town people just don't like change." Ella read my worried mind.

"You're right. Anyway, maybe I'll never see those men again." Unlikely in a small town. We took the sidewalk along the beach back to the store. The ice looked sturdier than the thin covering I'd seen on my first trip a few weeks earlier. In the distance, several pickup trucks were lined up at the lake access across the highway with fish houses on their trailers.

We stopped and looked out over the lake, "It's pretty, isn't it?" The lake was shaped like a wide heart, two big bays creating the top part of the heart. At the end of the bay stood a log-sided bar overlooking the lake, about a block away.

"Yep. Who'd have thought you'd be living across from a sweet beach like this?"

"Well, I haven't moved yet." Even as I said the words, I'd all but packed up my things and headed north in my mind. As we approached the store door, I caught a glimpse of movement off to my side. Standing near my parking lot was Mr. Negative Opinion, a stocking cap pulled over his big head. His hands arrogantly at his waist, legs spread in a firm stance, with sawdust hanging from his jeans and dirty coat. He looked like Superman in lumberjack drag.

I ignored him and fumbled for the key, wishing he'd go away. I was about to open the door when he spoke. "You're Celia's daughter, right? You'll want to call me when you're ready for firewood this spring. Rosie had enough to get you by for a while, but not enough for next winter. It needs time to dry so you aren't burning green wood." His voice was loud and deep.

Listen to Mr. Bossy pants! "Since I'll be lucky if I 'keep my business through the first winter,' I'm sure I won't be here to need any wood, especially from you." I reeled in my frustration. No need to let him think he was getting under my skin.

His face blanched. I was glad I'd gotten my jab in before Ella tugged at my sleeve.

"C'mon, let's go inside. Please." She was a pro at dousing my flame before it ignited.

Just as Ella pushed me inside and I slammed the store door, he shouted. "Fine by me."

It was all I could do to not yank open the door and yell back. Ella took the key from me and locked the door from the inside.

"Don't go there, Molly Rose O'Brien. Don't let him get under your skin."

Ella's warning was too late. And we both knew it.

Chapter 4

Back inside the store, Ella busted out laughing. "Steam is shooting out of your ears."

I threw my mittens on the counter. "Can you believe him?" I took a calming breath.

We stared out a window. "I've hardly seen any people on the street," she observed.

"I know. Supposedly the town swells to ten times its population in the summer. Depending on the weather in the winter, snowmobiling, ice fishing, and cross-country skiing are popular if the conditions are right."

I pressed my nose against the windowpane. "I'm concerned." I created a round patch of fog and leaned my forehead against the cold glass. "I don't have a plan for winter." My eyes closed at the image of a dreary, desolate winter here.

Ella nudged my side. "Hey, look; a human being. And what the heck…?"

I opened my eyes and used my sleeve to clear the foggy window.

We busted out laughing. "Is she walking a cat on a leash?"

"I'd say more like she's dragging the cat. Look at it, putting on the breaks with its paws!" The young woman made her way toward Main Street with her cat in tow.

It had been a good diversion from my possible meltdown. "This is crazy. What do I know about running a business? What will I do in a small town? What will I do without you?" Ella knew my insecurities, my fears, my dreams.

Yet one of my dreams was to make it on my own…reaffirmed when Nick moved out. I was long overdue for standing on my own two feet. If I could.

Ella leaned her head on my shoulder, my dark curls tangled with her golden-red waves. "This has a lot of possibilities and the land is a prime location. You'll figure it out."

The time bomb ticking for me at home—the inevitable move from the bank to evict me—was fuel to my spark. "You're right. And I have all winter to whip this place into shape. C'mon, I'll show you the house and backyard."

I opened the door and flipped the light switch in the small entry. Quaint and clean described the one-level home still stuck in colors from the 1950s and 60s. I didn't need a lot of room, and clean was high on my list.

We spent over an hour measuring the small rooms, talking paint colors, and measuring windows. We even made a brief trip to the dank, dirt basement. There was nothing there but a few bare wood shelves and water pipes…and probably a million spiders. My brain struggled to block flashbacks of the glossy, high-tech, cushy home I'd shared with Nick. *That life is over, Molly. Nick—and his money—are gone.*

It wasn't just his money, but it was easier to tell myself it was. Easier to forget about the fun we'd had the first few years. With no responsibility for children, no money worries, our life was just one big party when we weren't working. The higher up the ladder Nick climbed, the more pressure that came with it, including his pressure for me to play the high society part.

Until I'd become someone I barely recognized. We talked less, cared less, and loved less. Our precious weekends together became tense, boring, and forced. Did he sense the end of his job coming? He hadn't stopped spending, and never gave me any indication I should.

I blinked back regrets and opened the blinds on windows to show Ella the backyard.

"Wow, this is so beautiful and peaceful." Ella took in Love Creek which meandered through the woods behind the backyard. The town's intersection was landlocked by water, making this property all the more valuable—property solely taken up by Rosie's store and the gas station/mechanic garage next door.

In my research, I'd found it was still owned by an elderly man named Ernie Williams, who the realtor said purchased the property after Rosie opened her store several decades ago.

"If that Ernie guy sells, someone else could mow his shop down and put up a convenience store, possible competition for me." I'd found most businesses in town had been owned by the same people for years. It could change in a heartbeat. This sleepy little tourist town was prime for change, especially once the economy turned around.

"You've just got to think outside the box." Ella cheered me on.

"True. I guess I'll worry about that if it happens."

"What does your gut tell you? Can you see yourself living here and operating the store?"

I looked at the stark home but visualized the store. "Yes. I can see the shelves stocked with items cabin owners need, items the people hanging out at the beach will want, even the fishermen from the lake across the street, coming in for bait. What I can't see are the bleak winter months. Hopefully, I'll have that figured out by next winter."

"I can see you here too, Mol." She put her arm through mine as we walked toward the back door. We stepped out on the small deck outside and were surrounded by voices saturating the air. We looked at each other with our eyebrows raised. The town had come alive on the other side of the building while we'd been checking out the house.

"What in the heck?" We walked around the side of my house toward the front of the store where people were lining up along both sides of the street armed with folding chairs and blankets. I approached the first adult I found. "What's going on?"

There were more people lining up alongside the street than I thought existed in the town. Laughter, and the aroma of hot chocolate, permeated the air.

"It's the annual fish house parade." The woman rubbed her mittens together. "Are you new to town?" You could see her breath in the cold air.

"Yes." I wasn't ready to get into specifics. The pickups and fish houses we'd noticed at the boat access parking lot were now lining up. "So they just drive by with their fish houses?"

Another woman standing next to her chimed in. "Oh, it's more than that. Each fish house has a theme and they're judged for prizes." She pointed to a long table set up down the street from us, on the edge of the beach where two men and two women were seated.

Ella and I had planned to leave town, but no way in hell was I missing this. We ran over to my car, donned our mittens and ear muffs and found a space in the crowd to stand and watch. Fifteen minutes later, fish houses with crazy themes paraded by: Fish-Lips-Houlihan with a M*A*S*H theme, a Big B-ass theme where all the people had pillows in their pants, Fishing-in-the-dark theme with glow sticks and glow paint, an I'm Walking On Sunfish Sunshine float sparkled, and in-between all of the fish house floats were dancers, clowns, candy, and music.

This unexpected event slayed the negative outlook Ella and I had of the town just hours before. I stood there surrounded by people who would hopefully become my neighbors, my customers, and if I was lucky, I'd find some friends in the bunch too.

Toward the end of the parade was a fish house with women dressed up in gaudy, glitzy, dresses, and vibrant makeup, along with men in flashy suits throwing out quarters. Their theme? "Two-bit hookers." A stringer of rubber fish with a large metal hook through them hung from the front of the fish house. Right in the middle of them all sporting a pinstriped suit over his flannel shirt? None other than the Jackson guy from the café.

He spotted us in the crowd, smiled and blew me a mock kiss. I looked the other way, not allowing him to be a blemish in an otherwise fun event.

By the time Ella and I grudgingly pulled out of town an hour later, our attitudes were doing a happy dance. I couldn't wait to file the quit claim deed my dad had prepared, deeding me his interest in the property.

Soon, I'd be the solo, excited, and petrified owner of Love's General Store.

* * *

The next several weeks were a blur. I packed up my meager belongings and unpacked an ambition to succeed—one I'd neglected for too long. Nick was missing too. He'd changed his cell phone number and I was too proud to call his friends to beg for his new one. I told myself it didn't matter. I told myself I was done relying on a man. I told myself I didn't miss him.

By January, the bank had a buyer for my home. I had until the end of March to be out, which worked out well. I needed to have my store open as early as possible so I could get my feet wet before the summer tourist crowd bulldozed me.

I made so many trips to Love my car could've driven there without me steering. I scrubbed floors, stained doors and trim work, and brought a few of my things with me each time. The living room paneling got two coats of glazed ivory, brightening it considerably. Rosie's orange kitchen countertops from the 1950s were back in style. The kitchen walls got a fresh coat of ivory as well.

The first weekend in February, Ella accompanied me to help with some bigger home projects. None of my other friends could orchestrate a weekend away from their infants and toddlers. I understood. It was further proof my college friends had moved on and I hadn't.

Up bright and early Saturday, to the tune of boisterous grumbling from Ella, we walked the block to the hardware store to pick up the floor tile I'd ordered two weeks earlier, and the Rug Doctor I'd reserved for the day.

Tracie, the friendly clerk at the Ace Hardware was working. She'd been helpful in guiding me on tile selection during my last trip to town along with instructions on how to lay and grout the tile. She could have a fix-it-up television show for clueless women like me.

"Hey there, Molly, good to see you. I should've told you we can drop your tile and rug cleaner off with one of our trucks." Tracie's pixie style platinum blonde hair accentuated her large brown eyes, reminding me of Tinker Bell. She continued to ring up supplies for an elderly woman.

"And I should've driven over." I glanced at Ella whose expression told me that no way in hell was she carrying anything heavy for a block.

"I'll have them there within the hour. That way the driver can unload everything for you," Tracie offered.

"Thanks. Tracie, I'd like you to meet my weekend grunt, and best friend, Ella." I winked at Tracie before signing the charge slip. They shook hands.

I had removed the old carpet in the bathroom the previous week and my body was retaliating. I'd worked it harder physically than any aerobics class I'd attended over the past few years. I now built muscle for free. Well, not completely free, but the money I spent on improvements was minimal compared to the free home and business I'd received.

The carpet in the living room and both bedrooms was in decent shape, albeit outdated in a brown and orange pattern. I had more pressing things to spend my money on than new carpet.

"Thanks for all your help, Tracie. You'll have to come over sometime to see the finished product when I move here for good."

"That'd be great. I haven't been in Rosie's home for a number of years." Tracie put her fingers to her mouth. "Sorry, not Rosie's home. Your home."

"It's okay. I expect people will still call it Rosie's." I waved away her apology.

"Hey, are you two going to take a break at all? This weekend is our SnoGolympics." Tracie reached across the counter and grabbed a brochure.

"Bed races on the hill by the Pickled Perch Bar start at two, and barstool races follow at three. This morning was the smallest fish contest, and there are activities tomorrow if you'll be around." She opened the brochure.

"I'm game," Ella jumped on board. We had planned to take the night off and watch chick flicks. This sounded more entertaining. Plus, it was a rare calm and sunny winter day.

As I turned to walk out the front door, brochure in hand, I spotted that Jackson guy from the café. He was down one of the aisles talking to another guy as he picked up a couple of items and showed them to the man. No sawdust on his jeans now.

I looked at Tracie. "Do you know the guy down the aisle with the red shirt?" I assumed she did and was curious about her take on him.

Tracie leaned back to look down aisle three. "Jackson? Yes. He owns this place."

I nearly dropped the brochure along with my jaw. "Huh? I've never seen him in here before." I'd been in the hardware store several times. Ella's laughter blasted out.

"He's been out of town. He went to visit his parents and brother in Wyoming."

I yanked open the door, in need of fresh air.

"I'm surprised you haven't met him already," Tracie said.

"Oh, she has." Ella chimed in, chuckling at the irony of my situation. I was renting equipment from Jackson, and buying household materials from him… the man I'd sworn I wouldn't do business with for my wood-cutting. Clearly, that was a side job for him.

"We should get going. See you this afternoon, Tracie?" I held the door open for Ella.

"I'll be there. We close before two. Just follow the crowd to the hill across the bay from your store. The races are there by the Pickled Perch."

She referenced a log-sided bar overlooking the bay, one of the many local businesses I hadn't set foot in yet. I muttered my frustration as we walked back to my home.

"What's that?" Ella stopped.

"Aren't you funny? You know exactly what's eating at me," I growled.

"Not that, although him owning the store where you've been shopping *is* hilarious. I mean the hooting and hollering I'm hearing in the distance."

We rounded the block. Out on the frozen lake people were being whipped around on large inner tubes behind four-wheelers. "That looks like fun!" Ella's green eyes sparkled.

"It does." I'd almost forgotten what fun looked like these last several months.

It didn't take long for an Ace Hardware truck to pull into my driveway. A beefy man who appeared to be in his fifties laid down plywood over my deck steps. Using a dolly, he transferred the Rug Doctor and bathroom tiles in a matter of minutes. Ella and I went to work.

After four hours of manual labor and chicken tacos from Flap Jack Fever Café, we cleaned ourselves up enough to be presentable for our afternoon break.

"Didn't you bring anything warmer than those boots or coat?" I eyed Ella's high-heeled fashion boots and thin peacoat knowing full well a year ago I'd have dressed the same way for a cold winter weekend.

"I figured we'd be slaving away all weekend inside, boss. I didn't know we'd get time off for good behavior," she teased.

I held up my hand. "Fine. No whining if you get cold." I tossed her an extra pair of warm mittens I had. Everything I kept at my new home was practical. No need for bling or fashion in this town.

Gone were my French-tipped nails, replaced by trimmed nails sans polish. I laced up my warm Sorrell boots, zipped up my ski jacket, grabbed warm mittens and a sensible red stocking cap and scarf, and we were out the door. It was a short walk across the beach and lake to the hill by the Pickled Perch.

Tracie, dressed in ski pants and a snowmobile jacket, walked over to greet us. "Come meet my husband and son." We followed her toward the hill.

Tracie gestured toward a tall man with brown hair, holding a young boy. "Molly and Ella, this is my husband, Rick, and our three-year-old, Mr. Energy." She ruffled her son's blond hair as we shook hands with Rick.

Sunshine and no breeze offset the twenty-degree temperature, making it a welcoming winter day. Pine trees shaded the hill, keeping plenty of snow on it for the races. Screams of joy and laughter surrounded us as people went flying down the hill on bed mattresses.

"What a blast!" Ella gave me her "let's try it" look.

"No way. Plus, we don't have a mattress. Maybe someone else?" I looked at Tracie.

"Sorry, forgot my mattress." Tracie smiled.

"Fun-Molly would've tried it a year ago," Ella announced. She was right. But fun-Molly was packed up and locked away after Nick and his wallet moved out.

"I can't afford to break a limb right now." I didn't have health insurance. It was another thing on my to-do list. "I'll tell you what. We'll sign up for it next year, okay?"

Ella rubbed her hands together as if I'd said I was buying her a new car. I hoped a year from now Fun-Molly would be back.

The boisterous crowd reminded me of the fish house parade back in November. Maybe this wasn't such a sleepy little town in winter after all. The cozy idea enveloped me…until I spotted Jackson headed my way.

garage will not be sold or torn down while I am alive. I do not want a chain gas station in its place. It would detract from the character of the town."

I thought of the initial "character" that came to my mind of his old rundown business, and mine, when I first came to town. My attitude had changed as I'd come to work on the store and house, getting a feel for the town's personality. Ernie's station and Rosie's store gave the town quaintness. And yes, character.

"Did you ever meet my mom when she came to visit Rosie? Dad and I always stayed back at the cabin. Now I wish I'd have pestered her to let me come with her. I thought Mom would be around forever. I thought I'd have more time to ask her things."

"Yes, I sure did have the pleasure of visiting with your mother several times over the years. You remind me of Celia, although she was not as tall as you. Rosie always spoke of how polite and helpful Celia was in the store. I believe they were a great asset to each other." Ernie rubbed his protruding chin. "The first time I met your mother, Rosie introduced her as 'the daughter I wish I'd had.'"

His words reaffirmed the bond Rosie and my mother must have had. No wonder Rosie left mom her store. In a sense, I was the grandchild Rosie never had. Which made me wonder why we'd never met…an answer I'd likely never get.

We spent the next hour visiting over coffee and cookies until he glanced at his watch. "I am afraid I have kept you from unpacking, Molly. Would you like some help? It would give me great pleasure." He rubbed his hands together, apparently eager to work.

"I'm certainly not going to turn down free help. You are free, aren't you?" I teased.

"I have been told before by a certain lady that I was cheap, is that the same?" He winked at me as we both waded into the pile of endless boxes.

The afternoon slipped away while we unpacked my housewares. While we worked, Ernie asked me about my years growing up, where we lived, and what my dad was like. He offered useful information regarding life in a small town.

"Do not be afraid to tell me to mind my own business."

I wiped grime from my forehead. "Any input is appreciated. In fact, do you have any suggestions on where I should order my wood for next winter? For now, I'm using the electric heat. Honestly, I'm a little unsure how that wood stove works." I hoped the weather would soon turn warm enough to delay my need for heat until fall.

He explained how the wood stove worked by heating water which is pumped through the registers of the house and store. "Your stove is large enough where it needs to be fed only twice a day. You will want the wood cut small like Rosie had. She used to insist on filling her wood stove until she dropped a log on her foot while loading it. She was wearing slippers. The log broke a few bones in her foot and knocked some sense into her head." He cringed at the memory.

"After her mishap, her great-nephew, Jackson, or one of his friends, filled the stove. He owns acreage outside of town so he has always provided her wood. I can give you his number so you order early enough to allow your wood to dry over the summer."

My mouth went dry. "Jackson who owns the hardware store is Rosie's nephew?" There couldn't be too many Jackson's in a town this size.

"Yes, her great-nephew. Did he come and introduce himself?"

I told him about Jackson's comments I overheard in the café. They were all the more hurtful now after realizing he was related to Rosie. I stressed to Ernie I would not call Jackson to deliver my wood. "There must be other guys around here who deliver wood."

He shook his head. "Shame on Jackson for being unkind. That is not typical behavior for him. There are others you could call, but Jackson is the best. He will know how many cords of wood you need and will cut and split it too." Ernie was right. I needed to order firewood. I would be here next winter if nothing else than to prove Jackson and the old man in the café wrong.

We worked late into the afternoon as the winds died down, settling the remaining snow on the frozen ground. The sun hid behind gloomy clouds as it often did in February. Nearing suppertime, I offered to buy Ernie dinner at the café. It was the least I could do.

"I would be most honored, Miss Molly." He bowed slightly.

We shrugged into our coats and walked the short distance to the café, following the aroma of fried chicken. Being able to walk most everywhere was a convenience I appreciated already. Very few things had been within walking distance of my home in the Twin Cities.

Over bowls of wild rice soup and crusty French bread, we cemented our friendship. He relayed the few changes he'd witnessed over the years in town.

"Small towns do not like change. You will find that things happen gradually here."

The café was thinning out; they'd be closing for the night soon. Ernie reached over and patted my hand. "Do not let the store become your life, okay?"

"I promise. I just want to start out right and get through my first year or two."

"I recollect my experience was similar. This is a wonderful town. Enjoy what it has to offer." The café door banged open, interrupting our quiet conversation.

My spine straightened like a lightning rod when a familiar, deep voice boomed out.

I turned toward the door Jackson had just entered. "Hey, Scratch, don't forget we're meeting at Rick's fish house for poker." Mr. Bossy yelled into the kitchen. The big, bald, owner, nicknamed Scratch, told Jackson that he'd be ready soon. I forced my attention back to Ernie.

"Hey, Ernie! Got yourself a hot date?" Jackson joked as he came up behind me. "I don't suppose you want to give her up to join us in a wild night of poker?" Jackson's invitation died on his lips as he stood in front of our booth and realized Ernie's "date" was me.

I smiled up sweetly at him, batting my makeup-less eyes. My hair was pulled back in a loose clip, some unruly curls escaping. I pressed my lips together to keep my sarcasm hostage.

"Jackson, I would like you to meet my new neighbor and friend, Molly O'Brien." Ernie gestured at me as if he didn't know we'd already met. "As you know, she is Celia's daughter. She has been working hard and will have her place of business and home in shape in no time." He beamed as if I was his granddaughter. I wished I was.

Jackson's sky-blue eyes narrowed as he tucked his hands into weathered jean pockets and rocked back on his heels. "I met Molly recently, in this very café, Ernie." His smile had as much warmth as a glacier. "And at the bed races." His grin turned wicked.

"Molly and I were discussing earlier her need for wood for next winter. I recommended she enlist your help." Ernie seemed hell-bent to build a bridge between us.

I had to stop him. "I've got my wood lined up already with someone else."

"Oh yeah?" Jackson leaned a beefy arm on the table. "Getting it from Doug Delansky?"

I jumped at the name. "Yes, he's who I called. Doug said he's more than happy to deliver wood for me." I mentally filed his name so I could look it up later.

"Are you sure that is a good idea, Molly? Jackson here would be your best bet."

Jackson waved his humungous hand. "Oh no, Ernie. I'm sure Molly has checked around and found Doug offers the cheapest price for a cord of wood." There was no sincerity in his voice. "Anyway, I better get going. Stop out if you get bored later, Ernie. We'll be out on Woods Bay." He patted Ernie's shoulder, gave a curt nod to me, and walked back to speak with Scratch.

I stifled a yawn along with my frustration at Jackson interrupting our night. "It's late and I should get back to work. I really appreciate all the help from you."

"I have enjoyed every minute, Molly." Ernie's smile was sincere. "I will stop in tomorrow and see how you are doing. I would be more than happy to help again."

I thanked him again, not bothering to bring up his insistence I get along with Jackson. It was my own battle. One I didn't have the strength for right now.

"Are you kidding? I'm so glad to see another young woman move to our town that I'd lay a path of rose petals out for you."

It was all so much more than I'd expected. Ernie left mid-morning to go home and nap. When he came back later to help, I was surprised to see it was after two. "Have you been enjoying your day?" He set his hat behind the counter.

"I've managed to keep the wolves at bay." I joked.

Ernie and I were straightening inventory in the grocery section while he filled me in on more of the history of Love when another customer entered the store.

It was Jackson. I kicked away my vow to be sugar-sweet to all customers.

"What do you want?" It wasn't the right way to greet a customer but seeing him in my store the first day I opened took me by surprise. He'd shaved off his winter beard and mustache but was easy enough to recognize.

Ernie gently elbowed me. "Molly!"

I gave Jackson my most charming smile and batted my eyes. "I'm sorry, sir. If you're looking for sushi, I'm sold out."

Jackson busted out laughing, slapping his leather work gloves against his beefy thigh in amusement. "Okay, one point for you, Miss O'Brien." He turned to Ernie. "Actually, I'm here to see you about a new fan belt for my truck since Mike's out of town this week." Ernie's face relaxed now that a knock-down brawl hadn't developed between Jackson and me.

He moved from behind the counter to take down Jackson's information for the truck part he'd order through Ernie's Garage. They moved toward the door, stepping aside for an elderly couple who had just entered.

I welcomed the couple to the store but found it difficult to focus on them until Jackson walked out without acknowledging me further. Fine by me.

After the elderly couple left with their loaf of bread and quart of buttermilk, Ernie spoke. "You know, Jackson is a mighty nice man. He likes to joke; you cannot take him too seriously." His look nudged me to reconsider, not understanding my insecurity planted two decades ago.

Fidgeting with the receipt tape, I glanced out the window at the sunshine sparkling over the recently thawed lake. While it was just Ernie and me in the store, I confessed. "That day last November in the café, Jackson said I wouldn't know what to do without shopping malls nearby and cement under my high heels. And that I'll probably replace the bait section with a sushi bar." I studied my blunt fingernails. They hadn't experienced TLC in months.

Ernie's eyebrows rose with this "ah-ha" moment when my sushi comment registered.

"He had agreed with that man, 'Old Lloyd,' when he predicted I won't make it through my first winter in the store." It was embarrassing to repeat words I feared would come true.

"Many townspeople are stubborn to change." He patted my hand. "In Jackson's defense, when your mother passed away and Rosie sensed the store might end up in your hands, she may have spoken of you enjoying your exciting city life. Jackson likely could not imagine you leaving it all behind to come to our sleepy town."

He paused. "I do believe Jackson wants to make sure everything his great-aunt worked hard to build does not fall apart. And, unfortunately, Jackson's mother has not been enthused about the store and land not going to her. Perhaps she is clouding his judgment of you."

"She can't be angry with my mom or me that we inherited this. Did she think we should give it to her? Oh no, should we have? I mean, she's Rosie's niece, and I'm not even family." Guilt slathered my brain.

"Once you meet his mother, Nancy, you will likely have no problem relinquishing any guilt you may have." Ernie winked. "Lucky for you, she only comes to stay at their cabin during the summer. Jackson's family—his parents and his younger brother—live in Wyoming."

"Great. I can hardly wait to meet her. She sounds worse than Jackson." Maybe she'd never set foot in my store. "I understand how my reopening Rosie's store is a big change for townspeople."

"It will not be an easy first year, but I believe you have the gumption to make a go of it. This is your store now. People will adjust."

I squeezed his hand before turning my attention to the customers who'd entered the store.

After school, Adam took over for Ernie since there was no baseball practice or game that day. Adam high-fived Ernie before storing his backpack under the counter.

"Butt-draggin' yet, old man?" Adam teased.

"My butt is right where it should be." Ernie deadpanned. "It has been a great first day has it not, Molly? None of those mean locals threw eggs at your windows or smoke bombs inside. Seems like they might let you stay after all." He lightly pinched my cheek.

"Oh, get out of here. You know they'll wait until after I close so there are no witnesses around." I shooed him out the door as he reminded me he'd be back to help again tomorrow.

It was after seven when I turned off the OPEN sign and locked the door.

"My feet feel twice the size they were this morning." I groaned to Adam as I slipped my feet out of my tennis shoes. "I'm afraid my legs are going on strike from all the standing. They know biking. They don't know standing for twelve hours."

"When it's slow, sit down behind the counter," Adam suggested. His energy ignited the room. His night was just beginning. My body ached as if I was eighty and ready for bed.

"What're you going to do tonight?"

"First, a long hot soak in the tub, maybe an egg and cheese sandwich and a beer, and if I'm lucky I'll be able to stay awake to call my dad before crawling into bed."

As I closed the store and took the cash drawers back to my kitchen to count, I sighed several times in thankfulness for making it through the first day. When thoughts came crawling back of my fun, carefree nights in Minneapolis back when I wasn't completely mentally and physically exhausted…well, I chose to ignore those nagging thoughts.

A year ago, Nick had started the domino effect in my life—one I'd added many changes to—one I was determined to now make "my" life. No time for reminiscing now.

I'd promised Tracie that tomorrow night I'd go out with her and some friends to the Pickled Perch for a "Girls Night Out." A couple hours later as I snuggled under my covers, I decided the word "exhausted" should be added before the phrase "Girls Night Out."

Chapter 7

During my second day of business, I accidentally filled the coffeemaker with water twice. It quietly overflowed as curious locals filtered in, studying me like I was a creature from outer space. Ernie was scheduled to help me with the evening shift since cabin owners would be coming up for the weekend. I could handle it until then. I had to handle it. There was no Nick to bail me out financially, no mom to coddle me, and no dad I dared confess failure to.

I waited on men who'd been in earlier for minnows and were back for more. "Fish must be biting?" Fishing opener wasn't for another few weeks, but you could catch crappies and sunfish now.

"Yep, biting close to shore." They didn't point out as a bait supplier, I should've known that.

When I rang up their purchase, the till jammed. I took a deep breath and moved them to my main cash register and repeated ringing up their purchase. In my fluster, I knocked their bucket over, spilling the minnows and water all over myself, the counter, and the floor. They helped clean up as I replenished their bucket before they left me alone with my nerves.

I was as frazzled as the day Nick moved out. But considerably less pissed off.

Thank goodness my home was attached. All on one level, I didn't have to maneuver stairs as I ran back to change into a clean top and jeans and ran out to the store again.

I could've kissed Ernie when he arrived. "Busy?" His eyes took in my near-manic state.

"Did you know the crappies and sunfish are biting?" I nailed him for an honest answer.

"Yes, ma'am. I am guessing you did not?"

"Um, nope. How did Rosie keep abreast of fishing information?"

He didn't attempt to stifle his grin. "Jackson."

Wendy slid off her barstool. She sauntered back to the pool tables, right toward Jackson and some guy he was playing pool with.

"Who are the other guys besides Jackson and Mike?" I'd already filled Tracie in about my run-in with Jackson in the café my first day in town. She'd been doing her best ever since to persuade me her boss was a nice guy who had been fed the wrong information about me.

"There's Scratch, from the café, in the blue baseball cap," Charlee said. He looked different from the few times I'd seen him with his bald head wrapped in a red bandanna.

"You've met Drake, from the real estate office, right? And Curt? He works at the bank in Blue Bay, and also at our branch here." Tracie rattled off other names unfamiliar to me. I struggled to keep the locals straight, which was important as a business owner. My business may have only been open two days, but I'd lived in the town full-time for a few weeks.

"Most of those men are single. Exactly what Wendy is looking for," Charlee said dryly.

Wendy leaned in with a coy smile as she went from one man to another around the pool tables. I was surprised when Jackson turned his back on her.

"You've both known Jackson a long time. You think he'll lighten up on me once I've lived here a while?" I wondered how long I'd be an "outsider."

Charlee looked across the room at Jackson. "I knew nobody when I pulled into town at eighteen, other than Uncle Ernie. I married a man I never should have at nineteen and had four kids, bam, bam, bam, bam. After my husband left, I struggled to find two cents to rub together. Jackson helped me out." Charlee put her hand on my arm. "Jackson's got a good heart underneath his tough-guy image. I wouldn't be a nurse today without his help. He'd cringe if he heard me say this, but he likes to help people out. He's a lot like Rosie was."

"His mom, Nancy, is a bit of a bitch though. Oops, did I say that out loud?" Tracie snickered. "Thankfully, she doesn't spend much time in the hardware store when she's here for the summer. It's all sort of beneath her." She pointed her beer glass at me. "I wouldn't be surprised if she's been feeding Jackson false information about you. She's pretty pissed off her aunt didn't leave her the store."

"That's what Ernie said, minus the 'pissed off' part." We laughed. "I hope to never meet his mom." I rethought my animosity toward Jackson. Maybe it was time to offer a truce.

Wendy came back to our table, pouting. "They're too wrapped up in their stupid pool game." She fumed about the men trying to get her to play against them for money. "I'm not dumb. They're just looking for an easy target they can embarrass."

Wendy's whining gave me an idea. "So, Jackson's a good pool player?"

"They're all good," Charlee answered. "Most of them are in a pool league in the winter. Why? Don't tell me you're going to go challenge him."

I slid off my barstool, stuffed a few bills and quarters in my jeans pocket and grabbed my beer. "I am. Wish me luck." I headed toward the testosterone group. I planned to poke the fire and see if I got burned. Yes, I'd ask for a truce, but not before having a little fun at Jackson's expense.

I slid my quarters on the side of the pool table where Jackson was playing, selected a cue stick and stood against the wall to watch. My action raised a few curious glances from the men. Jackson ignored me and focused on his shot. In a matter of minutes, he beat Mike.

Mike, all cleaned up from his day working on cars, did a mock bow. "Good luck, Molly."

I thanked him before retreating back to my clueless, vulnerable image. It was easy to play. I'd lived it for six years with Nick.

The clueless look came in handy when Jackson acknowledged me. "Let me guess, you've missed me and want to spend some quality time together." He pointed his pool cue at me.

I batted my eyes. "It's your charming personality. I can't get enough of it." My lips formed a pout. "You guys have been hogging the pool tables. I decided it was a woman's turn. How hard can it be?" I challenged.

Jackson studied me, his eyes sharp. "I better warn you up front, Molly, we play for ten bucks a game. You lose, you pay. Got it?"

When Jackson called me by name, several of the men I didn't know raised their eyebrows. They likely were curious as to how Jackson knew me. "Do you want to break?" His dismissive expression told me he assumed I wouldn't know how.

I squinted at him as if the question pained me. "I'd rather you did." I stepped back, chalked my pool cue, and gave him full range for the break.

Jackson dropped a stripe and a solid on his break shot. "Lucky for you either way I've already sunk one of your shots." He tapped the cue stick against his oversized hand and checked out all his options. Deciding on stripes, he called his next ball and pocket. He made the next three shots as I blew out puffs of exasperation. Finally, he missed and turned with a smirk.

"You don't have to call your shots, honey, just remember you don't want to sink the eight ball until the end." I stepped towards the table. "It's the black ball." Jackson leaned in and whispered before he walked past me.

I made my first shots look like pure luck, sinking a solid with each shot. A few of Jackson's friends clapped for me as my mouth dropped in mock-shock. "I don't see what's so hard about this!" My eyes widened in innocence. A brief pang of guilt hit me for seeking revenge. Just this once, I promised myself. My offer of a truce would soon follow.

Dad had a pool table in our basement. It was one of the few things he and I did together when I was growing up. And my six years with Nick, a minor-league pool shark who taught me every trick he knew, were going to come in handy.

When I sunk one solid after another, his friends playfully jabbed Jackson. "Hey, she's gonna wipe the table clean with her beginner's luck. Better get your wallet out, Jackson."

Jackson laughed with them, but his face was tight. I missed my next shot and stuck my lip out enough for a bird to perch on it. When he stepped up to take his turn he eyed me up, likely reassuring himself I couldn't have intentionally left him without a shot. He attempted a bank shot and scratched. Swearing under his breath, he didn't laugh when Mike slapped him on the back.

"I'm putting my money on Molly. Looks like she's got you scattered about like marbles." Mike turned to another guy. "What do you think? Should we challenge Jackson on a side bet? Maybe I can win back some of my money."

I put my finger to my lip, studying the table as if I had no idea what shot to attempt next. Scratch took a couple steps towards me. His expression appeared as if he was going to offer me some advice. Jackson stuck out his arm to stop his beefy friend. "She's on her own, Scratch. She's the one who squeezed her little butt in here to break up our game."

Jackson's words barely left his mouth when I proceeded to sink each remaining ball of mine, calling the shot ahead of time with each one, and then gracefully sinking the eight ball. It was all over in a matter of two minutes. I took a bow to the group of men clapping for me.

"Pulling my chain all along, weren't you?" Jackson's words ground like metal in my ear.

"I never told you I didn't know how to play. You assumed it." My eyes narrowed. "How ironic that you'd *assume* something about me." I held out my hand, waiting for my ten dollars.

He reached into his jean pocket, pulled out a crumpled ten, and pressed it into my hand. His look—and touch—could've set me on fire.

"What's really going on here?" His back was to his friends, cutting me off.

I couldn't answer, couldn't admit to him, a stranger, how he'd fanned my insecurities that day in the café. If I spoke the words, it would give oxygen to my anxieties about my capabilities of making it on my own. Tracie was right—Jackson was probably trying to protect Rosie's store and reputation from total ruin.

Mike and Scratch stepped up to shake my hand. "Did you want to play again, Molly?" Scratch asked me politely. I had no interest in playing again. I'd merely wanted to make a point.

"No thanks, I'm good." I smiled at Scratch, a big guy who reminded me of a bald teddy bear. I'd have stayed to visit, but Jackson firmly guided me away by my elbow.

"Can we talk a minute?" He led me to the nearest, semi-quiet corner.

"Sure." It had been my plan anyway. I wasn't sure if I should offer the olive branch before he asked me why I'd done what I did. I decided to get it over with and focused my gaze on his work boots. "I'm sorry. I don't know what got into me." I'd hoped to whisper my confession but had to shout over the noise.

He reached over and tipped my face up. "Did I hear you right?"

His friends stole curious glances our way. Jackson removed his hand from my chin. "Wow, I didn't expect to hear that." He braced himself against an unoccupied Pinball machine as I leaned against the wall.

"Hey, if this has all been about what I said in the café, I'm sorry. I was fed a different impression of you. I was worried you'd destroy everything Aunt Rosie worked so hard for." He shrugged. "She put more than fifty years in the place." His blue eyes searched mine. "Rosie was more like a grandma to me than a great- aunt. That place was everything to her."

"It's also where my mom spent a lot of her time as a teenager. The last thing I want to do is run the place into the ground," I said.

"Yep. Rosie talked fondly about those years when her son, Tom, my mom's cousin, was alive. He was about your mom's age." Jackson shoved his hands into his jean pockets. "He died long before I was born, but it sounds like he was a great son to Rosie."

"I wish I knew more about those years. My mom never even mentioned Rosie to me. I was aware of her annual visits to her old hometown when we'd go to our cabin, but I didn't know who she was coming to see. I wish I'd have met Rosie so she could have told me about the years Mom worked in the store." Our conversation felt too personal to have in a crowded bar.

"She was a hell of a lady. It's hard to believe Rosie and my mom were related. Rosie was down to earth. My mom? Not so much." He rubbed his jaw. "Nothing pissed my mom off more than hearing Rosie refer to Celia as 'the daughter she never had.'" He grinned, and I experienced the pulse-stopping look my friend Ella must have swooned over months ago in the café.

"Since you brought your mother up, I hear she's upset she didn't inherit everything from Rosie. Is that true?"

He chuckled. "Yes. 'Upset' is an understatement. The thing is, she'd have never run the business, and Aunt Rosie knew that about my mom. She'd have just sold everything. Rosie wanted the business to keep going. Rosie and I talked about it before she passed away."

Jackson had moved next to me, our shoulders touching as we leaned against the wall. "Mom grew up in Alabama with younger brothers, a gambling father, a worn-out mother, and no money. Mom is the only one who left Alabama, and Rosie told her right to her face that no way could she imagine my mom running her store. She'd talked of leaving it to me, but once I moved here from Wyoming and bought the Hardware store, I didn't need it. My younger brother, Cody, is happy in Wyoming, and not interested in running a business."

"What did you do before you moved here to buy the Hardware store?"

"I worked for the Department of Natural Resources, in Wyoming. It was a great job, and I loved being outside. When Aunt Rosie told me about the Hardware store up for sale, I couldn't resist. We spent every summer at our cabin here when I was growing up. I loved the lakes, the fishing, hunting…and the quietness of a small town. It was an easy decision."

He took a swig of his beer. We'd been watching the pool games going on several feet away. Now, he turned to me. "Aunt Rosie said your mother felt the same way about the store and town as she did. After your mom passed away, I asked Rosie what she was going to do. 'I'm leaving my will as is, same with my life estate' she said. 'I hope that one day Celia's daughter will find her way here.'" He blinked his eyes several times. "Her voice was hoarse and tears ran down her gaunt cheeks when she told me that. She was suffering from cancer that took her in the end. It was her wish, and one I wanted to honor."

"Do you know if your mom ever met my mom?"

"I doubt it. She barely remembers her cousin, Tom. She was young when he died and had only been to Minnesota a couple times growing up."

Our conversation had become too cozy. I pushed away from the wall and offered my hand. "Truce?"

Dimples formed around Jackson's mouth. "Truce." He pumped my hand.

I turned on my heel and headed back to the table where Tracie and Charlee were, likely watching the whole Molly/Jackson show. Wendy was nowhere in sight. As they high-fived me for winning, my outlook brightened. Anger at Jackson had been a heavy burden to carry around.

Chapter 8

I'd developed a morning routine in the two weeks my store had been open. Clean the minnow tanks, bury the dead minnows in my backyard, bring in the newspapers from the store porch…and wave to the young man standing across the street at the beach. Sometimes his old-fashioned bike was parked next to him.

The first few days he hadn't waved back, just stared openly at me with a serious look on his round face. He looked to be in his early twenties. He had short dark brown hair and wore a striped shirt every day. Yesterday he'd waved back. Today, the same.

Each morning I had a number of early customers…men in for their newspaper and half-and-half, maybe a young mother in to pick up milk and bread for breakfast. When the post office opened, if I had no customers I'd jog the half block to collect my mail.

This morning the elderly man everyone called "Old Lloyd" stood inside the post office. I hadn't seen him since that first day in the café, but it was instant mutual recognition. His white hair stood up all over as if someone had stuck it in a blender and hit "swirl." His post office box was four rows over from mine. His solid bulk, impressive at his age, was hard to ignore.

"Good morning," I said in my sweetest sing-song voice.

My greeting was answered with a grumble and a shake of his head before he strode out the post office door. I'd have loved to challenge him as to what in the hell he had against me, but I needed to get back to the store on the odd chance I had another customer.

I was reviewing my delivery with the Coca-Cola supplier late in the morning when a disheveled man walked in. His filthy jeans were crusted with sawdust, and grease stains splattered his super-sized flannel shirt. I signed for the delivery and asked if I could help him.

"Morning, ma'am. I'm here to deliver the firewood you asked for." He bobbed his head as he stuttered out the words. His small pale eyes avoided mine.

This must be the man I'd called after Jackson offered up his name. I'd left him a message two weeks ago about needing ten cord of wood. "You must be Doug?" The man who never called me back. It didn't matter. He was here now.

"Got your wood out front here, ma'am." He gestured to the logging truck outside. *Holy buckets that's a lot of wood!* My arms and back hurt just thinking of loading it in my wood stove.

"Where do you want it, round back?" Doug held his sawdust-covered cap in his hands as he pointed behind the store toward my backyard.

"Yes, thanks. You do unload it, right?" I held my breath.

"Yep. That there is a flat-bed logging truck. See the hydraulic clam? It'll pick up the wood and dump it in a nice pile by your wood stove." He slid a crumpled piece of paper across the counter. "This here is your bill. No rush in paying it, beings you're startin' up here and all."

"Thank you. I appreciate this, Doug." I did appreciate him bringing me the wood. However, I didn't appreciate the idea I'd be working my ass off on it all summer long to get it ready for winter.

When I had a break between customers I went back to my living room and peeked outside. There sat my new wood pile, in an overwhelming mess. Nothing like the organized pile from last year. The trees were limbed and cut in lengths too long for me to lift. The pile was too far away from the stove. I didn't own a chainsaw or splitting maul…things I'd been told I may need. Even if I owned them, I had no clue how, or the strength, to use them.

My shoulders slumped as I shuffled back to the store. I sat on the stool behind the main counter, swallowed my pride, picked up the phone, and dialed Ernie.

"Well now, I suppose the polite thing for me to say is 'there, there, things will be okay.'" His velvet voice soothed like a salve after I'd dumped my wood problems on him.

"Why do I have a feeling I'm not going to hear the polite version?" Ernie had warned me, at least twice, I'd get what I paid for from Doug. I should've called Jackson. Since Doug never returned my phone call, I'd never canceled my order.

"Save your breath, I know what you're going to say." I huffed. "But, Jackson tricked me. He purposely threw out Doug's name, knowing I'd jump on it."

Ernie chuckled. "You are most likely correct. I do believe Jackson was attempting to teach you a lesson about ordering wood. Now you know." Although Jackson and I had buried the hatchet, I hadn't worked up the nerve to ask him about delivering wood for me.

Lesson learned. Ernie stopped in the store after checking out my wood pile. He rubbed his smooth chin. "We need someone to cut and split your wood pile. I will handle it, okay?"

"Oh Ernie, I owe you so much already. But I'm not even going to argue with you. You know everyone in this town and they'll listen to you. I'm afraid I'll get someone else who will screw me over." Doug hadn't screwed me over. I got what I'd be paying for.

He nodded. "Yes, it may happen. You will have to be firm and specific in your business actions, Molly. I do believe the townspeople will respect you. It will take some time, but you can do it. Look at all you have accomplished already." He opened his arms to encompass the store.

"You always make me feel better." I leaned my head down on his comfortable shoulder. "Did I tell you I hired a part-time person to help out when Adam and Logan are busy?" I was proud I'd found someone on my own, and that I'd made at least one right decision.

"And who might that be?"

"Her name is Susan. She's retired from the bank and her husband passed away last winter. She's been stopping in most days to pick up one or two things and we visit. She seems nice and smart—exactly what I was looking for."

"Ah, yes, Susan. A perfect choice. See, things are looking up for you already." He patted my arm as a handful of young men came in, purchased snacks and soda pop, and headed outside to sit at a picnic table on the deck. "Other than your wood problem." Ernie winked at me as he waved goodbye and left me alone with my customers.

* * *

The weekend was a non-stop tornado of activity, thanks to the warm late April weather. Adam and Logan were gone to their grandparents' house, so Susan worked most of the weekend with me. The saving grace was it was two more weeks before the fishing opener on May 15 and a month before Memorial Day weekend. It was a good test run for what was to come.

By Sunday night, I'd have sold my last pair of designer shoes for a foot rub. Take out from Flap Jack Fever Café kept starvation at bay. I collapsed into bed before dark.

In my exhausted state, my dreams were random and vivid. In that fog between wake and sleep, I dreamt someone was trying to saw me in half! The chainsaw revving, the bed vibrating… it was so real and loud, in my dream, I fought to scream for them to stop.

I woke myself up with the covers wrapped around my legs. My alarm clock read 5:24 a.m. and it was still dark out. Something had woken me up, and it wasn't my alarm. There it was again, that loud roar shaking my small home. It sounded like a chainsaw, but who in their right mind would be sawing logs in the semi-darkness?

I threw on my terry robe and went to look outside my back door. In the bleak early dawn, I could see a beam of light moving around my log pile, like a flashlight, but higher in the air.

Common sense told me someone was cutting up my logs, but who, and why at this ungodly hour? I wasn't concerned about my safety but I was upset they woke Ernie up since I could see his lights on in his kitchen. I slipped on my flip-flops and went out to investigate.

Jackson was attacking my wood pile while wearing a Miner's hat, which explained the beam of light. With all the noise, he had no idea I was heading his way. I stopped far enough away to avoid the sawdust spray from his chainsaw and waited until he paused in his cutting.

"What in the world are you doing?" I planted my hands on my curve-less hips, probably resembling a lazy woman who'd been interrupted from her nap. My curls formed a wild nest. My tattered robe and neon purple flip-flops downplayed the seriousness I hoped to portray.

Jackson stopped the Husqvarna chainsaw and took off his hearing protection. He turned to me with a wicked grin knowing his racket had woken me up.

"Didn't you think about waking Ernie?" I pointed to Ernie's kitchen light. "See? He's awake now. What're you doing here anyway?"

He took a dozen strides to stand in front of me and removed the ear protection he wore. The heavy machine dangled from his one hand, while the other covered my mouth with his dirty glove. "Shhh, are you trying to wake the entire neighborhood?" He must have read my lips while the light from his hat shone in my eyes as if I was being interrogated. "If you know what's good for you, you'll stop talking right now before I change my mind and leave you with this crap pile."

I removed his gloved hand from my mouth and wiped sawdust from my lips as I digested the truth. Jackson was doing me a huge favor—before six on a Monday morning. "I feel bad having Ernie woken up." I struggled to apologize for berating him.

He tossed his head back in laughter. "You don't know him any better than that by now? He's up by five every morning. I checked to make sure his kitchen light was on before I pulled in." He studied my face. "You think I'm that rude?"

"I don't know enough about you." I shrugged. "You didn't tell me you'd be here. I appreciate you doing this, and I'll pay you, of course. But I didn't expect you to help me."

"You know, instead of standing there stumbling over your words, you could go get dressed and come stack some of this wood."

"I should've thought to sleep in my lumberjack clothes." I thumped the side of my head. "Too bad I have to shower, clean out the minnow tanks, get the coffee going, open the store…" I sounded like a snobby, thankless bitch.

He reached over and lifted a large water jug from the tailgate of his old pickup, took a long drink, and wiped his mouth with the sleeve of his shirt. Without thinking, I reached over and wiped a sliver of wood stuck in his day-old stubble. I received a wicked grin in response.

"Can you get Ernie to cover for you in the store this morning?"

"Don't you have to work at the hardware?"

"Nope. I take most Sundays and Mondays off. I might go in later, but I want to get some of this cut up before the weather warms up too much."

I looked over at Ernie's home. "I hate to bother him, but if it's only for a few hours, I don't think he'll mind."

A morning outside sounded inviting—something I hadn't enjoyed in over two weeks since I'd opened the store. "I'll be back out in a bit," I promised.

After I cleaned up, knowing full well I'd get dirty again soon enough, I called Ernie. "You called Jackson, didn't you?" It was the only way Jackson would've known about my mess.

"I told you I would take care of your wood pile. And yes, I will be over shortly to work the store while you help Jackson." I could hear the smugness in his voice. He earned it.

He shuffled in the store shortly after I opened. "I appreciate your help—again. I'll be back to relieve you within a few hours." A four hour stretch in the store was plenty for my favorite eighty-four-year-old. I hoped to be as active at his age.

"I've got my cell phone on vibrate if you need anything."

"No hurry. I will sit a spell if needed."

I closed the door between the store and my house before hustling to change into the oldest pair of jeans I could find. I grabbed my old nylon jacket from when I'd played in a summer softball league. I had yet to invest in leather work gloves for handling wood.

Jackson eyed me up when I walked outside. "You sure you've got the pipes for this?"

"It's been a while since I've gotten much exercise; it's one of the downfalls of seven days a week in the store." I held up my bare hands. "Should I get my garden gloves?"

He shook his head, walked back to his truck and grabbed some extra work gloves which were two sizes too big for my hands. "These will protect your hands better."

He went over the routine with me. Fill the old wheelbarrow which stood next to the wood stove with the cut and split wood he'd tossed on the ground, wheel it over to the existing woodpile by the wood stove, unload and stack it. "Got it?"

"Got it. I'm actually glad to be outside. I love these cool, sunny mornings." I had initially planned to bike in the morning before opening the store, but the days had become more physically and mentally draining for me than I'd planned, and it was still too dark out at 5:30 a.m.

"Besides, I need to build up these pipes if I'm going to be feeding the fire all winter." I held back my sarcastic comment on whether I'd make it through my first winter or not. Jackson was being kind. It was time for me to play nice.

After only an hour of working—on my part, I'd worked up a good sweat, and appetite. I looked over at Jackson standing on top of the pile of logs, like the king of the mountain with his chainsaw, his flannel shirt off and his old gray T-shirt sticking to him.

I had placed a large water jug on the tailgate next to his and stopped to take a drink. He spotted me and came down off his mountain to join me for a drink of water. "Hungry?" I imagined he would be after mowing through the wood pile for a couple hours.

"Yep. It's more important to stay hydrated though."

"Do you want some breakfast?" I, for one, was hungry. My body was used to a light breakfast and was not used to so much physical exercise.

"Maybe in another hour or so." He reached over and chucked my chin. "You aren't done yet, girl. We need to get after this while we can."

For the next two hours, we worked methodically, stopping for occasional water breaks. My body was shaky. "I need to eat. You ready for breakfast?" Jackson was splitting a log.

He tipped his head sideways, his eyes narrowed. "Don't tell me you actually cook?"

"Why are you surprised? What did you think I ate?"

He picked up an old rag lying on his truck bed and wiped his face. "I don't know. Since you lived in the Twin Cities I figured you went out to eat all the time."

"I'd have gone broke if I did." I laughed. "I guess I did anyway, didn't I?" It wasn't painful to joke with him this morning—maybe because he'd saved my sorry ass by coming to cut and split my wood. For a price, I was sure, but at this point, I didn't care.

"So, were you surprised when Ernie called to tell you about my predicament?"

He rolled his eyes. "Hardly."

"You set me up in the café that day. You threw Doug's name out there, knowing I'd bite." I elbowed him as we leaned side-by-side against his pickup.

"And you might have deserved it." Jackson's words held no malice.

"Eh, maybe." I kicked at the gravel in my driveway. "I have some bacon and eggs in the fridge and can whip us up some omelets if you'd like." I'd invite Ernie back to eat with us.

"Sounds good." He rubbed his flat stomach before following me to the house. Standing on the deck, he brushed off his dirty T-shirt and stained jeans, toed off his work boots and left them on the deck. "I'll go wash up." He stepped inside and headed for the bathroom, comfortable in Rosie's old home.

I peeked into the store. Ernie was organizing tackle on the pegboard wall.

"How about some breakfast, Ernie? I'm whipping up bacon and eggs for Jackson and me." His eyebrows rose and his mouth hung open.

"What? Even the devil has to eat." I winked.

Ernie patted the slight paunch beneath his red suspenders. "Thank you for your invitation, but I am good. I had my oatmeal before I came over and packed myself a sandwich in case I am here for lunch." He nodded toward my kitchen. "You two enjoy your breakfast."

"Thanks for everything, Ernie." I shook my head as I headed back to my kitchen. If someone would've told me last month I'd be making breakfast for Jackson in my kitchen, I'd have sworn I was on Candid Camera. Sometimes I even surprised myself.

Chapter 9

"I like what you did with Rosie's old paneling. The paint lightens things up." Jackson looked around. My home felt cozy and inviting to me, but I was surprised Jackson was okay with me making changes to Rosie's home.

"Mind if I make coffee?" He asked as he washed up at the kitchen sink.

"Sure, go ahead. Filters are up there." I pointed to a corner cupboard as I got the coffee beans out of the fridge along with the bacon, eggs, milk, and cheese.

"It must be hard coming in here now." I separated the bacon in the pan.

"It feels kind of weird, but I'd already been in here a few times after we donated most of Rosie's things to charity, which helped." His eyes took in all of my changes.

We worked together in silence. Jackson grinding coffee beans and pouring water into the coffee maker, me frying bacon and whipping eggs, cheese, mushrooms, and seasonings in a large glass bowl. He set the table for two.

"You must have spent a lot of time with Rosie." I turned over the bacon slices.

"Yep. I'd come load her stove. If I was gone my friends covered for me. Most Sunday nights my friends and I came here for dinner with Rosie and Ernie. She'd come to my house on hot summer nights to cool off even though she had the beach right across the street. I live on a small lake a few miles from here." Jackson poured us each a cup of coffee. "She was a special lady. It's too bad you never got a chance to know her."

Our eyes met. "So I've heard." There was something I'd been meaning to tell him. "I know you're worried I'm going to run Rosie's business into the ground. I'll do everything I can to keep this place alive and kicking. My future is at stake too."

His pale blue eyes stood out in his already-tanned face. "I know." He studied the kitchen cupboards as if they could backup my words. "You wouldn't believe the crap I've been fed about how your family had taken advantage of Aunt Rosie."

I turned the burners off as we loaded up our plates. "From your mother?"

His eyebrows rose. "Have others told you about the infamous Nancy Brennan already?"

"Honestly, not much. Feel free to fill me in."

Over heaping plates of cholesterol, he explained his mother's deep-rooted money insecurities. "Dad makes plenty, but she grew up poor. I think for her, she can't stash enough away, although she has no problem spending it too. Mom nearly burst a blood vessel when her aunt left this place to a non-relative, instead of her. Rosie's husband died when their son was young. Then Tom died in Vietnam. Mom's brothers are younger and haven't been to Minnesota for decades and have shown no interest in Rosie's business."

He fiddled with his fork. "By deduction, Mom figured this place would go to her. I think Aunt Rosie knew my mother would have turned around and sold it without a second thought. Dad hasn't been back here for years, even though he enjoyed our time spent at the cabin when Cody and I were growing up. Now, he's too busy."

"What does your dad do for a living?"

"He's an executive at Baker Hughes. They're a big GE company in Wyoming. When we were growing up, he'd use his vacation time to hang out at the cabin and take Cody and me fishing and waterskiing. As he's climbed up the ladder, I think he spends his vacation time behind his desk. He should retire, but that would mean spending more time with my mother."

He winced at the thought. "When I go back to Wyoming, he's good about taking a couple of days to hang out with me. I enjoy his company. He doesn't stress me out like Mom does."

"I feel bad that your mom is so upset over it all. But if Rosie thought she'd sell the place, then I don't blame her for not giving it to your mother."

"Rosie put Celia on a pedestal, and Mom wants to knock her off it, even though it shouldn't matter now. She's been squawking non-stop about how your mom's family snuck out of town in the middle of the night and couldn't be trusted, so we shouldn't trust you either." He forked a large bite of omelet into his mouth. "She can't seem to let it go."

I forced myself to swallow the bacon I'd been chewing. "What did you mean when you said my mom's family couldn't be trusted?" Clearly, his mom was telling tall tales. "My mom never did anything even remotely untrustworthy. Her family moved from Love to the Twin Cities after she graduated from high school. After college, Mom taught underprivileged children and traveled all over the country to work in underfunded schools. She moved back to Minnesota after she met my dad. She was about as honorable as a person can be."

He nodded. "I believe you. I'm only saying my mom has tried hard to paint a dark picture of your mother and her family. It doesn't matter. Whatever happened is in the past and has nothing to do with you now."

I could've spent hours telling him what a great person my mom was, but it wasn't him I needed to convince. And I had no desire to ever meet his mom, much less talk to her.

After we set our empty plates in the sink, I checked with Ernie to make sure he was still doing okay before Jackson and I went back outside.

"Hey, do you realize we've been together for three hours and haven't maimed or killed each other yet?" He twitched his eyebrows. If he'd had a mustache, he'd be stroking it.

I laughed. "Didn't you notice I've kept my distance from you when you have the chainsaw or splitting maul in your hand?"

"Wise woman. The previous victims who got too close to me while I was cutting wood are buried out in the woods behind my house." We walked side by side toward the woodpile. A tan and white cat skittered in front of us. "Yours?" He arched an eyebrow.

"No. She's been hanging around my yard though, digging up the dead minnows I bury." I wasn't a fan of cats, but she kept her distance and I kept mine.

"She'll keep the mice out of your house."

"I have mice in my house?" I stopped walking.

"No…I'm sure you don't." He fought to tame his smile and his eyes twinkled.

I made a mental note to keep the minnows buried close to the surface. As long as I kept the cat fed, she'd stick around.

We put in another hour splitting and stacking wood before Jackson took off his gloves and stretched. "We've got a good start. I'll give you notice next time before I show up."

My back screamed for joy at the news we were finished for the day. I probably wouldn't be able to get out of bed tomorrow and would've quit long ago if it was just me. Jackson had made an impressive dent in the woodpile after working his way through it like a steam engine.

I stretched and rubbed my lower back. "I'm glad we're done for today, I don't want you dropping over of a heart attack in my yard. I'd have to bury you with the dead minnows."

He leaned against the handle of the splitting maul. "I do this all the time. It keeps me in shape. Sorry to squash your dreams of an early death for me." He tossed the splitting maul in the back of his pickup.

"I'll come back some night soon when it's cooler to work on the rest of the pile."

"I appreciate all you've done. At this point, I'm at your mercy so you can charge me what you want." Dollar signs spun in my head, like a revolving door. *This is what you get, you stubborn mule.* I only had my foolish pride to blame.

Jackson yanked his grimy T-shirt over his head. I avoided studying his torso. He slammed his tailgate up and turned to me. "You feel indebted to me?" His grin was wide. "You make it hard not to say something dirty just to tick you off."

I gave him my best steely glare.

He reached over and squeezed my upper arm. "You've got some pretty good pipes there, Molly. Maybe you aren't such a city wimp after all."

It was as close to an apology for his initial opinion of me, as I could expect from him. He waved goodbye and I dragged my already tired body back inside to clean up, again. I had another seven hours ahead of me in the store.

* * *

The first week of May snuck up like a clever joke. My Grand Opening was scheduled for May 9 and the following weekend was the fishing opener. Thinking about it made my heart race. So I avoided it, much as I'd managed to avoid remembering how much easier my life was when I lived with Nick.

I was done doing easy. My focus now was on rewarding.

"Snowbirds" flocked back to their cabins for the summer months, and the increase in business helped the work days fly by. Each night I fell into bed more exhausted than I'd ever been in my partying days.

Tracie's thirty-third birthday was May 5. She reminded me that she and Rick were hosting a Cinco de Mayo party on Friday night. "I know you're beat, but this will give you a chance to meet more young people. It'll be fun, even if you stay for just a couple hours."

"I can't guarantee I won't fall asleep face-first in the guacamole dip."

Tracie giggled. "Well, that would make a lasting impression on everyone."

As temperatures rose in early May, people returned to open their cabins. It was a welcome relief to have tourists sprinkled in with the locals, some who asked too many nosy questions without so much as buying a loaf of bread. Thankfully, most locals were welcoming.

Tourists stopped in for random items like towels, flip-flops, toothbrushes, Coleman fuel, and sunscreen, among other things. Love had a small grocery store, but it was two blocks off the highway. When cabin owners came in, they also bought their bread, eggs, and milk. My pocketbook had been on a diet for too long and was ready for a thick, juicy meal of cash.

I leaned against the locked store door and sighed after another long day. I craved my recliner and an ice-cold beer. Instead, I showered, and let my hair dry into its usual curls. The idea of blow-drying and straightening my hair now seemed like a waste of time. My meticulous grooming of facial scrubs, French-tipped nails, and professional highlights were a distant memory…one I couldn't imagine resurrecting in my new blue jeans life.

I picked out a multi-colored top, zipped up a red hoodie, and stepped into my ballet flats without a minute of downtime before driving the few miles to Tracie and Rick's home.

Their brown rambler-style house was overflowing with people when I arrived. Sliding glass doors opened from the living room out to their large patio and backyard. Making my way through the crowd, I walked outside praying I'd recognize at least a few new friends.

Rick was tending a small outside bar and offered me a margarita. I thanked him for the drink I could easily down. Maybe if I had a couple, I'd loosen up and talk to these people who lived in the town I now called home. I'd been lulled over the years by hanging out with the same friends in Minneapolis. It was now up to me to extend my hand and friendship to new people.

When we went out as couples, Nick and I had always hung out with his friends and their significant others. If I went out with my girlfriends, it usually consisted of Ella, and a few other friends if they could maneuver a night away from their little ones. Here, I was outside my comfort zone. Another reason it had been too easy to stay with Nick.

Tracie gave me a quick tour of her home before leading the way back to their patio where picnic tables overflowed with Mexican-style food. Tracie spotted Wendy in a circle of men and introduced me to the guys before she excused herself to attend to other guests. Wendy barely acknowledged me.

When Charlee appeared, and tapped me on the shoulder, I was glad for the break from Wendy's circle. They'd had plenty to drink. I felt like an uninvited college kid crashing a frat party. Charlee and I went to sit with a few other women who introduced themselves. After a bit, I excused myself to go inside and use the bathroom. A strong arm reached out and grabbed me as I walked into the crowded living room. It was a good-looking man I'd recently met at our local bank branch. I couldn't remember his name.

"Hello again, Molly. Remember me? Curt Adamson, from the bank." His well-manicured hand gently squeezed my elbow.

My eyes followed his tanned arm up to his green eyes and short, wavy, blond hair. He resembled a surfer dude who cleaned up well. "Yes, I remember. How's it going?" I stayed to exchange polite talk for a minute before excusing myself. I headed down the dark hallway to the end where I remembered their main bathroom was.

The bathroom door was shut, so I stood in the hall, my back to the living room crowd. My mind counted down the minutes until I could politely leave. Bathed in exhaustion, the one yummy margarita had already given me a fuzzy brain.

As I reached up to rub my temples, a hand clasped over my mouth from behind me. Another strong arm wrapped around my waist, and in an instant, I was dragged into a dark room before the door quickly shut behind me.

Oh my God, oh my God! My eyes blinked in rapid succession to adjust to the dark. I recognized the extra bedroom from Tracie's quick house tour. He had my arms pinned to my sides, his large, sweaty hand still clamped over my mouth. I regretted not wearing stiletto heels as I stomped on his feet and kicked him in the shins. My ballet flats did little damage.

"Nobody wants you here in this town. Nobody!" He hissed. "You better leave while you can." His words were enunciated and gruff. A harsh whisper that raised every hair follicle on my body. As my brain tried to digest what was happening, he shoved me hard, in the opposite direction of the door.

I fell to the floor, narrowly missing an exercise bike. By the time I pushed myself up and turned around, he was gone. Horror pumped adrenaline through my veins as I shook in disbelief. How could that have happened in a house full of people?

Perspiration glazed my body. My hand shook as I opened the partially-closed door and looked down the empty hallway. A mere fifteen feet away, people were laughing and partying in Tracie's living room. I scanned the faces I could see. Not a single man appeared to be watching the hall for me to come out and recognize him.

The bathroom was still occupied, and a few seconds later a woman I didn't recognize walked out, smiling as she walked past me. I went in and locked the door, leaning against it as if someone would try to break in. I should've stopped her to ask if she heard anything, but of course, she wouldn't have. My legs bounced with jitters as I went to the bathroom, my hand over my mouth in disbelief.

When I was done, I looked at my face in the mirror. What a mess. Smudged mascara below my dazed eyes, smeared lipstick, and matted curls where his arm had been. *Do not cry, Molly. Get yourself under control. Walk out of this bathroom as if you had not a care in the world. Whoever it was, they'll be watching you.*

Chapter 10

With Herculean courage, I weaved through the crowded living room and out to the patio pretending to be the same person who'd walked through just minutes earlier. The reality of what had happened followed me like a ghost I couldn't shake. I should've met each pair of male eyes with a challenge. Instead, I focused on getting the hell out of there.

Tracie and Charlee were still sitting at the same table I'd left a few minutes earlier. Or fifteen. I had no sense of reality. Charlee smiled up at me for a second before her smile was replaced by furrowed brows. "Hey, you okay?"

Whoever threatened me was wrong. Tracie and Charlee wanted me there. And Ernie too. That might not be very many people, but I'd only lived full-time in the town for a month. Apparently long enough to make an enemy. My words couldn't get past the panic clogging my throat and it was futile to think I could stop my tears.

"What happened?" Tracie jumped up and put her hand on my shoulder.

My eyes darted around. Where was my purse? I should've stopped and combed my hair and put fresh lipstick on. And seriously, where had I left my purse? I couldn't leave without it. Charlee leaned in next to Tracie, trying to get me to focus.

"Molly, did something happen inside the house?"

I dabbed at my eyes. Damn, why couldn't I have just left? Oh yes, I needed to find my purse. "Um, do you know where my purse is?" My words squeaked out.

They each hooked an elbow through my arms. "C'mon, we'll help you find your purse. You aren't leaving already, are you?" Tracie's voice was soothing, but I could tell she meant to uncover what happened.

"When you got here, where did you go first?" Charlee quizzed me.

"To the bar. Rick poured me a margarita."

Tracie led the way to their outdoor bar. Rick was talking to a small group nearby. "Honey, did you see a purse sitting around at the bar?" She looked to me to describe it.

"It's red. About the size of a sheet of paper." I was glad I'd brought my red purse; there couldn't be too many red purses sitting around.

Rick excused himself from the group and reached under the bar. "Is this it? It was left on a bar stool." I eyed Rick's hands. I couldn't help but inspect every guy's hands at the party as if by some miracle I'd recognize them even though the room had been dark.

"Thanks. I appreciate it." I clutched my purse to my chest like a shield. Tracie poured three margaritas. Apparently, I wasn't leaving or else she was really thirsty. Charlee put her arm around my shoulder and Tracie led us to the corner of their backyard where an empty table gave us privacy.

After we sat down, I stared at my frosty margarita. "I should go home. I'm exhausted."

"Drink up. You aren't going anywhere right now. And if you need to go home after this, we've got sober drivers who can bring you home," Tracie said. "Now tell us what's wrong. I might not know you that well, but I do know you're trying to keep it together and it sure isn't because you thought you lost your purse." She stared me down. My tears welled up.

My hands shook as I took a big swig of margarita and swallowed my pride along with it. "When I went to use the bathroom, I was waiting in the hall and some guy came up behind me and dragged me into your extra bedroom."

"Oh my God!" Charlee's hand flew to cover her mouth. "Did he…hurt you in any way?"

For the first time, it dawned on me what could have happened. I shivered. "No, he didn't try anything, and I'm not hurt physically." But mentally? Shaken like an earthquake.

"He told me nobody wanted me around here and that I better leave town while I could." My leg hammered up and down, my knee shaking the table.

"That's awful, and so not true!" Charlee's hard-working hand clasped my trembling one.

Tracie stood up. "Son of a bitch! I'm telling Rick. He'll know what to do."

"No! Please don't tell Rick. I don't want anyone to know. People will think I'm making it up, or that I'm a sissy city girl."

She harrumphed while her eagle-eyes studied the crowd before sitting down again. "Do you remember anything specific? What did his voice sound like?"

"He whispered so it was hard to tell." I closed my eyes, concentrating. "He was taller than me and strong. It doesn't narrow it down much, other than any guy shorter than five foot nine is probably off the hook."

"Oh, Molly, I'm so sorry! I can't even imagine who would do that." Tracie plopped her trim body back down on the picnic table bench and drummed her fingers. "Whoever it is, they're wrong. We're glad to have you in town, glad to see Rosie's store open again, and glad to have another young woman around." Tracie reached out and added her hand to Charlee's and mine.

"You two might be fine with me living here, but I've had a few locals stop in, check me out, and leave as if I was under suspicion of a crime and the jury was still out."

"Some small-town people grumble at change. I went through it when I moved here." Charlee shook her head at the memory. "I had hoped having Uncle Ernie living here would help pave the way. But he was still being judged himself."

Charlee had been judged by people's pre-conceived ideas about her. Now I was too.

"Let's walk through the house. I'd like to see if any guy looks guilty and see who all is here." Tracie stood again, and Charlee helped me up, my body wilting with emotional fatigue.

Tracie located paper and a pen in the kitchen and wrote down every guy's name as we worked our way slowly through the crowd, eyeing up each man as a potential suspect.

I mentally picked out the men I knew by name. Curt, from the bank, was still here. Scratch, from the café, Drake, one of the realtors, Mike, owner of Ernie's Garage, and Jackson. Jackson was here? Of course, he would be. I just hadn't seen him before this. Was he here when I'd come in earlier to use the bathroom?

My stomach churned at the idea of suspecting Jackson. We buried the hatchet, didn't we? Why would he threaten me when he'd come and cut up my wood pile for me?

Charlee rubbed my back. "The best thing you can do is stay. Don't let people think you're going to turn tail and run. Plus, we can observe people and see if we hear or see anything unusual." She kept me close to her side as I was introduced to another dozen or so people over the next hour. I inspected each man's hand I shook, and looked them right in the eye, especially if they were taller than me.

Little by little the crowd made their way inside or went home as the night grew cooler. I helped clean up outside while some of the men packed up the outside bar. I was hours past exhaustion.

A few tiki lamps illuminated the now empty backyard when I went out to gather the hoodie I'd left on a chair. Shadows danced from the lamps as I walked back to the house. And there, in the shadows, stood Jackson. I hesitated by the sliding glass door. He reached for my arm.

"Can I talk to you for a minute?" My heart raced again. I wasn't sure if it was from seeing Jackson in his form-fitting black T-shirt or being taken by surprise…still on edge from my earlier encounter. In the shadows, he appeared sinister. I reminded myself he wasn't.

He gently took my hands. "Are you okay?" I raised my eyebrows. "Yes, Tracie told me what happened. I want to help find the asshole so I can set him straight," he said.

I took a deep breath. Of course, it hadn't been Jackson. I'd have sensed it. "I didn't know you were here until I walked through the house with Tracie and Charlee."

"I didn't get here until late. You three looked like you were on a mission, so I asked Tracie what was going on." He squeezed my hands. "So, this guy was taller than you…were his hands rough or smooth? His voice deep or high? Did you feel long sleeves on his arm or facial hair when he had his face against yours?"

My brain whipped through his questions, trying to focus in on exactly what I'd experienced in that minute. "You should be a detective. I didn't think about any of those things."

He leaned against the outside of Tracie's house and pulled me toward him, still holding my hands. "Close your eyes. Let's walk through this together."

I closed my eyes as I focused. "His hands were kind of smooth." The palms of Jackson's hands were calloused. "Not like yours."

He rubbed my hands against the roughness of his day's growth of stubble.

"Did he have a full beard? Whiskers? Smooth shaven?" He continued to gently rub my palm against his cheek. It tickled, but I wasn't pulling away.

"Smooth, and I don't remember smelling aftershave or cologne."

"How about his hand…any scent?"

I concentrated, reliving the hand clamped over my mouth. "It smelled like salsa."

My eyes flashed open and met his. "I guess it doesn't narrow it down much at a Cinco de Mayo party, does it?"

"You're doing great. How 'bout his voice?"

"He whispered, so it was hard to tell. It was deeper I guess." I shrugged. "A sleeve brushed across my cheek, so he had long sleeves on, but I don't know how much that helps. Most of the guys were wearing long sleeves. Believe me, I looked."

Jackson's next move surprised me. He let go of my hands and enveloped me in a hug, pulling me against him. The warmth of his body was comforting, and I found myself laughing.

"What's so funny?" He asked, not letting go. He rested his forehead on mine.

I pulled back so I could look at him. "The other day when we were eating breakfast in my kitchen, I thought if someone would've told me the first day I met you that I'd be eating breakfast with you in my kitchen a few months later I'd have split a gut." I smiled.

He traced a finger along my jawline, resting it on my chin. "Then I'm guessing you'll find this hilarious." His hand guided my face to his before his full lips softly kissed mine. There was no brain function on my part, only instinctive responding.

I cleared my throat to rid the emotion coating it. "Well…that was unexpected."

He gave me a half-grin before pulling me back in as if I might back away. I could've saved him the worry—I wasn't going anywhere. The heat of his torso radiated my front as his hands wrapped around my lower back, sliding into the pockets of my jeans.

My mouth welcomed his kiss, now anything but soft. Every lost hormone of mine from the past few years danced full blast through my body, pouring out of my lips in response to his firm body and sexy mouth. I was certain at any given second our bodies were going to fuse together as our kiss skyrocketed to just shy of a get-us-a-room level.

Until the screen door slid open a few feet away from us. "Oh, I'm sorry!" Tracie jumped as she stepped outside. "I—I was just going to get my camera I left out here." She stammered as if she had been caught trespassing in her own yard.

I was barely working my way back out of a steamy fog to think of stepping away from Jackson. Tracie hustled to a picnic table, retrieved her camera, and avoided looking our way as she breezed back inside her house.

Jackson slipped his hands from my pockets and stepped back to the wall. "Let's talk about what happened earlier. I want to find who threatened you and rip them apart. And I'm following you home to make sure nobody is waiting for you there."

I hadn't thought about being threatened at my house. Now the idea of going back to the store and empty house made me nervous.

He led the way back inside and we helped Rick and Tracie finish cleaning up. Rick took a stack of bowls from me. Tracie showed me the list of names they'd come up with so far. "There's about thirty. Some hadn't been invited, but that's the way it is in a small town. People just show up." Rick's mouth was grim. "We will get to the bottom of this, Molly."

"I appreciate it. You can scratch any man shorter than me off your list." I offered.

Tracie hugged my shoulders. "It could've been someone who was here for a minute and left. We'll ask everyone if they noticed someone pop in and then leave."

"Molly said his hands weren't rough, so we can count out any loggers," Jackson said.

My mind jumped back to our kiss, and Jackson's hands. Hands I'd been more than willing to have on my body.

We said our goodbyes, and Jackson followed me home in his pickup. When we pulled up my driveway, he took a flashlight from his glove compartment even though I had left my outdoor light on. "You stay in your car until I walk around the outside."

I did, and he was back in a minute. "All clear. I'll go inside first." He held out his hand for my key. I handed it to him and followed behind.

We turned on every light in my house, walked through every aisle in the store, and although my heart raced, I found comfort in Jackson's presence. When we made our way back to the kitchen, Jackson asked for my cell phone. "I'm keying in my cell number. You sleep with your phone next to your bed, okay? You hear anything, you call me right away."

I nodded. "Thanks for everything." A softball of emotion lodged in my throat.

"I was wrong, Molly. You're a lot tougher than I gave you credit for." He took my face in his hands. "Be careful. Keep your eyes and ears open, okay?" His kiss was quick before he walked out; making sure the door was locked before he left.

I spent the better part of the night in bed replaying each minute detail of those horrifying seconds…wondering if I'd have been better off staying in Minneapolis.

Chapter 11

The store's Grand Opening on Sunday was a welcome diversion after Tracie's party. Ernie served donuts I'd purchased from the local bakery. We served a lot of coffee, people signed up for prizes, and I was pleasantly surprised at the number of locals who showed up. Every man I'd seen at the party was scrutinized by me, but I didn't notice any unusual behavior and never felt a vibe of anger toward me.

I was glad to have the Grand Opening behind me. A couple days later I was unpacking inventory, crouched down, stocking cereal on the bottom shelf when someone came up behind me. There stood Curt Adamson, all decked out in cream dress pants, crisp white shirt, and a pale green tie to match his eyes. His bleached blond hair was gelled up enough to transform the beach-dude look into reserved banker.

"Hello, Molly. I figured I'd catch you here." Curt's voice was as smooth as his face.

I forced a chuckle. "Well, besides Tracie's party the other night, I rarely leave this building, so your guess was pretty good." I kept stocking Cheerios on the shelf.

He got down on his haunches. "Do you have a minute?" He grasped my arm and I automatically stiffened. Curt's hands were smooth. He was on the list from the party.

I stood, hoping he'd get right to the point. "What can I help you with?"

He stood too, towering over me. "I'd like to ask you out."

My smoldering kiss with Jackson was still front and center in my brain. I tried to kick it aside but it wouldn't budge. Curt was nice looking and polite. I should say "yes." Maybe if we spent time together, I'd know if he was the one who'd assaulted me. Although it didn't make sense that a man who wanted to date me would also be trying to drive me out of town.

"There's a beautiful restaurant in Blue Bay on a point that overlooks two lakes. They've got great food. How about dinner there this Sunday night?" he asked. I was tempted to grasp Curt's well-manicured hand and study it. "I know, it's the opening of fishing and you'll be exhausted by then, but a relaxing meal would be a great way to unwind after your weekend."

More than likely I'd read something into Jackson's actions at Tracie's party since I hadn't seen or heard from him since then—not even at my Grand Opening. I reflected on the night at the Pickled Perch when Wendy implied that Jackson was just out for a good time. I didn't want to be a "good time" for someone.

I meant to say "yes." "I'm sorry, Curt. I don't think so." My answer surprised me.

Curt's smile fizzled. "Are you sure? We can go somewhere else if you'd like."

I had a feeling tangling with the dating scene again would be like walking into a giant spider web—another reason I'd stuck it out with Nick. Dating had been a hassle years ago. It wouldn't be any easier now. "I'm too busy now, and don't have time for dating." My smile was weaker than my mom's tea, but it was the best I could do. "I'm sorry."

Curt was diplomatic. "I understand. Maybe another time." He gave me a small nod and left me alone to question what had taken over my tongue.

I was sweeping the floor that afternoon when a skinny, elderly woman dressed in purple polyester pants hiked up over her tiny paunch, hustled in like a mini-tornado. Wiry gray hair poked out from under a white news cap with a plastic purple tulip sticking out the side. A pencil was tucked behind her long ear. Ruby lipstick and penciled-in eyebrows stood out against her pasty face.

"Daisy here, looking for any dish to report in my column this week." She stuck out her parchment-paper-skinned hand to shake mine in a grasp far firmer than I expected.

"I beg your pardon?"

She nodded as if she expected me to be clueless. "I'm here for my Dishing Daisy column I write for *Up North* newspaper." She smacked her lips. "Like if anything exciting happened in your store, or you had company for dinner…scoop like that." She winked.

"Um, I can't think of anything right now. Sorry." There was nothing in my personal life I wanted to air to the locals.

She handed me a hot pink business card. "Call me if you do. I'll check in now and then." Her words were as hurried as she was. She yanked her stretch pants up and bustled out the door.

By the end of the fishing opener weekend, I had dragging-ass-syndrome. It had been an initiation I wouldn't have survived without Adam, Logan, and Susan. After I closed Sunday night, I called Tracie. We hadn't talked since Curt asked me out.

"I bet you're wiped out as much as I am." I had her on speaker phone while I mixed myself a vodka lemonade. After two large gulps, my shoulders relaxed.

"Ugh, you said it. After I put our little guy to bed, I'm kicking back with a drink and my feet up. I'm lucky I've got tomorrow off from the hardware store. I'm guessing you don't."

"Nope. I've got a bitch of a boss," I joked. I took my drink and kicked back in the recliner. "I have a question for you. What do you know about Curt from the bank?"

"He's nice. Kind of full of himself though. Why?"

I took too big of a drink and coughed my words out. "He asked me out for a date."

"What? You've got a date with Jackson?"

"Ah, no, Curt." I swallowed what was hopefully my final cough. "He asked me out and I couldn't think of a good reason to say no. But I did."

"Curt Adamson, not Jackson?" I could feel her confusion through my phone.

"I know, I know. What you saw was just Jackson comforting me." *Those sizzling kisses that could've burned a tattoo on your weak mind…they were comforting?*

Tracie snorted. "I've known Jackson for years, before I was married, and he never 'comforted' me like that."

"Anyway, I am rethinking my decision with Curt. Plus, Jackson has made no attempt to contact me in the past week." I sounded like a pouty teen. *Grow up, Molly.*

"Jackson was gone all last week and just came back Friday night in time for the busy weekend. He went to help a college friend move to a new home," she explained.

"Why didn't he tell me that?" It explained why he wasn't at my Grand Opening.

"Um, because he's stubborn and probably just as confused about his feelings as you are."

I couldn't argue with that.

* * *

After nine days and ten hours since our kiss I'd thought about way too often, Jackson sauntered into my store.

Lucky for me, I could ignore him. The young man who'd made it a habit of watching me from across the street while I brought in the newspapers had just walked in the store.

He had yet to speak to me, but his aunt, Susan, told me his name was Travis. "Travis is on the autism spectrum, high functioning, and lives at home with his parents. I live down the road from them and he loves to come and visit."

He often rode his bike around town, shaking maracas to whatever tune played in his head. If you overlooked his unusual behavior, he'd appear like any other clean-cut young man. In the past several days, he'd made a new habit of walking over from the beach each morning, silently walking up and down the aisles, hands behind his back as if he was making sure all was in order.

Jackson and I watched Travis walk around for a few minutes before he left in silence.

"Is Travis coming in every day now?" Jackson broke our silence.

"Just this past week. My goal is to get him to talk to me. Susan warned me it could take months." She'd told me of the importance of routine for him, and his wariness of people.

"I think he's got a crush on you," Jackson said. "Guess I've got competition. Speaking of competition, I heard Curt asked you out." His arms were crossed over the chest I'd leaned into over a week ago. Although I didn't know him well, his feigned indifference didn't fool me.

Sarcasm itched to roll off my tongue. "I forgot how quick word spreads in a small town."

"When did he ask you out?"

About five days after your kisses burned a brand on my hormones. "Last week. Why?"

I wanted to hear his reasoning.

He pushed himself away from the wall with his shoulder. "Just wondering if he'd already asked you out before Tracie's party. Curious about why you kissed me."

"Why *I* kissed *you*?" My mind hit instant replay. He kissed me first, didn't he? *Please God, tell me he made the first move.* "Same reason you kissed me. There was a lot of emotion that night."

He took the few steps between us until he was close enough for me to smell his shampoo, close enough to see he'd shaved that morning, close enough to feel a lightning bolt melt my core.

"You're going out with him because I was gone? Is that how you city women think?"

His words stung me as his eyes turned ice-blue. I wanted to say *no*, at least not this "city girl." He left as two customers came in. Where were they a minute ago?

I wanted to tell him about the night we played pool together when Wendy had indicated Jackson toyed with women until he tired of them. It was a comment stuck on repeat in my head. *Yet you kissed him like he was a hot fudge sundae you'd been denied, Molly.*

* * *

Gentle rain moved in late Sunday afternoon on Memorial Day weekend, which cut down on the last-minute customers for the night. I'd let Susan and Adam go home after a day where I felt I'd been stuck in the eye of a tornado, I counted down the minutes until I could lock the door. I planned to eat everything in my fridge before a long soak in a bubble bath with the window wide open to take in the cleansing scent of rain. I'd light some candles, enjoy a glass of wine…

"Are you the new so-called owner of Rosie's?" A high-pitched voice jolted me from my dream. It belonged to a well-coifed woman, probably early sixties, meticulously dressed, with each strand of her short, tinted blonde hair in place. A small designer purse hung from her elbow as if she were perusing items at Tiffany's. Her umbrella dripped on my counter.

"Yes, I'm Molly. Can I help you?" And I don't sell fine jewelry.

Her eyes dissected me. "Hmmm. You look pretty much like I thought you would. Taller than I expected though."

"Excuse me, but do I know you? What did you say your name was?"

"I am sorry. I'm Nancy Brennan, Jackson's mother."

I got the vibe this woman had never been sorry in her life. If she could lie, so could I. "Nice to meet you. Did you know my mother?" My pleasantry was strangling me.

"I'm not from around here." She wrinkled her nose as if a dog had defecated at her feet. "I've seen pictures of your mother from when she was employee of my dear Aunt Rosie."

I waited to hear the purpose of her visit, wishing a last-minute customer would come in and interrupt our tense non-conversation. "Is your cabin close to town? Jackson didn't say what lake it's on."

"Talk to Jackson a lot, do you?" Nancy's eyebrow reached an impressive height. Her fake tanned face didn't move a muscle other than her pale pink lipsticked mouth.

I swallowed all the sarcastic words pleading to be said.

"My cabin is just a mile from town. I stay here each summer so I can visit my Jackson." Nancy pursed her lips as if she should never have to stoop to answer a question. Her cat eyes perused my counter…church cookbooks stacked up for sale, a coffee can with a slit on top advertising the latest area fundraiser. Her arm flinched as if the items might bite her.

"Is there something I can help you with? Did you want to look around at the changes? I tried to keep the feel of Rosie in the store, and other than fresh coats of paint and a few flooring changes, the store and house haven't changed much."

"Don't act as if you knew my aunt." Apparently, Nancy was skipping pleasantries.

I could stand there for an hour until she decided it was time to state her purpose. Honestly, I couldn't take another minute. My feet were killing me. It was time to close.

How had Jackson grown up with this wretch? It explained a few things about him.

"I will not tolerate you causing problems in this town like your mother and family did, and then up and leave, just as they did. It will tarnish my dear aunt's name and the reputation she built over the years at her store. My son has warned me you've been a trouble-maker already." Nancy leaned forward and pointed one manicured finger at me. "I am here to warn you. I'm watching you, and Jackson and I will *not* put up with you trashing this place that you were so generously *given.* Understood?"

If I hadn't been so positive it was a man's hand at Tracie's that night, I'd have put her at the top of the suspect list. I was shocked, and yes, offended, by her words. By the time I thought of an equally rude comeback, she'd opened the umbrella she'd let drip all over, turned on her pink high heels, and sashayed out.

I stomped over to the front door and locked it behind her. "Who the hell wears high heels in Love?" I shouted to the empty store. I yanked the OPEN sign chain and the neon words went dark, letting everyone outside know, in no uncertain terms that I was *not* open anymore.

All the outside lights that had been flipped on in the graying rain were now shut off. I took the two cash drawers out of the tills and headed back to the kitchen table. Before doing another thing, I poured a glass of wine, picked up my phone and called Ella.

After hanging up with her an hour later, I missed my friend even more. We called each other often since I'd moved in early April, but it wasn't the same as living by each other. And we were both heading into the busy season at our jobs. She promised to take a few days off during the week to visit me soon, and my chest unclenched a bit. I needed her wisdom in person.

Chapter 12

Susan covered for me the following morning, my first day to sleep in since I'd opened the store six weeks ago. I spent part of the day shopping in the closest town with a Target store, nearly an hour away, stocking up on items not found in Love. I also indulged myself with a spruced-up coffee from Starbucks, a treat for me now…one I'd taken for granted living in Minneapolis. Yes, I could drive to the small coffee shop in Blue Bay on my day off, but you'd have to have a fierce coffee craving to make that half-hour round trip.

I'd researched the possibility of a future coffee bar. And I wished for the hand-dipped ice cream Rosie had. I promised myself I'd have them both, eventually. One thing at a time. Today was a day for relaxing. Charlee had invited me to her home several times. I finally had the chance today.

After supper, I rode my bike five miles west of town to Charlee's small hobby farm. Mother Nature had been itching for a real storm since the gentle rain a few nights before. The air was heavy, clouds rolled in, and the humidity did a number on my curly hair. On any given summer day my hair resembled Roseanne Roseannadanna's wild style. Dressed in old cutoff jean shorts and a tank top, I'd have worn my bikini if I'd dared. I clipped my hair up to keep it off my neck and filled my water bottle.

I'd met Charlee's other children, both young teens, the first time she stopped by the store after I'd hired Adam and Logan. As I pedaled up their long gravel driveway, I spied Charlee with her daughters, planting seeds in their enormous garden.

"Hey, Molly," Charlee called out. All three wore knee pads as they crawled along, digging a few inches down and placing seeds in holes before covering them. Charlee stood up, rubbing the small of her back. "Are you here for your gardening lesson?" She teased.

"That's about the only thing you *don't* need to teach me." If there were ever an Apocalypse, I was going to live with Charlee. She was a survivor. "My mom was a teacher. She planted a garden every spring and I enjoyed helping her. She never got into canning though, too busy in the fall with teaching."

Charlee glanced at my tank top. "You aren't dressed for digging in manure. Let's get you an old shirt of mine." She pulled off knee pads from her muscular legs and led the way to her house. In her backyard were rows of neatly stacked, split wood. Currently adding to the piles were Adam, his younger brother…and Jackson. Shirtless and gleaming with sweat.

"Hey there, Molly," Adam called out. "Did you come to help us stack wood?" He joked as he continued hauling and stacking.

"Thanks, I'll play gardener instead. You guys are crazy to be working in this heat and humidity." As I spoke, I remembered Jackson's promise to finish my woodpile when the weather was nice. Well, if his mom was right and Jackson had a bone to pick with me again, that would explain why he was out here instead of at my house. He surely didn't owe me. I owed him.

"It's our mother. She's a slave-driver." Adam called out. I barely glanced at him. Instead, I watched Jackson wipe the sweat from his face with a towel before lifting a large jug of water and tipping it back for a long drink, wiping the dribble off his chin with his forearm as his eyes locked on mine. It was a replay of the day at my house, only about forty degrees warmer now…which must've been the reason heat now ran from my cheeks all the way down to my toes.

I forced myself to turn and follow Charlee inside. She dug out a clean, old top for me. "Do you want to change your shorts or are those okay?" She eyed my frayed jean shorts, not sure if they were new but meant to look old, or if in fact, they were old shorts.

"No, these are fine. Thanks." I changed my shirt while Charlee retrieved a pitcher of lemonade from the fridge and some plastic glasses before we headed back outdoors.

Charlee walked the lemonade and cups over to Jackson and the boys as I looked around at their quaint setting—the fertilized, earthy scent from her two tilled gardens, the chickens clucking in their pen—while not a single car drove by on the gravel road.

"Does Jackson usually help the boys?" I asked as we walked back to the garden.

"We buy our wood from him. He's been great about helping ever since my ex-husband left years ago. My sons consider him like a big brother. I think he enjoys 'teaching' them a thing or two."

Charlee's ex-husband had left for a fishing trip to Alaska when they were married and never came back, leaving her with four small children and no money.

Eventually she was able to obtain a Divorce by Publication and get on with her life. "I'd have picked a cooler night for 'class.'" I took my own glass of cold lemonade and held it to my face.

Charlee laughed. "I agree. The boys don't care, they enjoy being with Jackson. He's usually so busy that I gladly take his help whenever he has time."

Back inside the fenced garden, I took a bag of green bean seeds from Logan and started planting a new row. There was little conversation between us as we worked in rhythm planting seeds. I was so deep in relaxation mode I didn't notice the dark clouds.

Charlee stopped and stood to stretch her muscles. "As much as I enjoy having you here and appreciate the help, you might want to start heading home. It's looking pretty dark in the west." She pointed to the ominous clouds making their way toward us.

I marked the place where I'd stopped planting and set the rest of my seeds back with the other bags before standing to stretch. I said goodbye to the girls before walking with Charlee to my bike. The air was so thick you could slice it with a knife.

"I can throw your bike in the back of Adam's truck and give you a ride," Charlee offered. "I'm afraid you won't make it back to town before those clouds open up."

"That's okay. You've got work to finish. What's the worst that can happen to me? If I get wet, it will be refreshing."

"How about Jackson? He'll be heading back through town soon. He can give you a lift."

My heart did a little jig thinking about sitting with him in his pickup. "Nope. Thanks though." Her eyebrows rose at my answer. I'd have loved to tell Charlee about my conversation with Jackson's mom but didn't want to discuss it with her kids around. Or Jackson.

I gave Charlee a sticky hug goodbye, refilled my water bottle, and promised to send the top back with Logan after I washed it. I hopped on my bike and was a mile from her home when the sky opened. Hard raindrops pelted my eyes, making it nearly impossible to see.

Thinking it wouldn't last long, I rode into a gravel driveway and took shelter under a large oak tree. I was drenched, and cold. The temperature had taken a quick dive.

I was reaching for my phone in my shorts pocket hoping to call Charlee before it got too wet when a dark pickup drove by slowly, its headlights illuminating the gray. It slowed after passing me, backed up, and stopped. The window rolled down, and above the thunder of the rain, I heard a man shouting for me to get in the truck. Jackson.

"That's okay, I'll wait it out. It shouldn't last much longer." I shouted over the downpour, praying my stubbornness wouldn't give me pneumonia.

He turned into the driveway, leaned over and opened the passenger door. "Don't be a fool, Molly. Get in this truck. The storm could last an hour and then it'll be *really* dark." I could hear the exasperation in his voice. He was right, I was being childish.

I swallowed my pride. It was nearing sundown anyway so even if the storm let up, it would be dark soon. And I was chilled to the bone.

I went to the back of Jackson's truck and loaded my bike into the truck bed. The passenger door was still open, but the window was now rolled up. I slid onto the wet seat. Jackson had the heat blasting and as soon as I shut the door, I sighed with relief at the warmth enveloping me. I'd gone from sweating to freezing. This was bliss.

He sat there with the truck in park, resting both his arms on the steering wheel and staring at me as if waiting for something.

"You didn't even get out to put my bike in the back." I itched to pick a fight, so I could bring up what I really wanted to ask—why he'd labeled me a troublemaker to his mom.

Instead of firing back, he sighed. "Now what's crawled up your butt, Molly?"

"What do you mean?"

"I mean what's eating you this time?" The rain and wind whipped against the truck, making it necessary for him to shout. Or maybe I frustrated him.

"I beg your pardon?"

"You're acting like a stubborn mule. You want to tell me why you'd rather stand out in the cold rain instead of accepting a ride from me?"

His eyes searched my face which had to resemble a raccoon with my mascara running. My hair felt messed up like a wet bird's nest. His eyes moved down past my neck. I looked at my top which appeared painted on, allowing my small breasts to show how chilled I was.

Jackson's weathered hand now rested mere inches from my shoulder. His T-shirt was stuck to his muscular torso, and golden-brown hair on his arms still held beads of moisture.

"I'm guessing that, like the store, you assumed I couldn't make it home on my own. Well, I've got every intention of making it in the store. And," I reached over and poked him in the chest, "I could well have made it home tonight without your help. I'm not some weak damsel and I'm *not* a troublemaker!" My chattering teeth didn't help convey my anger.

He held up his hands and stifled a smile. "Whoa, girl."

My annoyance was steaming. "You think it's funny, don't you?"

"Hey, calm down. I don't know what the hell you're ranting about." He reached over and wrapped one of my curls around his finger. "What happened to our truce?"

"That's what I'd like to know." My anger mellowed a bit. "Why do you say mean things about me?"

His thumb moved slowly across my face, wiping at my mascara streaks as he frowned. "Other than when you first came to town, I haven't said anything about you."

I turned to watch the downpour. "Did you know your mom came to see me in the store?"

"Hell, no! What was she in there for?" He pulled his hand away as if my words were full of electricity. His surprise was too genuine for me not to believe him.

"She stopped in and sort of threatened me."

"About what? Oh, I probably don't want to hear this." He rubbed his face and shook his head. "I should've warned you she was back for the summer. She normally doesn't grace me with her presence until early June. I have a feeling she came to town early because her curiosity of you got the best of her."

I relayed my conversation with his mom.

"Holy hell, Molly, don't listen to her. She's a bitter, greedy, unhappy woman."

"But she's your mother."

"I know. And I love her, but I'm also well aware of her flaws. I'm sorry. I did *not* call you a troublemaker. She feels you took her inheritance and believes your grandpa snuck his family out of town, leaving a lot of unpaid bills in his wake, along with unpaid workers. In her eyes, you are somehow responsible for your families past transgressions."

Jackson stifled a snort. "She doesn't see the irony in that. Mom came from a tough upbringing, really tough. It would be like people blaming her for her father's actions years ago. But she doesn't see it. Everything is money driven for her. Dad has sunk a fistful of money into renovations of our old family cabin to meet mom's high expectations as if she'd been born with a silver spoon in her mouth." He shrugged. "I know she wasn't, but she doesn't want anyone else to know. She's so worried what people will think of her."

We sat in silence. I went from being angry at him to feeling sorry for him. I didn't want to feel anything for him. "Are you going to take me home or are we going to sit here all night and talk about our feelings? I know men love that."

Jackson laughed as he unwound his finger which had found its way back to my curls—too distracting for my peace of mind. He shifted the truck into reverse and backed out of the driveway. "Okay, princess, we're on our way." We rode in silence, pulling into my backyard driveway minutes later. The storm had let up a bit, but it was still raining hard.

There sat my woodpile. "You need to tell me what I owe you for the work you've done so far here. I'll pay you, I promise." I batted my eyes and gave him a cheesy smile.

Jackson grinned before hopping out to lift the bike out of his truck bed. Apparently, we weren't going to talk about my woodpile.

I got out of his truck. "Thank you." Raindrops dripped from my hair onto my face.

"You're welcome." He held onto my bike just as I did, waiting for him to let go, even though we were getting more waterlogged by the second. "I'll come over sometime this week and finish the wood. And I'll talk to my mom. There, am I back in your good graces?"

"Don't push it, Brennan. You're still a burr in my butt." I pulled my bike away from him and started for my back door.

"And might I say what a nice butt it is." He yelled as he climbed back into his truck.

I smiled as I ran inside to the dry comfort of my house. Scratch that…my home.

Chapter 13

Ella took a couple days off from work in early June to visit, and I scheduled help to cover for me in the store. Early Tuesday morning, I rustled her awake. "Let's grab some coffee and head across the street to the beach." Sitting on the sugar sand as the sun rose over the rippling lake and listening to the call of the loons was a gift I rarely allowed myself. Mornings were too rushed since I opened the store by 6:45.

"Crazy girl. I'm on vacation." Ella's auburn hair was strewn over her pillowcase and face. Fifteen years as best friends told me I was pushing it. Morning was Ella's nemesis.

I bounced on the edge of the bed in the guest bedroom until she caved. We filled travel mugs with coffee before walking across the empty street in our cotton shorts and tank tops. We'd missed the sunrise, but the mist hovering above the calm lake still made giving up sleep worthwhile. "You're so lucky to have this right at your doorstep."

"I am, but I haven't had much chance to enjoy it yet." It was comforting to have Ella beside me. There was no friend like an old friend. "You sure you and Rolf don't want to move up to this area? You'd make a great realtor over at Blue Bay. They have plenty of gazillion-dollar homes you could sell there on the chain of lakes."

"That *is* tempting, but I think you forget that Rolf would struggle to find a scientific engineering job in this area."

"He can come visit you on weekends." I nudged her.

"Yeah, right. Not to change the subject, but is there any update on the asshole who threatened you at Tracie's party last month?"

"Nothing yet. Rick even went so far as to call or visit every guy they saw at the party. Of course, nobody confessed. They're now wondering if it was some uninvited guy who snuck into the party, which I guess is normal here since word gets around about parties."

"No trouble since then?"

"No, thank goodness. I'm hoping it was just some drunk playing a mean prank."

"Some prank. I hope you're right though."

We sat for over two hours, relaxing and catching up on life. "We should go shower and get ready to pick up Tracie." Tracie had the day off from the Hardware store and the three of us were making a half-hour drive to meet Charlee for lunch at a café close to the clinic where she worked in a nearby town.

* * *

The concept of raffling off meat seemed bizarre to me but one that was a common event at local bars. According to Charlee and Tracie, it was time for Ella and me to experience one.

During our lunch, Tracie and Charlee had suggested we all meet at the Pickled Perch for their weekly meat raffle…a local event I'd yet to attend. After Charlee was done with work, she joined the three of us at a small table in the crowded bar. We ordered a pitcher of beer and buffalo chicken wings.

A large table full of packaged meat sat on display. Nearby was Drive by Daisy—Ms. Sleuth who'd badgered me before Memorial Day with such boring questions like what I'd had for dinner the night before. She held a purple megaphone and her canary yellow polyester pants glowed like a thin ray of sunshine in the packed bar.

After purchasing our meat raffle tickets, we visited as I took in the crowd, recognizing a few faces. Right before the meat raffle was to start, spritely Daisy walked around with her megaphone to each table "shushing" us and usually getting a round of laughter in reply.

As she neared our table, she leaned in. "I'll stop by your store next week for news." She did a loud stage whisper as if we were conspirators on getting the gossip out to the public. Daisy might not weigh more than ninety pounds, but her tenacity for juicy news packed a big punch.

Ella practically rolled on the ground when people started winning in the meat raffle. I was torn between mortification and surprise as each winner chose their meat prize, and then had to take the megaphone and do a voice impression of the animal. We heard everything from pig oinks, turkey gobbles, cow mooing, and chicken clucking—out of the mouths of big strapping young men and nicely-dressed middle-aged women. Nobody brought their pride to a meat raffle.

And when I won and had to cluck like a chicken, I figured *what the hell.* I went all out flapping my arms like wings and strutting like a proud rooster.

This crazy town was rubbing off on me.

* * *

Ella and I walked to the post office before she left the next morning. There stood Old Lloyd again, chewing the fat with a lady at the counter. I'd given up saying hello to him each morning, knowing I'd get nothing but a glare in return.

Not Ella. Clearly, she didn't remember him from the café last winter. She flashed him her professional smile as she waited for me to empty my post office box.

Her cheery "hello" was answered with a grumble.

"I remember you." Old Lloyd studied Ella's unusual copper-colored hair.

"You do? I live in Minneapolis." She gestured toward me. "I've been visiting my friend Molly here." Even though Old Lloyd's mouth resembled a ruler, Ella continued to smile.

Old Lloyd's white hair flopped over one eye as he muttered under his breath.

"Have you lived here all of your life? Molly's family is from here. Maybe you knew them." Someone must've fed five buck's worth of quarters in chatty-Ella. I locked my post office box and headed for the door, never expecting to hear his voice.

The gravelly sound bounced off the wood-paneled walls. "Sure have. Knew her family too. Collins' family was no good."

I spun around, one hand on the door and the other clutching my mail. "Excuse me?"

My mother's maiden name was Collins.

"Your grandpa was Carl." He huffed out an accusation.

"Yes. You remember him?" I braced myself for his answer. I'd never met my grandpa. He'd died before I was born.

"Wish I wouldn't have. He owned the lumberyard and left all us loggers high and dry as he snuck out of town with our money." Old Lloyd stuck up his overgrown nose and huffed, reminding me of Grumpy from The Seven Dwarfs.

I sucked in enough air to float away like a balloon. "My grandpa wouldn't do that!" *How in the hell would I know? I knew nothing about him. Thanks, Mom.*

Ella, speechless for the first time ever, tugged at my hand and led me out the door.

I continued to rant all the way back to my kitchen where I tossed the mail on the table. "I doubt Old Lloyd is the only old person here who remembers my grandpa. Now I'm going to have people cop an attitude about me for something my grandpa supposedly did?" Each word matched my stomping back and forth. Ella let me go on until I ran out of steam.

My frustration was followed by watching her pack. I wanted to jump inside her suitcase.

"Call your dad. He must know *something.*" Ella zipped up her luggage.

"When can you visit again?" I whined like a two-year-old as we walked out to her car.

"Hopefully soon. I don't want to miss out on more beach time." She hugged me hard.

I waved goodbye long after she pulled out of my driveway.

I collected my overloaded thoughts before I picked up my cell phone to call my dad.

It was mid-morning. He'd be done golfing by now. When he answered, we discussed the weather in both of our states and other pleasantries before I laid out Old Lloyd's accusations.

His sigh sounded like a deflating balloon. "I don't know much more than you do, Molly. Your mom's parents both died before I met her. Her three sisters have lived out east since before we met and there were very few visits between them. I can only tell you that your mom said things were hard for them before her family moved from Love. Her father's sawmill business was failing and your mother had just graduated from high school. The rest of her family moved out east, your mom stayed in Minnesota and went to college in the Twin Cities."

I digested this information as I made myself some iced tea and took it out to the back deck steps. "Your grandpa needed help with your aunts, so he moved with his younger daughters to Maine where his sister lived." Dad's voice dragged. "That's about all I know."

"Mom never said anything about him leaving town because he owed people money?"

"Well, I imagine he did. That area was big into logging, and I understand your grandpa's sawmill had mechanical problems that he didn't have the money to fix. Between that and trying to raise four daughters without their mom, I'm guessing it all took a financial toll." He paused. "Why are people giving you grief over something that happened fifty years ago? See? That's why I've never been a fan of small towns. People have long memories there. They shouldn't be badgering you about something better left forgotten."

I closed my eyes as the sun warmed my face. Distant voices from people enjoying the beach across the road danced in the air. I tried picturing the town as it was fifty years ago. "I feel sorry for Grandpa; I can't imagine what he went through. Poor Mom. I remember her talking about taking care of her younger sisters after Grandma died. It had to have been tough on all of them, and with no money, and Grandpa losing his business…wow."

Fear of not making it in the store gnawed at me. Still, if that happened, it would only bring me down. I didn't have the weight of responsibility for children, the way my grandpa had.

"Yes, well, now you understand why Rosie was probably so important to your mom."

"Do you know if Grandpa ever paid any of the people here back?"

"Once she started teaching, your mom saved as much as she could and sent checks to the workers and businesses she'd remembered her dad owed. She paid some of the bigger accounts she was aware of. That was about seven years or more after they'd moved."

I walked around the backyard needing to release some frustrated energy. I remembered her telling me she'd traveled for years, teaching in the poorest schools, helping children who were getting very little help from anyone else. Back in Minneapolis, teaching at a low-income school, she'd met my dad, and that was the last of her traveling to teach. She couldn't have made much money during those early years, yet she'd managed to send what she could to cover Grandpa's outstanding debts.

I'd ask Lloyd if he heard from my mom. If not, it wasn't for lack of trying on her part.

After Dad and I hung up, I glanced at my watch. I had another hour before I needed to relieve Susan in the store. I went inside and made a tuna sandwich, poured some more iced tea, and walked across the street to the beach, finding a secluded area to sit and enjoy the breeze off the lake while I rehashed this news about my mom. My family had a history in this town, just like many other locals. I had as much of a right to be here as anyone else.

And as soon as I found out who threatened me at Tracie's, I was going to let him know I had no plans to leave this town unless it was *my* decision.

* * *

On Sunday night, Ernie came over and we barbequed burgers. Closing at six on Sunday nights gave me a few hours of daylight and a chance to enjoy the late spring nights. Starting next week—mid-June—I'd change my hours and close at nine every night but Sundays. Summers were short. If I didn't capture the beach business while it lasted, I'd be sorry.

Over our juicy hamburgers, I relayed my conversation with my dad to Ernie.

"You knew all of this already, didn't you?" There'd been no surprise reaction from him.

He gave me a small nod before taking a long drink of his lemonade. "I am glad your father informed you about your mother paying back some of her father's debt."

"Do you think I should say something to Old Lloyd?"

Ernie leaned back and slipped his thumbs under his suspender straps. "I have known Old Lloyd a good many years. Some people have a hard time leaving the past where it should be left. If it will make your heart feel lighter, I recommend you share your thoughts with Old Lloyd. You may change his mind. If you do not, it is through no fault of yours."

"I'm being judged for something I have no control over."

He put his dark hand on my pale one. "I understand, all too well."

We moved on to other subjects, and before Ernie made his way across the field back toward his home, he reminded me, "This town is worth staying in. Put your head and heart into things and it will work out. And don't forget to have some fun once in a while."

I stooped to hug him and reminded him I'd had plenty of fun with Ella this past week. But Ernie was right. On Tuesday, I planned to go exploring on my bike. There was so much of the area I'd yet to see.

I left home mid-morning with a small cooler strapped to the handlebars of my bike. After two hours of pedaling on various side roads, I came to one that wound around a small, secluded lake. Stopping at the deserted boat access, I parked the bike and slipped off my tennis shoes. Not quite noon, it had to be nearing ninety degrees. I walked the gravel access to the lakes' edge and waded in knee-deep, the coolness offsetting my upper body, damp with perspiration.

Before stopping at the landing, I'd heard what sounded like someone chopping wood, likely out in the middle of the woods—too far away for me to worry about them. All was quiet now. I didn't see any sign of life at the only home across the small lake. The water felt too good to not take advantage of it. I slipped off my shorts and tank top. *Better leave the bra and underwear on, just in case.* Diving into the water, it was a sharp contrast to the heat of my body. I surfaced a few yards out, feeling exhilarated and refreshed.

After floating on my back for several minutes, I spotted an eagle swooping down in the distance to retrieve a fish from the lake before he flew away. A flock of ducks landed at the other end of the lake, making a fluttery splash-landing. I stood waist deep and breathed in slowly, closing my eyes as the June sun warmed my skin.

A pair of loons yodeled nearby and the serene setting filtered its way inside me, calming me in a way I hadn't experienced for a long time. I could've fallen asleep standing mid-waist in the water…until a man yelled from behind me.

Chapter 14

I swung around, my eyes wide. "What in the world?" I ducked under the water up to my neck when I spotted Jackson. "You scared me half to death!"

He smiled and stepped closer to the waters' edge. "Curiosity got the better of me and I just had to find out who the intruder was. Damn horsefly bit me and gave away my spying."

"Intruder? Please tell me you don't own this lake."

Jackson laughed. "Nope. Wish I did though. This is Whispering Lake, and I'm the only homeowner on it. Most of the lakeshore is tax forfeited."

His eyes kindly stayed focused on my face. "I was home minding my own business when I noticed movement across the lake. I needed to check it out and make sure nobody was casing my place from over here." He winked.

"Yeah, right." I pointed to my clothing hanging from my bike handlebars. "Would you please toss me my top and shorts?"

Instead of listening to me, he peeled off his T-shirt and bent down to unlace his boots.

"What're you doing?" I eyed him like he was a boa constrictor ready to strike.

"What do you think?" He toed off his boots and pulled off his socks.

"Oh, no you don't. Go swim at your own place." I backed up further into the lake.

"What? Are you saying you now own this side of the lake, Miss O'Brien? I do believe this is a public access, and I have every right to the water over here too." He looked down at his legs. "You're lucky I forgot a towel. If I take these jeans off, I'll never get 'em back on over my wet legs." He looked unhappy about it.

Before I had a chance to exit the water, Jackson made a run for it and dove in. Surfacing, he let out a howl. "Wow; that feels good!" He raked back the wet hair from his face. My body stiffened.

"Relax," he said as he swam toward me. "I'm not going to do anything…unless you want me to." He grinned.

"Don't even think of coming near me. You want to cool off, do it over there." I pointed to several feet away. "How did you get here? And aren't you supposed to be at work today?" I didn't see a bike, hadn't heard a car.

"Business was slow this morning so I took the day off to cut wood. When I glimpsed activity here at the boat landing, I went in my house, grabbed my binoculars, put my black lab, Trigger, inside so he wouldn't follow me, and walked the four-wheeler path along the shoreline over to here." He smiled. "I went through a lot of effort just to come and bother you."

"Gee, thanks." I was smiling too much to even pretend to be upset.

"When I saw you with your barely-there bra and panties on, I felt it was my duty to come over and warn you about the big fish in this lake that like to nibble on pale, tender skin."

"Hmmmm…now you're telling me?"

"I'm here to protect you now. I was too busy dodging the horseflies and mosquitoes on my way here. All warnings I was going to give you fled my brain."

He dove under, swam toward me and grabbed my shins. My yelp vibrated off the water as he surfaced. "Sorry." He looked anything but sorry. It would be a huge mistake if he touched me anywhere above my knees.

A fistful of heartbeats happened as we stared at each other. He took the small step needed to pull me to him. Shoulder-deep in the water, he closed the gap between our mouths. The tenseness in my body liquidated to a warm pool of desire.

This was different than the night at Tracie's. That had been an unplanned kiss fueled by alcohol and emotion. I'd convinced myself he'd been comforting me then. He wasn't comforting me now. He was stirring up a whole slew of hormones in me. It was becoming painful, not comforting. His hands settled on the small strip of material on my panties. The muscles in his legs touched mine. I itched to wrap my legs around him.

When our lips parted, he whispered, "I'm not going to apologize for that." Sun sparkled against the top of the lake, shimmering sun-diamonds around him. The last thing I wanted from him was an apology. In fact, I didn't care if he uttered another word.

"I suppose the decent thing for me to do is bring you your clothes." He looked to the shore where my clothes hung over my bike. "I'm struggling to be decent."

I didn't want decent. "Thank you." He walked back to shore, picked up my shorts and tank top, and walked them back. Turning, he waded back to shore allowing me to walk out of the water to dress while his back was turned.

I met him at my bike, fully dressed. "Why even bother wearing those underthings? My dental floss is bigger than that string on your panties."

"We wear them simply to torture men."

"Well, you do a damn good job of it." He looked across the lake.

"If you have time, do you want to come over and see my place?"

"I've got the whole afternoon off. I'm curious to see where you spend your time thinking up ways to torment me."

"Let's not talk about tormenting." He rolled his eyes before leading the way as I walked my bike behind him on the trail. We sped up the pace, fighting to keep the mosquitoes and biting flies at bay. Soon, we made it to the clearing of his property. His log-sided home sat at the top of a meticulously groomed gentle slope overlooking the lake and creek.

Jackson led the way to the back door. As we entered the mudroom, we were greeted by a loud bark from his black lab whose size resembled a small horse. "Back off, Trigger." He playfully pushed the hundred-plus pound animal out of the way before I stepped inside.

"Just a second here. I'll put the big lug back outside where he belongs." He looped a finger under Trigger's collar and led him out the screen door. "Trig is just a big overgrown baby who assumes every person who comes to my house has shown up to play with him."

He walked from the mudroom, down a small hall, and into his spacious home. He waved his arm casually to encompass it all. "Here it is; where I spend all my waking hours trying to figure out how I can be a thorn in Molly O'Brien's behind."

Full-length windows stretched over the entire length of the living and dining rooms, giving a person the feeling they could reach out and touch the lake. A tongue and groove vaulted ceiling tied the open rooms together and a center island separated the spacious kitchen from the dining area. Simple, masculine furniture was strategically placed in the living room offering a person the best of views. Hardwood flooring covered the home along with a few throw rugs.

"I like it. And you can't beat the view. I haven't noticed a voodoo doll lying around here yet that resembles me." My eyebrows rose.

He chuckled. "I keep the voodoo doll in my bedroom for all the evil thoughts that come to me at night." He walked to the refrigerator. "Can I get you a beer or something?"

"That sounds great." I followed him into the kitchen, taking the ice cold bottle he offered me. "Do I need to check for poison?" I held the amber bottle to the sunlight.

He took the beer from my hands, took a quick swig, and then handed it back. "There. No poison, at least not in that sip. Maybe it all sunk to the bottom." He gently tweaked my cheek.

"I'm going to run upstairs and change out of these jeans. Be right back." Jackson jogged up the steps and was back with shorts on in less than a minute. He reached for my hand and led me outside. The deck wrapped around most of his home giving a full view of both the creek and lake. When Trigger heard us, he bolted up to join us.

I glanced across the lake to the access. What a calming, gorgeous view.

"So you knew that was me across the lake?"

He pulled out a chair for me at the patio table and sat down next to me. "Not until I looked through my binoculars." Jackson studied my face. "You know, sometimes you look so fearless, like you could take on the world. Other times, like when I watched you in the lake, you look so vulnerable that I forget about that sharp-tongued side of you."

I kept silent. "I guess sometimes with you I can't tell if I'm moving two steps ahead or three steps back," he confessed.

"We haven't made an attempt on each other's life yet. I'd say our truce is leading toward friendship, don't you think?" Friendship was a far cry from how turned on I was in the lake.

He focused on his beer bottle. "Is that what we are, friends?"

I leaned back in my chair. "Aren't we? I'm a big enough girl to admit I was defensive at first, but we've been getting along now. I shouldn't have let your mother get to me. Have you talked to her about what she said to me?"

"Yep, I went over to her cabin that night after I dropped you and your bike off. It's like arguing with a wall. I don't know if reason will ever penetrate through her closed mind."

"I want to prove to your mom she's wrong about her preconceived notions of me."

"Good luck. You seem to be making headway with the locals though and that's important. Once the tourists and cabin owners are gone in the fall, you'll really appreciate the townspeople, so don't forget about them—which is easy to do when you're busy in the summer with tourists." He paused as if searching for words. "Like Curt Adamson. Did you go out with him yet?"

I burst out laughing. "You sound like a preteen trying to find out if a girl likes you. He asked me out. I said no. Although he seems like a nice guy."

"He's okay. If you don't mind settling for just 'okay.'"

I shrugged. "Eh. I've had 'okay' before. I'm looking for spectacular now."

His shoulders relaxed. He took my hand and led me out of my chair. Reaching up, he placed a hand on each of my hips and pulled me onto his lap. I wrapped my legs around either side of his, leaned in, and kissed him, plunging ahead with the passion I'd been holding back.

He moaned, reached his hands around to my lower back, and I smiled against his lips. He'd controlled himself to this point. I gave him credit for that. My lips moved to his cheek and neck. I lost track of time and where I was, but not whose lap I was sitting on. So when Jackson leaned back and put a distance between our bodies, reality stung me.

"You make it damn hard to think, Molly. You smell good, you taste good, you feel good…" He took a few deep breaths as if he was trying to calm himself.

"And…what?" I attempted to reel in my own overzealous emotion.

"And I'd like to ask you out. Wine and dine you, go for a ride and talk about our feelings, build you a bridge…whatever you want." He closed his eyes a second. "Because I can't seem to wipe out the image of you standing peacefully in the lake, drops of water glistening on your skin." He opened his eyes. "I'm trying to do the right thing." His voice was gruff with emotion.

I leaned back in, softly kissing his lower lip. "I think I'm available."

He took my hands that had been caressing his face and held them firmly between his.

"Molly, I've been in relationships before that have moved too fast and crashed. I don't want that to happen to us." He helped me off his lap and stood up, stepping away to put some physical distance between us.

The last thing I wanted was to go home.

The last thing I wanted to do was leap into a relationship like I had with Nick.

I was ticked off at Jackson for dousing my desire.

And yet, I respected him for it.

Chapter 15

Wednesday morning I turned on the store lights and found the minnow tank overflowing. Minnows had knocked out one of my plastic pipe intakes, thereby damming up the water until it overflowed onto the store floor. I lost most of my minnows and probably damaged the subflooring under the indoor/outdoor carpet. I called my bait distributor to bring more minnows—two days earlier than my normal scheduled delivery.

That was Wednesday. Thursday, a little girl plugged up the bathroom toilet in the store with a full roll of toilet paper until that also overflowed.

Friday brought a torrential downpour. Some of the ceiling tiles fell from a leak in the roof, which dumped water on the grocery shelving and ruined most of the cereal boxes. By that night, the rain turned to muggy, sticky, sweaty heat. My before-bread-was-invented air conditioner couldn't keep up. I propped open the front door of the store, hoping to capture a bit of the minimal breeze coming off the lake.

Logan was by my side. Shortly before we were ready to close, my feet and legs begging to be propped up in my recliner while I downed a cold beer, the shit hit the fan in the store.

"Ohmygodohmygodohmygoddddd!" Logan screamed down a grocery aisle toward me, an eight-pack of toilet paper held over her head, her face resembling a *Friday the 13th* horrified teen. Above her head circled a small black airplane—heading right toward me!

I dove for cover. "What was *that*?" I yelled to Logan from behind the counter. With my eyes and brain focused at high alert, I reached up to the counter and grabbed the phone. "Stay where you are, Logan. By the way, where are you?" What kind of employer was I? Letting her get eaten alive by a ginormous flying critter while I hid like chicken-liver.

"I'm behind the twelve-packs of pop display."

"Okay, stay there. I'll call Ernie." I hoped he was still awake.

Logan shouted from her hideout. "We need to get to the broom. Once the bat lands, we can sweep it into a bucket, cover it up with the broom and release it outside."

Ernie answered his phone and I relayed Logan's experienced wisdom. He snickered at my expense. "Do as Logan said, shut your front door, and I will be there in a few minutes."

My mind digested the word "bat." What in holy hell was it doing in my store? This one was surely genetically crossed with a 747 plane.

I wasn't budging from my hideout. I heard a rustle and saw Logan poke her head around the counter, toilet paper pack still held above her head.

"I'll get the broom and shut the door. You'll have to get up and help me find the bat."

"Over my dead body. Ernie will be here in a minute. He can help. That thing looked like it could eat us for dinner." City-girl was back, oozing from my every pore. I was closing in ten minutes and that flying vampire had better be out of here by then.

Logan had shut the front door and I heard the overhead bell ring as the door opened again. I peeked over the counter and released a sigh as Ernie walked in.

I stood up as Logan came around the corner with the broom from the kitchen and Ernie greeted us both with a shit-eating grin. "Save it." I held up my hand traffic cop-style.

"Is it only one bat?" He took the broom from Logan.

"What, one isn't enough? Have they been in here before?" I would never sleep again.

"Usually not until August. This hot, humid weather brings them out. You cannot leave the door open when it gets dark out." Ernie's old eyes scanned the ceiling of my store.

"My air conditioning can't keep up." I went over and turned the OPEN sign off.

Ernie shut off the light in the grocery section. "They usually do not fly if the light is on."

"Well, it did!" My brain filed that useful information. I could sleep if I left my light on.

Ernie found an empty box, and slowly walked up and down the two grocery aisles. I had locked the front door and was taking the drawers out of the cash registers when Ernie came up to me with the broom laying over the box opening. "Can you unlock the door for me so I can let this poor, confused thing go?" His mouth twitched.

"Why can't you just kill it?" I was overseeing this release to make damn sure that thing didn't make a U-turn and fly back in.

"They eat mosquitos, Molly. Bats are our friends."

"They aren't *my* friends." I unlocked the door and made sure Ernie went several feet away before releasing the bat. As I stood outside, a car pulled up with Logan's friends inside. "Have fun. See you in the morning." I waved goodbye as she got in the car.

I thanked Ernie a thousand times before he rounded the corner of the store to head back to his home. I opened and shut the store door at lightning speed while eyeing the sky and had no more than locked the door again when I heard a banging on the door behind me.

I whirled around as if the bat had come back with its humungous wings beating down the door. There stood Jackson, holding a take-out bag from Flap Jack Fever, and a twelve-pack of Michelob. Maybe my storm cloud week had a silver lining after all.

After renting the wet/dry vac from Jackson's store three days in a row while he'd been at a buying show, Tracie must have filled him in on my week.

"My sources tell me you've had a shitty week. They also divulged that you had no plans for tonight other than a hot bubble bath—so I invited myself over. And I'm even willing to help you with that bath if needed." His smile was charming, one I'd thought of ever since Tuesday.

"How do you know I don't have plans for tonight?" Why was I making this difficult?

"Easy. I asked Tracie." He leaned in, whispering in my ear. "You should pick better friends who won't cave so easy with your personal information."

There had to be a straight shot from my ear to every nerve ending in my body. He hadn't touched me—yet. But I was as aware of Jackson as if he was lying on top of me naked.

I willed myself to turn and give him my best poker face. "I guess you can stay, only because I smell Scratch's awesome stir-fry. Plus, I'd kill for an ice-cold beer."

"What you meant was, 'thank you, Jackson, I don't know what I'd do without you,' right?" He helped shut off the lights around the store. I picked up the cash drawers and locked them in the safe. I'd balance the drawers before I opened tomorrow.

We entered my kitchen and were greeted by the outside cat who had been hanging around and had somehow wormed her way into becoming a mostly inside cat. Nobody was more surprised than me that I'd become attached to a cat, whom I'd named Pixie. She gave Jackson a good once over. I'd have scolded her for not keeping the bat out but remembered she was in the house and the bat was in the store. I could see a bed for her behind the counter in the near future.

He twisted the cap off a Michelob for me. "Wow, what service." We washed our hands before he pulled out my chair and leaned down to softly kiss my cheek.

I eyed up a cleanly shaven, damp-haired Jackson. "Did you clean up for me?" I felt like a grubworm after a long day in the store, especially sitting next to pretty-boy.

A blush crawled across his face. "If I didn't know better, I'd think you were trying to court me, Mr. Brennan." I rocked my shoulders back and forth, batting my eyes.

He deflected the attention from his appearance to the food still in the to-go bag. "Remember, I did ask you for a date." He pointed to the to-go diner containers. "This isn't it. I thought we'd take a couple of chairs and go sit on the beach and eat."

"Great idea. I'd love to get outside and cool off." Now that darkness had set in, the temperature was bearable. I cleaned up, changed into a tank top and running shorts, and slipped on my flip-flops. Jackson filled a cooler with ice packs and beer.

We went through the back door, around the house and store, and walked to the beach, finding a secluded spot on the sand. "I've got a couple lounge chairs in the back of my pickup, I'll be right back." Jackson set the cooler down, and I unpacked the stir-fry. We were only fifty feet down the beach from the main stretch across from my store, but other than a handful of people walking along the sidewalk, it was deserted.

I sunk my feet into the cool, soft sand and sighed as the stress of the past few days evaporated from my body. Jackson returned with the chairs and we settled in, the cooler used as a small table between us. "Mmmmm, this is good." I mowed my way through my first plate.

"This is one of my favorite meals Scratch makes." Jackson waited for me to dish up my second helping before he filled his plate again. "I'm glad you were hungry. I was afraid you'd already eaten." He settled back into his chair and took a swig of beer.

"I hate being interrupted, so I usually just snack throughout the day. This is the most I've eaten at one sitting for a long time." I licked the hot sweet and sour sauce from my lips.

"Why was Ernie at the store tonight? Were you so busy you needed Logan *and* Ernie?"

I groaned. Should I lie? He'd find out the truth eventually from either Ernie or Logan.

"What? Was it that bad?"

I cringed, hoping to avoid honesty. "If I say I don't want to talk about it, will you agree?"

He leaned toward me. "Hell no. Now you've got my interest. If you don't tell me, I'll bug Ernie until he does."

I filled him in on the supersized Dracula bat, downplaying my sissy ways.

He clapped as if I'd described an Oscar performance. "I could've told you they'd show up sooner or later." Jackson's smile was stretched to the giddy point.

"They? You mean I should plan on this critter coming back with his aunts and uncles?"

He pointed to the tall pine trees lining the road and surrounding much of my yard. "Bats like to be near water, and like the pine trees. You've got the perfect environment for them."

"That's great news. I suppose snakes and spiders love this setting too?"

"You had the front door to the store open, didn't you? Don't do that. They might sneak in with a customer at night, but if you leave the door propped open, it's a free for all."

"I need a new air conditioner in the store. I could switch it out with the one in my house, which so far seems okay, but I get so little breeze back there, I hate to give it up."

"I'll swing in sometime tomorrow and take a look at the air conditioner. Maybe it just needs Freon. I tried to get Rosie to replace it a few years ago, but she was sure it would outlast her. As usual, she was right." Jackson set his empty bottle in the sand and pushed off his chair.

He stood and stretched, facing the lake. Jackson had a nice rear—there was no arguing that bald fact in front of me. He turned around and kneeled in the sand at the end of my chair.

He slipped off my green flip-flops. "What're you doing?" I trusted him about an inch.

"You've had a tough few days, I thought you could use a foot rub."

"I've been on my feet all day. I'm pretty sure you don't want to touch them."

He raised an eyebrow. "I can fix that." He scooped me up. My arms circled around his neck as he carried me to stand in the tepid lake. Our feet sunk into the sugar sand. He put his arms around my waist, his body flush behind me while the silvery moon reflected on the calm water. Even my toenails sighed. "Better?" He kissed me below my right ear.

I turned around and kissed him as if I'd been waiting days to do it. I had.

"Wow, remind me to stop by more often with food and beer."

"That was just to ensure I get that foot rub, Mr. Brennan."

"At your service, Princess." He scooped me up out of the water, carried me back to our chairs, and gently massaged my feet, enveloping them in his warm, strong hands.

"I'd moan, but I don't want you to get the wrong idea." I slid further down the lounge chair melting from his touch.

"Believe me, every idea I have right now is wrong." His voice was husky.

I had closed my eyes, enjoying the stress leaving my whole body via my left foot. When Jackson spoke, I opened one eye and looked at him. He wasn't smiling.

His look sent goosebumps dancing on my body, much as his massage was doing. When he reached for his beer, I sat up, grabbed his T-shirt, and pulled him on top of me. If I took him by surprise, he recovered well, as he barely skipped a beat by responding and taking the lead.

"Hell, if a foot rub does this to you, I can't wait to see what a back massage brings out." He leaned back and smiled.

"You're so funny." Kissing him was on a level similar to bungee jumping—exciting, scary, and addicting. Nothing like I'd ever experienced before. Including my years with Nick.

I slid my hands underneath his shirt, feeling the firm warmth of his skin. Right in the middle of my fantasy world, Jackson's strong arms pushed his body up and off me. His eyes were closed as he mumbled some stupid words I was sure had come out wrong.

"Huh?" I was trying to get my brain back to the twenty-first century.

"I said I should go." He pushed himself all the way up, his eyes rimmed with an apology.

"You can't be serious." I wiped my tangled hair out of my face and wrapped my arms around my suddenly chilled body. I sat up and tried to keep the hunger from my voice. "You look like you want to leave about as much as I want to step in front of a runaway train."

"Remember, the whole dating thing? I've been burned before, Molly, by jumping too quickly. Don't make this any harder than it already is." He leaned down and folded up his lounge chair, packed up the cooler, and waited for me to gather my wits and fold up my chair.

My electrified hormones were totally fine with take-out stir-fry and beer qualifying as a "date." Unfortunately, my hormones didn't get a say in the matter. I kept my chin up as we walked across the street, packing up my pride with our chairs.

A chill ran up my spine as we walked across the street in the dark and I found myself looking around. Streetlights softened the darkness, Jackson's hand was firmly on my back, yet I couldn't shake the sudden feeling we hadn't been alone on that beach.

I was too ticked off at Jackson for shutting me down to voice my paranoid instinct.

So I kept my feelings tucked inside me as he walked me to the door, kissed me, and then drove away in his pickup.

I slept with my bedroom light on.

Chapter 16

Ever since Pixie wormed her way into my house and heart, we'd developed a morning routine. She came out to the store while I cleaned out the dead minnows and then followed me outside while I buried them. Saturday morning was no different.

Except when I opened my door and we stepped out on my back deck, I noticed my car sitting unusually low to the ground.

I hurried down the steps, minnow pail in hand. All of my car tires were slashed.

Fear and anger enveloped me. Fear that whoever had done this was sneaking around my property during the night, and anger at the expense of replacing four tires.

Laughter bubbled out when I noticed my ten-year-old car had also been keyed. Didn't the person notice the dings all over this steal I'd bought last year?

I dug a hole for the dead minnows, left a few out on the ground for Pixie, and walked, shoulders slumped, back inside to open the store.

It wasn't long after I turned the key before Jackson sauntered in, a tool belt hanging from his waist. "I'll take a look at your sick air conditioner before I head to work."

He set his coffee mug down as he studied my grim face. "You still angry with me?"

I finished pouring water into the coffee pot. "Who said I was angry?" Fatigue clipped my words. My eyes focused on his Minnesota Twins baseball cap.

He burst out laughing. "You looked like Puff the Magic Dragon last night. Smoke was coming out of your nostrils when we walked back here from the beach."

It wasn't one of my proudest moments. Right now though, it was way down on my list of concerns. I closed my eyes, seeing dollar signs. A hot tear slid out of my right eye.

Jackson came around the counter. "What is it, Molly?"

"Someone slashed my tires." My chin quivered.

"Are you kidding? I didn't notice it last night, so they must have done it after I left." He shook his head. "Dammit! This isn't good, Molly. That guy was right outside of your house while you were sleeping." He closed his eyes and rubbed them with his thumb and forefinger.

"I know. What I don't know is if I should call the cops? It seems so trivial…"

"Not when you put it together with being threatened at Tracie's party. Who do you have scheduled to help you in the store today?"

"Adam and Logan will be in soon. When they arrive, I'll call the sheriff's department."

"That's a good idea." His brow furrowed. "So, besides coming to look at your air conditioner, I came over to talk about a date. We can discuss that later though." He leaned in and kissed the tip of my nose. "I'm worried, Molly."

I nodded. I was too, but saying the words would only give them strength.

As I waited on customers, Jackson tinkered with the air conditioner. I heard him swear a few times as he dissected it and then begrudgingly put it all back together again.

"It's dead." Jackson delivered the obvious news. "You want some help in looking for a new one? I can show you what models I can order through Ace, or help you find something online. You're going to end up spending at least seven hundred for a decent one."

"I'll stop by the store later to order an air conditioner. I can't go through the summer without one." It was only mid-June. We could have another two months or more of hot weather.

I thanked him and gave him a quick kiss before a group of teenagers walked in the store.

After Logan and Adam arrived, I took my cell phone outside and paced alongside my car while I relayed what happened to my car to a Sheriff Deputy.

"Also, I was threatened over a month ago by some guy at a party, but we haven't been able to figure out who it was, yet."

"Did you report it?" The deputy asked.

"There wasn't much to report. An idle threat from a man I never saw, who didn't injure me. I didn't exactly have much information to pass on to you."

"We'll dispatch a deputy. We've got two crimes against you. They may not be related, but it's worth documenting everything in case something happens again. I'll start an ICR."

"What's that?"

"Initial Complaint Report. It's a case number. Some call it a CFS, which stands for Calls for Service."

Whatever they called it, it made it all too real. "I'll be here all day." I'd run to the hardware store now, before a deputy arrived.

Before leaving to order an air conditioner, I dug out my notes from Tracie's party.

As Jackson and I poured over air conditioner options, he also drilled me about making sure my windows and doors were locked all day and night. So much for fresh air.

"Yes, mother." My heart was heavy and my pocketbook light.

"I'd say we should order you a security system too, but with your budget, I'm guessing you want to wait…?" Jackson studied me as if I may cough up a wad of cash.

"Yes. I've got tires to order now, too. I promise to lock everything up at night."

Almost a thousand dollars later, I walked home to wait for the deputy.

* * *

I met Mike and Ernie at my car after the deputy left. Ernie deferred the ordering to Mike as he went over a few tire options for me. I decided on a midgrade tire. I thanked Mike for his input and help—one of the great assets of living in a small town. Quick, helpful service.

Jackson stopped in after lunch for an update on what the deputy said. "Keep notes, that's about it. I told him I've done it, showed him the list of names from the night at Tracie's, as well as printing out photos of my car to keep in a folder with my notes."

We went on to talk about a date for the following Tuesday.

"Where are we going on this official date?"

"Wherever you want. Fancy dinner out? Movie? What do you miss doing in the cities?"

"It's sad to say, but Nick and I rarely went out the last few years unless it was for one of his business events. I usually went out with my girlfriends."

"Where to?"

"We liked First Avenue if we wanted the social, dancing scene. I did a lot of biking around the Lake Calhoun area, and we'd also rent paddleboats or canoes. I love Como Zoo, and every year I hit the State Fair. In the winter we'd go cross-country skiing, I was in a pool league with Nick…" I poked his flat stomach, reminding him of our pool game a few months ago.

He rolled his eyes. "No pool. How about kayaking down the Crow Wing River? There are some great sandy spots to swim and an excellent Mexican restaurant nearby."

"It sounds perfect." It was just what I needed to take my mind off of someone lurking in my backyard at night.

* * *

A sunny, light breeze and an expected high of about eighty greeted us on Tuesday. I packed a picnic lunch for us, and we rented kayaks from a shop a block off the river. We'd been kayaking for an hour when black smoke billowed in the distance. "Good thing the wind hasn't picked up. It looks like a forest fire to the east," Jackson said.

"We need rain. I can't believe I'm even saying that since it puts a damper on my business. It can rain at night," I bartered.

"I've been called out twice in the last couple of weeks for grass fires."

"You're a fireman?"

"Yep. In towns our size, we depend on mutual aid from nearby departments. One of our grass fires was eight miles away. Surrounding townships got called in for backup."

"Even *talking* about fire makes me hot. How much further to the island so we can swim?"

Suddenly the back of me was wet. I screamed and turned to see Jackson smirking. "Oops, sorry. I'm having a tough time controlling my paddle."

"Oh yes, you look really sorry." My life jacket had somewhat protected my bare back.

"The first sandbar is just around the bend. We can stop there for a while."

A few minutes later we'd pulled the kayaks up on the beach, unpacked our picnic lunch from the cooler and spread out our towels. We had the place to ourselves.

"We can take our life jackets off here. We're out of the current as long as we stay between shore and the point of the sandbar." Jackson shrugged out of his. I blatantly stared at his farmer's tan torso with a light covering of chest hair darker than what was on his head.

"Do I pass inspection?" He held his arms out wide.

My face warmed. "You'll do, I guess. I'm not so sure about that farmer's tan. I think you should cut wood more often without a shirt on." I felt his eyes inspecting me too. I was the last person to criticize. I resembled a boy in a bikini.

Jackson reached out and put his hands on either side of my hips. "And may I ask what you did with your womanly curves, Ms. O'Brien?"

I chuckled. "I knew that was coming. I guess I asked for it. God forgot to paste my breasts and hips on me before he shipped me down."

Jackson peeked down at my swimsuit's attempt at cleavage. "Well, there seems to be a little something going on there…"

I pushed him away. "Yes, it's called padding." I needed to break our contact, finding the need to ease my desire. I turned and dived into the clear, cool water.

Jackson joined me. We swam around the little inlet of water protected from the undercurrent…which was nothing compared to the current between us. He pulled me to him and planted a kiss where my cleavage should've been, working his way up to my mouth. I wrapped my arms around him. He smelled of summer and sunscreen.

As he nibbled behind my ear, his body flush with mine, he mumbled, "I'm hungry."

"For food?" We all but had our swimsuits off in my mind.

"Of course." His smile told me he was lying.

By late afternoon, we were waterlogged, a little sunburned, and famished. We changed into the dry shorts and T-shirts we'd brought before hopping on a tandem bike and peddling to eat at Jesse's Oasis. After scarfing down overflowing enchiladas and jumbo margaritas, I felt like a bloated wood tick.

We struggled to push ourselves off the comfortable chairs on the deck overlooking Crow Wing River. Jackson took me by the arm. "Okay, let's do it. I need the bike ride to wake me up before I drive us home." He paid the bill before we hoisted our legs back on the bikes.

"Whose bright idea was this?" He grunted behind me as we attempted to synchronize our peddling again.

"It seemed like a good idea yesterday." Clearly, I hadn't taken into consideration a day on the river paddling, swimming, and breathing in all that fresh air.

It was dusk when we returned the bike. My legs were like rubber bands, my arms, dead weights. We had an hour drive home. I hoped to stay awake for nighttime activities.

Instead, I gave up the fight and fell asleep like any exciting date would do. I was jolted out of my peaceful slumber by what sounded like a police radio.

"Shit!" Jackson pulled off the highway to listen to his fire pager. "Can you find a piece of paper and pen in the glove compartment for me?"

I found them, and he replayed the announcement, something about a structure fire.

"It's south of Love, about twenty miles north of here. You can drop me off and take my truck back to your house. One of the guys can bring me home when we get back to town."

I was still feeling fuzzy-headed, my brain playing catch-up. "Okay."

He pulled back on the road, going much faster than the speed limit. "I'd hoped to have you come back to my house with me. But a structure fire usually takes hours." He reached over to take my hand. "I'm really sorry."

"Me too." I was exhausted. Maybe this was for the best. I wanted to be fully alert when I explored Jackson's body.

Chapter 17

It was a chaotic week preparing for the upcoming Fourth of July weekend. Jackson installed my new air conditioner while I ran around fueled by coffee and nerves. During the summer chaos I'd misplaced my house and car keys. I found them two days later—on my stove. And, I swear I was losing pairs of underwear. I'd heard of people accusing their clothes dryer of eating their socks. I wondered if mine had a thing for women's panties.

Also missing was my birth control pills. I'd been off them for several months but started up again a few weeks ago, fairly certain I'd need them any day. Now I'd have to explain to my new doctor my absent-mindedness.

The word was out about my "car crime" with the additional information about me being threatened at Tracie's party in May. So much for secrets. Yet as much as I wanted to be angry at the townspeople for gossiping, their support and help in spreading the word for possible suspects gave me confidence that at least some of the community actually cared if I stayed in town or not.

The consensus from the deputy was I should keep as much of the facts from the public as possible, in hopes someone would slip up and say something they shouldn't know. It was hard to do in a small town. If people had their information wrong, I tried not to correct them.

Travis arrived for his morning walk through the store. He'd added whistling, but as yet, no words. It was time to change that. I headed to the bait section and "accidentally" tipped over a box of bobbers, scattering orange and white bobbers all over the bait section floor.

"Oh no!" My eyes widened in feigned surprise as Travis turned around at the noise. "Can you help me, please?" I shrugged, as if I didn't know how to pick up bobbers. He eyed the mess I'd made before he knelt and silently picked them up, one by one, carefully placing them back in the cardboard box. I studied his meticulously combed dark brown hair, chubby cheeks, and light brown eyes up close—finally. "My name is Molly O'Brien. What's yours?"

I wasn't sure he'd answer. He was focused on the bobbers. I knelt beside him and put out my hand to shake his. "What's your name?" I knew it, but we'd never been formally introduced.

"Travis Franklin Osvold." His voice was hoarse, as if they were the first words he'd spoken today. "People call me Travis. You can call me Travis."

"It's nice to meet you, Travis. I appreciate you helping me." He avoided my eyes, likely unsure if I was being kind or teasing him. I imagined he'd been teased a lot in his life already.

He slowly looked up. "It is nice to meet you, Molly O'Brien." He shook my hand, and my heart beamed. I thanked him for his help and he left a few minutes later, whistling.

I was working on my candy order when Curt walked in.

"Hey, Curt." I hadn't seen or heard from him since he'd asked me out last month.

"Hello, Molly. Do you have a minute?" Curt's smile gleamed from his tanned face.

"Sure." I put my order aside and we stepped away from the counter.

"First of all, I wanted to tell you how sorry I was to hear about your car being damaged. Hopefully, they'll catch whoever did it soon."

"Thank you." I was pretty sure he hadn't stopped in for that reason, and I braced myself for what I feared was coming.

"Do you have plans this weekend? I thought we could go to the fireworks after your store closes. I'm sure you've heard they have booths and other activities at the park and beach."

The idea he'd ask me out again hadn't occurred to me, my mind now focused on Jackson. This could get uncomfortable. I had to pull out the "honesty is the best policy" motto.

"Thanks for asking, but I'm going to the fireworks with Jackson," I said kindly.

"I should've asked you before this. I was out of town last week on a business trip." He studied me. "When he's done with you, come look me up, Molly. I'll wait." His well-shaped mouth clamped shut as he turned and strolled out the door, leaving me alone to pick at his words.

* * *

The week of July Fourth featured more hot and humid weather.

"Any scoop for me?" Drive by Daisy swarmed in on Saturday morning, pencil clenched in her hand in case gossip dropped like rain when she entered the store. Her high-pitched voice plucked at my nerves. She leaned over the counter, too far into my personal space.

"No, sorry, Daisy." *Nosy old lady.*

"No scoop on your tire-slashing thug?" Drool escaped as she waited for a juicy answer.

"I'm afraid not." I averted my eyes to a young man juggling pop and ice, standing behind her, struggling to set his cold goods down on the counter.

As she made her exit, her shoulders drooping in disappointment, I wondered why everyone couldn't just mind their own business.

The fireworks would be launched from Love Point, across the lake from the beach. Jackson walked in shortly before I closed the store. I locked the door to the sound of raucous laughter on the beach and was antsy to get out and join the party. He handed me a beer he'd brought in.

"I don't suppose I could talk you into another one of those amazing foot rubs?" I sighed before taking a long drink of my beer.

He put his arms around my waist. "You can talk me into pretty much anything. I think you know that." He bent down and started kissing me under my earlobe, making me forget I even had feet. My brain reminded me we were standing in the store, and although it was closed, it was still light enough out where people could see in through the windows.

I reluctantly pulled away and took the till drawers out. Jackson followed me back to my home. "I'd be happy to give you a foot rub at my place afterward."

"What?" I set the tills on the kitchen table for Jackson to help me balance them. If I understood him correctly, he wanted me to spend the night at his place. Finally.

He sat down and pulled me onto his lap. "I want a sleepover with you, only the fun kind, not the individual sleeping bag kind." He took one of my curls and wrapped it around his index finger, watching me with intent.

A week ago, after our date was cut short due to a structure fire, I could've used someone to hose me down and cool my desire. But between then and now, Curt had planted that seed of doubt. If I went to bed with Jackson, would I be history in a few weeks?

I pulled up a chair next to him. "I like you. A lot. But I need to be honest here. I've slept with one guy in the last seven years." I fiddled with the stack of tens in front of me. "If I sleep with you, it means something to me. And I'm not sure it will to you," I said softly.

He took my hand, caressing each individual finger. "I don't know what you've heard about me, but I'm not using you, Molly. I want to sleep with you because I care about you." His thumb rubbed the top of my palm. "Hell, if I didn't give a shit about you, I'd have made a move the night I gave you a foot rub. And I sure wouldn't have bothered with your feet." His eyes told me exactly where he'd have started.

My willpower drained. "Good point." Someone who was just looking to get laid would've taken me up on it right then and there.

We quickly balanced both tills before I locked them in the safe. Jackson waited while I changed into jeans and a red, white and blue Rolling Stones T-shirt. We had an hour or more before the fireworks, and after locking my house door, Jackson and I walked hand in hand across the street to the crowded beach to find Tracie, Rick, and some of the others.

We met up at the beer garden. As Charlee, Tracie, and I visited, Wendy walked by with Drake. They looked like polar opposites—Wendy was a stunning, if flamboyant, beauty—Drake was button-up-shirt seriousness. She was pasted to him like another appendage. His serious "land is a great investment" personality was not what I'd pictured Wendy was looking for when she'd boasted at the Pickled Perch how she was all about having a good time. To each his own.

Shortly before the fireworks were to start, a group of us headed to the beach. As we settled on the sand, I leaned against Jackson and listened to the group talk about organizing an inner tube floating trip down the Crow Wing River, where Jackson and I had kayaked.

I found my mind distracted by their conversation, already visualizing the relaxing float, nearly tuning out the noise around me. Children ran around wearing glow-in-the-dark necklaces, families sat on blankets, the elders nestled in their folding lawn chairs, all patiently awaiting the colorful display. The light breeze carried the scent of corn dogs, popcorn, and yeasty beer. Mosquitos were kept to a minimum thanks to the mosquito squad who'd sprayed earlier in the day. A thousand stars blanketed the sky.

After dark, everyone stood as spotlights lit up the flag in the park. A senior citizen band played an introduction before the crowd joined in to sing "The Star-Spangled Banner." Jackson's voice behind me bellowed out the words in a tune so off key I struggled not to giggle.

After the anthem, the crowd erupted in applause and settled back in for the fireworks. I elbowed him in the side. "I think I found your flaw. You're an awful singer!" I kissed his cheek to offset the sting of truth.

"Yep. I got my god-awful voice from my dad. He brought me up to sing loud and proud no matter if I make the neighborhood dogs howl. You should hear us together, it's a musical nightmare." Jackson grinned.

And for some reason, his confidence made me like him even more. This was a guy I wouldn't have to constantly build up. The fireworks were an impressive half-hour display for such a small town—big, loud, and colorful, extracting waves of oohs and aahs from the crowd.

When it was over, Jackson and I excused ourselves and walked back to my house. "You sure about me staying overnight? I'll have to get up early…and it's late already."

"Yes, I'm sure. I'm an early riser anyway," he replied. I grabbed an overnight bag and tossed a few things in it. "I'll bring you back in the morning, no need for you to drive."

I left my car with its new tires, hopefully safe, in the driveway while we both hopped in Jackson's truck. A few minutes later we pulled into his driveway, hearing echoes of Trigger barking in excitement at our arrival. I'm glad someone was excited. I was nervous as hell.

After giving Trigger his deserved attention, we made our way to the living room. I was still clutching my red canvas overnight bag.

"You want to bring that upstairs?" Jackson eyed my bag.

His bedroom was in the loft. His suggestion that I take my things upstairs made my nerves tingle. What if some new rules had been written about sex that I'd been clueless about in my time with Nick? And Jackson was going to see me naked. Slow breath in, slow breath out.

"Um, hello, earth to Molly?" He stood waiting for my answer.

"Sure, I'll take it up." *Now? Were we getting down to business right away?*

As I turned to walk up the wood staircase, Jackson asked, "Are you hungry? Thirsty? I've got beer, iced tea, juice, whatever you want. I can make us sandwiches, or I've got some chips and dip…" His words tumbled out, almost as if he was nervous too.

Was I hungry? "I'm kind of beered out. Maybe just a glass of ice water?"

"Sure. How about a ham and cheese sandwich?" He stood at the bottom of the steps.

"Wow, you know how to woo a girl, don't you?" Jackson offering me food helped deflect my jitters. "I'll be back down in a minute." I unpacked my few things in his bathroom—makeup remover, night cream, toothbrush, and toothpaste. I dug out the clothes I'd thrown inside in haste. A pair of lacy underwear, socks, my faded green Lake Calhoun T-shirt, and two more pairs of lacy undies. Definitely not my quickly-dwindling-everyday-underwear.

Clearly, I had underwear covered. Why did I throw socks in? I'd worn flip-flops to his house. And who could resist me in my T-shirt from the 1990s? Yet what else would I have packed? The lacy underwear was a hopeful gift from Ella on my last birthday.

I went back down to the kitchen where Jackson had glasses of milk and water poured, and ham and cheese sandwiches on fresh bakery buns. "I didn't put any mustard or mayo on yours. I wasn't sure which you wanted." We sat at his counter and I squirted mustard in my sandwich.

"Mmmm, I didn't realize I was hungry. This really hits the spot."

"I got to thinking you probably didn't have time to eat supper with the store so busy."

"You're right. I don't think I've eaten since noon, other than some popcorn with my beer at the beach." I tried to not wolf my sandwich down in front of the man I'd soon be ravishing.

Jackson chuckled.

"What?"

He reached over and wiped mustard from my cheek. "There. You're back to perfect."

I had a feeling he'd see just how imperfect I was in a few minutes.

We rinsed our dishes and put them in his dishwasher, and as I turned around, Jackson took my hand and pulled me to him. "You okay with this?" He whispered.

How could I want something so bad, yet be so afraid of it? Still, in that instant I knew—I wanted to be with him—and I trusted him completely. In response, I took his hand and silently led him up the staircase with me.

We walked into his bedroom and he stated he was going to shower, as if we'd discussed our bathroom habits a hundred times. I heard him brush his teeth before the shower turned on.

"You don't need to reinvent the wheel," I mumbled before walking in to brush my teeth and wash my face while he showered. His shower curtain of forest green was disappointing. Why didn't he have one of those see-through shower doors? *Oh, what the hell, Molly, don't you think it's time to follow your heart…or your gut…something? Make a move!*

"Want some company?" I raised my voice over the noise of the shower, keeping it light as if I didn't give a flying toad what his answer was. Even though I was bare-ass naked.

Jackson peeked out behind the shower curtain with bear and moose imprinted on it. His grin resembled The Grinch riding on his sleigh of presents. He gently pulled back the curtain and offered me his hand. As I stepped into the steaming water, Jackson's body enveloped me, creating our own steam.

It was the longest shower I'd ever taken in my life.

Chapter 18

I hadn't fallen asleep with a man's body wrapped around mine for a few years. Cuddling with Nick had faded from our relationship, much like the laughter.

After Jackson and I had become better acquainted in the shower we laid next to each other in his king-size bed as moonlight paved a glimmering path across the lake outside his full-length windows. We told stories of our high school years, favorite vacations, best friends, and the pros and cons of living in a small town versus a big city.

It was after two when he snuggled up behind me, spooning his length around mine, his large hand comfortable around my waist. And I couldn't sleep. I couldn't stop thinking about how much my life had changed in the past year, couldn't believe the feelings I was experiencing with Jackson and hoped every decision I was making was the right one.

His alarm rang at six. "Let's call in sick," Jackson mumbled in my ear.

"I don't know about your boss, but mine's a bear." I longed for weekends off again as I snuggled in deeper under the covers. We'd left the crank-out windows open and the gentle breeze carried cooler air.

After a few minutes, Jackson pushed against my back, guiding me toward the edge of the bed. "C'mon, lazybones, *you* need to get up so I can drive you home so you can open your store while I come home and nap."

I sat on the edge of the bed and pulled my T-shirt over my head. "You don't work today?"

He leaned up on his elbow. "I was dreaming. Of course, I'll be at the hardware running my ass off just like you will." With the Fourth of July on Sunday, most people took Monday off.

"I've got Adam and Logan working all day with me so that helps."

"Let me know if you're up to doing anything tonight."

I looked over my shoulder at Jackson with an eyebrow raised. What exactly did he mean?

He shook his head. "I didn't mean that. If you want to rent a movie and make a pizza or sit at the beach, take a pontoon ride…whatever you want to do, I'll wait to hear from you." He threw his legs over his side of the bed, reached down for his boxers and put them on. "That is assuming you are willing to see me again." He stepped into some gym shorts.

I was more than willing to see all of him again, fatigue or no fatigue. My actions over the past six hours answered his question.

* * *

"We'll be fine, stop worrying." Susan all but booted me out of my own store on the following Sunday morning. "If we have any problems, we'll call Ernie. Now go have fun."

She sounded like my mother would have as I shut the door between the store and my home. Susan and Adam would run the store until it closed at six.

And for six of those hours, I'd be unreachable. It was tough to let go.

Jackson and I picked up Tracie and Rick. We were going to what apparently was an annual event in mid-July. A group would drive to the Crow Wing River, rent inner tubes and float the river—the same one Jackson and I had kayaked on our first date.

Over two dozen of us gathered in the city parking lot before caravanning to the river an hour away. Charlee rode over with Scratch, Wendy, and Drake. Charlee and Scratch were just good friends. I wasn't sure about Wendy and Drake. I was surprised Drake wasn't wearing a dress shirt with his swim trunks. Every time I'd seen Wendy, she was wearing very little.

At our first float stop, everyone relaxed on a sandy beach, unpacking the drinks and waterproof food we'd put in coolers floating in their own tubes.

An hour and a half later, when we stopped again, the booze which had been consumed under the beating July sun, was taking its toll on a few. Wendy was one of them. Watching her perfect body, barely covered in a hot pink bikini, sway in front of Drake in a seductive dance was one thing. When she pushed Jackson into the water and fell on top of him, it was another.

From the first time I met her, I had a hard time visualizing her as a paralegal. Supposedly she was smart and a hard worker, but when she drank, all hell broke loose—along with her morals. It took an extra helping of willpower to not stomp into the water and drag her wet, slithering, nearly-naked body off of Jackson.

Thankfully, Jackson did it for me and he was back to tossing the football in a matter of seconds. I tried to concentrate on my conversation with Scratch and Drake. "How do you like the store? Is it how you imagined things would be living in a small town?" Drake asked.

"Some things are better, some worse. It's a lot of work but I like being my own boss."

"I think you're doing great," said Scratch. "It all takes time, and people just need to get to know you." He threw his beefy arm around my shoulder. It helped me forget Wendy.

At the end of our float, we drove to a chicken shack boasting the best fried chicken around. Sunburned and exhausted from the float and fresh air, we were famished.

Wendy sat at the picnic table next to us, leaning so far onto the table I was sure her breasts were going to drag through the puddle of ketchup left on her plate.

I had Jackson on one side of me and Charlee on the other. Tracie and Rick sat across from us. Wendy stumbled over to our table and whispered something in Tracie's ear.

"No, Wendy!" Tracie shot up and grabbed Wendy's arm. "C'mon, let's get you a cup of coffee while we wait for everyone to finish."

Tracie wasn't quick enough. Wendy unhooked her bikini top and leaned over the table to Jackson, her breasts dangling in front of his face. "Oh Jacksy-boy, don't you miss these girls?" She lifted her breasts—apparently the "girls"—so close to him he could've licked a nipple.

I was rooted in shock, and surprised that Jackson didn't jump up, shove her away, and tell her what she could do with her "girls." I silently pleaded for a rebuttal from him.

Instead, he pulled his body back. "Wendy, you're pathetic and drunk. Do yourself a favor and let Drake take you home."

Tracie had already thrown her hoodie over Wendy. Rick jumped up and firmly guided Wendy back to where Drake was standing, visiting with others. There was a scuffle and a lot of swearing before Rick, Mike, and Drake guided Wendy to Drake's car and the two drove away.

Charlee and Scratch caught a ride home with us. For a pickup crammed with six friends, our ride home was unusually quiet. I was seething.

Jackson had some explaining to do.

Chapter 19

I was in no mood to see Jackson's mom fly in on her broomstick Monday morning. It was much earlier than I figured a diva would drag her body out of bed.

Jackson and I didn't have a chance to talk last night on the way home. If he was sending his goon in to defend him, he'd chosen a poor representative.

I continued working on my bait order. It was 8:15 and they'd be calling at any minute.

"I see you're up early working." Nancy's smile reminded me of the Joker on *Batman*. Yes, she was beautiful, but her demeanor could chase the devil out of hell.

"I'm up every single morning, working long before this." If she planned on insinuating I rarely put my time in, I'd strangle her with the twine from the daily newspapers.

"Yes, I'm sure you are. After all, when one is given something as generous as this, one should put some effort into making the most of that gift." Nancy's thin arm swept the store as if she was Vanna White presenting me with a Porsche.

I wanted to tell her this "one" was overtired, underpaid, and short on patience. Instead, I matched her plastic smile with my own. "What can I help you with this morning, Nancy?"

"I want to know more about you since Jackson seems to be spending more time with you than his own mother."

Great. Jackson now owed me another foot rub. And a month's vacation in Hawaii.

"What would you like to know?" Obviously, Jackson mentioned me enough for her to feel it was time to interrogate me.

"For starters, have you ever been married? Any children? Do you plan to stay here in Love, or is this just a passing phase for you? Do you have any money or are you going to drain this business dry? And finally, why aren't you living wherever your father is?"

With each question Nancy shot at me, my intestines twisted like a tornado. When the phone rang it was a welcome replacement for her shrill voice. I took my time giving my bait order, asking the bait supply owner about his wife, their new grandbaby, how their business had been over the weekend, and anything else I could think of to delay my conversation with Nancy.

As I hung up I prayed for an onslaught of customers. But it was too early for the beach crowd. Damn.

"No, no, yes, and I'm sorry; none of your business." It had been a few minutes since she'd asked me the questions, but I remembered the order they'd been fired. I don't think she did by the furrow of her perfectly arched brows.

"I beg your pardon?"

"I haven't been married, don't have any children, I plan to stay here, and the rest is not your business. Actually, *none* of it is your business." If my mother was here, I'd get scolded for being rude. Nancy set my teeth on edge, especially on this exceptionally-bitchy-mood day.

"Wouldn't you rather know that I'm a good, honest person? That I'm a hard worker, am nice to your son, and doing my best to make Rosie's store thrive?" They were things I'd want to know if I had a grown child who was dating someone.

Nancy's tight face softened a bit as she drummed her coral-colored nail tips on my counter. "I do care about that, yes. I don't want my son getting hurt, or him being sucked into a toxic relationship again." Her dark green eyes challenged me to ask her to explain.

I folded my arms over my chest. "Is that the kind of person I seem like to you?" *And what toxic relationship are you referring to?*

"I don't know what you are like, that's why I'm here." Nancy slapped her hand on the counter as she stepped back to leave. "But Wendy seemed fine, and she dragged Jackson through the mud." Her finger pointed in my direction. "You pull that on my son, and you'll be sorry."

The door opened and Travis walked in, causing Nancy to turn with her nose in the air and strut out. He'd taken to lining up my various bobbers in neat rows in their boxes every day. Sometimes I had to mess them up before I opened the store so he'd have a job to do. He was in the tackle section by the time I tucked away the aggravation Nancy had created. I was tempted to plant a thank-you kiss on his cheek. I owed him for his impeccable timing.

He stood by the minnow tanks, his back to me. "Good morning, Travis," I said, before approaching him. He didn't like to be surprised.

Travis turned around, a shy smile on his face; clutching a bouquet of wildflowers he'd clearly plucked from the nearby ditches. "For you, Molly O'Brien." He proudly held them out.

It was the first time he'd brought me anything. I had a sneaking suspicion Jackson had been right weeks ago when he said Travis had a crush on me. I was honored to be a person Travis trusted with his emotions. "Thank you, Travis. That's so kind of you. I'll get a vase."

"You have to put them in water. Don't forget to put water in your vase, Molly O'Brien."

I smiled. "I won't. Thanks again." He straightened some bobbers before leaving as an elderly woman entered. I'd heard she had recently lost her husband of sixty years. We visited after she made her purchases and I silently wondered how a person got over losing someone they'd loved for so long.

I tried to keep that perspective in mind as I phrased and rephrased in my mind what I'd say to Jackson tonight after the store closed. He'd offered to come over so we could talk. I said I'd rather go there. I wanted to be in control of when our conversation would be done.

He likely didn't know about his mother's visit this morning. He would tonight.

* * *

I showered and dug out my "good bra" from Victoria's Secret. After getting a birds-eye view of Wendy's "girls," my own girls deserved a boost. I primped longer than I had since moving to Love. I hoped it was worth it. It was dark when I pulled in Jackson's driveway.

Trigger got to the door before Jackson did, his big tail wagging so hard it sounded like a hammer on the door. I gave him his deserved attention before Jackson nudged him aside, pulled me inside his house and shut the door behind me. He smelled of shampoo and fresh air.

With an arm braced on either side of my head, he leaned in, his forehead touching mine. His brow furrowed as if a painful headache brewed. I guessed he was deciding what to say, how to say it. Instead of words, he conveyed his emotion by tenderly kissing the tip of my nose before making his way to my mouth.

We'd yet to say a word. He didn't need to. Here was my answer.

An hour later while we lay side by side on his couch, Jackson's finger traced my face. We'd already discussed his mother's visit and had moved on to Wendy. "Wendy is needy," he said. "She needs everyone to love her, needs attention, and sucks the life out of a relationship. At least with a guy." He reaffirmed they'd dated a while but he felt nothing for her. Or her "girls."

"Good trick with that push-up bra of yours though. For a minute, you had me fooled." He kissed my neck and I responded with a punch to his shoulder.

"A girl has to pull out all her moves when she's up against someone with a body like Wendy's." I'd never been insecure about my lack of curves until now. I struggled to erase the images of Jackson's hands on Wendy's perfect body. Hard not to think about what Wendy could have possibly done to drag Jackson "through the mud" as Nancy had said, hard not to think of why I cared about his past with Wendy…and hard not to wonder if there was a future with us.

Chapter 20

I scrambled to get home in time to shower and change before opening the store. Poor Pixie, she was probably meowing at gunfire pace, wondering where I was. She'd gone from living outside, to camping out in my living room, to sleeping on my bedroom floor.

I stepped out of my car and was choked by a horrific stench.

I looked around to find the culprit in the early dawn. On my deck, pushed up against my door, lay a dead, bloated, maggot-infested, bloody deer. *That son-of-a-bitch, whoever he is!*

I heard Pixie mewing on the other side of the door.

I whipped out my new cell phone, one with a camera I'd splurged on since I'd sold my expensive Nikon camera on eBay last year. I snapped a few pictures of the deer, from a safe distance as I covered my nose with my arm. I called Jackson as I made my way around to the front of the store and back to my house to rescue Pixie.

"Don't touch a thing," Jackson instructed me. "I'm on my way."

As if he needed to tell me not to touch the deer! I took more pictures of the poor creature from inside my living room before scooping up a distraught Pixie and bringing her into the bathroom with me while I showered. When I was dressed, I spotted Jackson in the yard and on the phone. I waved to him before going outside to meet him via the store.

He pocketed his cell phone as I walked up. "Poor doe was obviously hit a day or two ago. In this heat, it doesn't take long for them to bloat." His face was grim as he wiped a bead of sweat from his forehead. It was going to be another sweltering July day. "I called the sheriff's."

"Is that who you were talking to?" I wasn't sure it was worthy reporting. I wouldn't have called them, fearing I'd sound like a scared city girl.

He had backed up his old truck close to my deck. He dropped down the tailgate, slid cardboard flat to line the bed of the truck, and donned gloves. "Can you hop in and slowly back it up until I tell you to stop? It'll be easier for me to hoist the deer onto the bed that way."

I climbed into the old truck he used for hauling wood. It was perfect for hauling a smelly deer carcass. Once the tailgate was close to my deck, Jackson yanked the carcass inside the truck bed.

"You'll want to hose down your deck with bleach water, get rid of the smell and germs." He looked at his watch. "I'll do it. It's almost time for you to open your store."

"Adam will be here soon and I can clean it up then."

"It will only take me a minute." He leaned in for a quick kiss. "The deputy I spoke with gave me an email address for you to email photos. I explained you'd been at my house all night and this was here when you arrived. They're adding it to the other information they have."

"What good will it do? It's not like we're going to have them dust the deer for fingerprints." I was frustrated at the veiled threats against me that couldn't be traced.

"Every bit of information will help in the long run."

I hoped so. Every time I felt in control of my life, it seemed to be followed with me fighting to keep from falling, or being pushed, into a gaping hole.

Travis was standing next to the store door when I unlocked it. His early visits were common now, the comfort level between us increasing each day. "Good morning, Travis."

"Good morning, Molly O'Brien. I'm here for my mother. She needs some eggs. Two eggs, over easy, for her. Two eggs for me, over hard. I don't like runny eggs." His round face was serious, as if he was giving an order to a waitress instead of explaining why he was buying eggs.

"Hey, Travis, how long have you been standing across the street this morning?"

"I left my home at 5:23. I arrived at the beach at 5:29 and saw a beautiful sunrise." He studied his oversized watch. "It is now 6:55. You are late in opening the store."

"Yes, I am, although technically my store hours state I open at seven." He was nailing me to the wall for being late in my normally early routine.

"But every day you are open between 6:37 and 6:42."

Initially, it creeped me out being watched so carefully. Now I was thankful he kept an eye on me. "Do you know why I'm late, Travis?" I didn't want to upset him, but he'd hear about the deer eventually anyway. I explained and his eyes widened in horror.

"Did you notice anyone drive out from the road in the back?" It was a long shot. The deer had likely been put there during the night. I'd ask Ernie if he saw headlights, but if he had, he'd have called me. Someone hoping to scare me wouldn't have driven in with their headlights on.

"Only you, Molly O'Brien. You arrived at your home at 5:47 and then you walked around to the front door of your store."

This young man should go into private detective work. If only he had the social skills. I'd just rung up his eggs when Jackson walked in.

"Good morning, Travis." Jackson gave him an absent-minded nod. His eyes told me he had news. He watched me put the eggs in Travis' backpack. "Tell your mom hello for me."

"Yes, sir," Travis said. I chuckled. For some reason, Jackson was "sir" to him, yet he was only a couple years older than me.

As soon as Travis left, Jackson spoke. "Scratch said there was a bloated deer down County Road 65 yesterday, a few miles east of town. It sounds like about the same size as what was left on your deck. He spotted it on his way to work. Once his staff showed up, he drove back out east of town to load up the deer to dispose of it before it baked in the heat for another day. It was already gone."

"So someone stored this yesterday and last night? Yuck." I couldn't imagine the smell.

"Yup. They had this planned out." Jackson scratched his day-old stubble. My phone call likely messed up his morning routine. "We need to get cameras on the outside of your place."

"I thought of that. All I can see are dollar signs though." I'd finally been able to add to my savings for the slim winter months ahead. The idea of spending any of my nest egg was almost as scary as not feeling safe in my home.

Jackson took hold of my shoulders and looked me in the eyes. "I'll loan you the money, Molly. It will be worth it for my peace of mind."

"I appreciate the offer, but I want to do this on my own. I'll look into the cost of a system." I didn't want to start the slippery slide of allowing a man to take care of me financially again. Jackson hadn't offered *that*, but borrowing money from a man I'd just started dating? No thank you.

When Adam arrived to work, I made some calls to security system companies. There was just no way I could afford anything decent. I compromised and decided on motion detector lights for my backyard. Ernie's home was far enough away through the trees so the lights shouldn't bother him. It was all I could afford right now.

I'd tossed around the idea of getting a big outside dog but it wouldn't have stopped a person from depositing a dead deer on my doorstep. Or stop them from threatening me at a party. Or stop them from slashing my tires.

If Jackson was disappointed with my decision when I called to order four motion detector lights from his store, he was smart enough to keep his mouth shut.

After my phone calls, Adam and I unpacked my shipment of beach towels and T-shirts, replenishing my dwindling inventory. We discussed the upcoming town event…"Eight-One."

For the past forty years, the town held a celebration every August 1, no matter if it fell on a weekday, no matter the weather. Townspeople would gather in the park that night at six for many fun events, the main one being a unique food item for sale. If you managed to choke it down, you'd get an "Ate One" T-shirt.

Signs and flyers had been plastered around town since Fourth of July announcing Love's "Fun-in-the-Sun-Eight-One" annual event. "I'm a little leery of whatever they plan on serving this year. I'm not sure I'd classify eating something disgusting as 'fun.'" I grimaced, remembering the previous year's food of choice I'd heard about.

"Do you know who came up with the idea for this event?" I asked Adam.

"Rumor has it some loggers years ago challenged each other to eat disgusting things like pickled pigs feet. After a few years of these challenges, they made it an annual event."

"Have you heard any hints about what this year's food is?" The food preparers were sworn to secrecy. I couldn't believe anyone would pay money to eat their choice this year. But I'd been here long enough to know that townspeople did some crazy things for fun.

"We never know until that day. Each year they pick an eight-person committee for the following year. The committee chooses the snack and orders the food. They make enough money to pay for the food and buy the T-shirts."

"Do you usually eat their selection?" Adam was a typical teenage boy who I imagined would eat just about anything you put in front of him.

He grinned as he broke down the cardboard boxes for recycling. "Duh."

I was pretty sure I would *not* be eating the mystery snack.

* * *

After sleeping with a tennis racket by my bed ever since the first bat sighting, it was a welcome break to stay several nights at Jackson's until my motion detector lights were installed. He agreed I should bring Pixie with me. After two days of her bossing Jackson's dog around in his own house, Pixie was delegated to the garage at night.

I was still staying at Jackson's house when the "Eight-One" event rolled around. August 1 fell on a Sunday. The crowd at the beach rivaled Fourth of July;

only most of these people were locals since the majority of cabin owners had left for home for the upcoming work week. Food stands were set up in the park, some featuring the Ate-One selection—Cajun-fried grasshoppers on a stick. It could've been worse. I'd caved and choked one down. I was now the proud owner of a lime-green Ate-One T-shirt. Another way to get the shirt was by entering the frozen T-shirt event…now front and center at the park's bandstand.

At eight o'clock it was time for the big highlight. Contestants paid twenty dollars to select their T-shirts the day before, with the strict instruction the shirt had to actually fit and not be too big. Each contestant was given a number corresponding to their shirt, and those shirts had been twisted tight and frozen until now.

The shirtless men had to untwist the frozen T-shirt and put it on. The first one with his shirt on won half the pot they all paid to enter. The other half went to next year's committee.

The women went next and had to don a swimsuit cover-up over their swimsuit instead of a T-shirt. It was painful to see Wendy up there shimmying into her frozen cover-up over her silver bikini that would've fit a Barbie doll. My only shallow redemption was watching her stumble around in her stiletto heels as if she'd been spun around blindfolded.

Seeing Jackson shirtless on stage ratcheted up my desire. Even Old Lloyd was up there rocking his attempt to wiggle into the frozen shirt with surprising enthusiasm. In the end, it was Adam who took away half of the earnings. I wasn't surprised. He never sat still while working in the store. Of course, he'd have an abundance of energy and determination to win the prize.

The firemen water hose fights were next. If Jackson's mother would have been on a team, I'd have signed up to play against her. An empty keg hung on a long cable between two tall posts. The firemen and townspeople broke into teams with a fire truck on each end of the cable. The teams took turns using the high-pressure water stream from the hose to push the keg to their opponents' end. Jackson's team lost to Scratch's in the finale and most of us in the crowd were drenched from the overspray of the powerful fire hoses, the water warm in the cooling dusk.

Afterward, Jackson walked Ernie home. A handful of us stood on the beach listening to a funny story Mike was telling, describing a teen who'd tried to drive away without paying for gas, but also forgetting to take the gas nozzle out of his gas tank. I looked across the street at my closed store, the lights inside the coolers shining inside, the red and white umbrellas closed up above new wood picnic tables on the deck, the colorful planters along the front of the store…and a sense of pride swelled inside me like a happy balloon ready to burst.

I swear I could hear my mom whisper in my ear, *You done good, Molly. You done good.*

Chapter 21

Over the past two weeks, I'd heard plenty of theories as to who put the deer on my doorstep. I'd nod and file away their "helpful" information on the odd chance it *would* be helpful. That people wanted to help warmed my heart. When my store door opened the morning after the town's Eight-One event, I was shocked by who greeted me.

There stood Old Lloyd, his weathered hat in his hands. "Don't suppose you have any fresh whippin' cream for my strawberries?"

My jaw could've hit the counter and bounced back up before I could speak. "Do you mean regular whipping cream or Cool Whip?" I'd been a Cool Whip kind of girl until I moved to Love. Most of the townspeople wanted the real deal.

His oversized nose wrinkled above his grimace. "Not that plastic-tasting Cool Whip!"

I bit my tongue to keep from reacting to his biting tone and led him to the cooler. He grabbed a pint of whipping cream and followed me back to the counter.

I rang up his purchase and he paid me. Then he stood with his arms folded over his massive chest and studied me. "I don't suppose you've figured out who's bugging you."

It wasn't a question and I wasn't sure whether he implied I was too dimwitted to figure it out, or if he already knew the suspect hadn't been caught. It was tempting to say 'you' in response. "No. Why, do you have a tip?"

"I have my own ideas, but I'm keeping them to myself for now. I don't aim to accuse anyone if I'm wrong." He puffed up a bit as if this piece of news made him worthy of a medal.

I couldn't stop my comeback. "You didn't have any problem accusing me of following in my grandpa's footsteps, or blaming me for something he may have done decades ago…"

His lips opened and closed a few times before clamping shut. I wasn't backing down until he said something. We could have a staring match all day.

He cleared his throat. Several times. "Yes, well, that's why I'm here. You seem to be trying to do right with Rosie's store. I may have been wrong about you."

His semi-apology was muttered in his gruff voice, but his words soothed like a salve. I was tempted to hug him.

He turned and walked out the door before I had a chance.

* * *

The wiring had been done for my outdoor motion lights. There was no excuse for me to keep staying at Jackson's house. As wonderful as it was to wake up with a lake view, I missed the convenience of being at home, mere steps from my "day job."

"It's supposed to hit the low nineties. Why don't we hang out here for the day before you move back to your place tonight?" Jackson asked as we lay in bed. It was Tuesday, my day off.

I was all for a relaxing day in the cool lake. I moved my things back home, picked up my swimsuit, some steaks from Jimmy's Meats, and was back to Jackson's place by noon.

After swimming and floating around in inner tubes, Jackson fired up the grill. We'd worked up a good appetite. Dinner was followed by a walk with Trigger along the gravel road. Jackson's home was the only one on the road. It was an odd feeling to know there wasn't a soul around for probably a mile. Deer stood camouflaged among the trees, steadily watching us walk by, their white tails twitching to ward off insects. Squirrels scurried through the woods, creating noise in the stillness. Trigger chased them, along with a bunny, without success.

We showered when we got back to his house. Jackson reminded me the sun would set any minute and it would actually cool down. "Did you bring any long pants?"

"I packed some sexy gray sweatpants and a hoodie. You won't be able to keep your hands off of me." I pulled my soft Ate-One T-shirt over my head.

Jackson dressed in an outfit similar to what I'd brought. Were we already at that point in our relationship where we chose comfort over ooh-la-la?

He lit a number of bamboo citronella torches around the railing of his deck, which was illuminated by the moon shimmering on the lake in the background. I packed an ice bucket, filling it with ice cold beer and water bottles from the kitchen.

I stepped out on the deck. There was a large air bed blown up with a sheet draped over it.

"What's with this?"

"I blew it up while you were showering. It's a full moon tonight. It will be a perfect night to lay out here and enjoy the view."

No mosquitos, the air cooled to a pleasant temperature and a gorgeous view of the moon over the calm lake. We lay down, eyes to the sky, the moon just starting to peek above the tall pine trees to glisten across the lake.

"Tell me about your family—other than your mother." I turned and looked at his profile. "Does your brother or dad ever come to visit?" I was curious about their family dynamics.

"Cody comes every fall to duck hunt. By then Mom has moved back to Wyoming. He's happy to visit when she's not around. I go there once or twice in the winter to ski. I miss my dad, who never makes it back here, thanks to work, but I spend time with him when I go home."

"What do you think attracted your dad to your mom? From everything you've said, they seem so opposite. Yes, she's an attractive woman, but it had to be more than that."

Jackson tucked his hands behind his head. "From what I was told, they didn't date long. She was a stunner, dad had money, and they both liked to go out and have fun."

I lay back down, turning toward him, and observed the strong jaw and cheekbones he'd inherited from his dad, judging from the pictures I'd seen of the man. "What do you suppose went wrong in their marriage?" I didn't feel I was being nosy. Jackson hadn't held back about the animosity and tolerance his parents shared.

"Dad's money hasn't made mom happy, and mom's neediness has probably drained dad's physical attraction to her over the years." He sat up and took a swig of his beer. I studied his broad back. His voice was pensive. I wished I could see his face.

"I'm sorry." I felt bad for him. I was positive my parents loved each other…even if I never experienced the fatherly love I sensed Jackson had with his dad.

He turned and faced me. "Don't be. I had a good upbringing. Nobody's life is perfect. Was yours?" He flopped back down and reached over to brush away a curl from my cheek.

"Close. My mom did everything for me, probably loved me too much, if there's such a thing. She worked hard to allow me to play sports and not have a job during high school."

"What's your dad like?"

I wasn't sure how much to divulge. Jackson knew my dad had a heart attack years ago, knew he was a microbiologist, knew he loved to golf, knew he was nine years older than my mom…but he didn't know my dirty little secret.

He'd opened up about his childhood. I wanted to do the same.

"My dad is smart. He believes in hard work and I think it bothered him how much Mom coddled me. Looking back, I see I took advantage of it." I shrugged. "Mom always wanted more children. When that didn't happen, she focused all her love on me."

"And your dad?"

"He tried to be strict and expected the best from me…which I had a hard time delivering." A lump was snowballing in my throat, each layer built on memories.

Jackson was patient; likely sensing I was about to cough up emotions better left buried in the cobwebs of my memories.

"I still remember what pajamas I was wearing. They had a photo of the TV show *Full House* cast on the front. It was winter and my feet were cold as I stood in our hallway upstairs, on my way to the bathroom." My voice faltered. "I'd been in bed a while so I'm sure they thought I was sleeping. I stopped because I heard them raise their voices from the living room below—something they rarely did."

Painful shame coated my throat. "I'd failed a science test that day in school. It was my worst subject, and I was sure dad was disappointed in me. I stood still, listening to my mom plead with my dad to 'try harder.' I didn't know what she was talking about but I could hear in her voice how upset she was. And then dad said 'I just don't have it in me, Celia. I can't make myself feel the fatherly love you want me to. Stop pushing me to feel something I can't with her.'" A cool tear slid down my flushed cheek. Jackson wiped it away with his thumb.

"I'm sure your dad loves you. Maybe he was just having a bad day." Jackson whispered.

"I know he does, but I also think his disappointment in me has restricted his depth of love. My mom over-loved me, and I remember they continued to argue over his feelings toward me until I heard my dad leave, slamming the outside door, and my mom sobbing loudly." I had tiptoed to the bathroom and sat on the edge of the bathtub with my fists stuffed in my mouth to drown out my matching sobs.

"My mom was still so upset the next day she had her nervous hiccups."

"What are those?"

"I guess my mom inherited them from my grandma. Whenever they'd get really nervous, they'd get a full-blown case of the hiccups for hours. It's never happened to me though."

Jackson let go of my curl and reached over to hold my hand.

"From that point on, I recognized my glaring inability to grasp science and math the way my dad did…and the way my best friend in grade and high school did. I set low expectations so I wouldn't disappoint myself." I closed my eyes, remembering the feelings of inadequacy. "I'd allowed myself to second-guess my ability to succeed. Which is why making it in the store is so important to me."

Success came in all forms. Mine would come in the shape of a store.

I leaned in as Jackson's strong arms enveloped me in reassurance and comfort. We'd opened a can of worms I'd buried for two decades. As painful as my memory was, a slice of it had been lifted simply by sharing it with him.

Chapter 22

I didn't have to count the days until Labor Day, Logan and Adam were doing it for me. Less than three weeks until Labor Day weekend. Susan would be my only employee after that since both Logan and Adam were in fall sports.

Jackson stopped by Wednesday on his way to work. "We should take advantage of your help and get away for a couple of days before Adam and Logan go back to school."

I clapped like a kid getting a birthday present. "I'd love to! Where are we going?"

"I thought maybe you'd like to go to the State Fair. The Twins are home for a few games the end of August too if you're interested in taking in a baseball game."

"The State Fair?" It was an event I looked forward to every year, one I'd thought I'd have to miss. It was a great sacrifice for Jackson. He hated crowds. And I loved him for the offer.

Our conversation was interrupted by an elderly couple and their young grandson, in to pick up the package of powdered-sugar donuts they bought every time their grandson came to visit. Jackson wandered up to the tackle section while I waited on them. When I made my way to him, I saw Jackson holding his baseball cap against the pegboard where the tackle hung.

His hat was moving.

I slowed my steps. "What are you doing?"

His face said it all. He wanted to lie, but the truth was obvious.

"Are you hiding a bat under there?" I shivered at the thought of the creepy creature being unleashed in the store.

"Busted. Now if you could get me the dustpan, I think I can slide it under my cap to trap the poor guy until I can release him outside."

I hurried to get the dustpan, in case the bat broke free from Jackson's hat. Like a sissy, I ran to my house and shut the door before yelling approval for Jackson to make his move.

A minute later, he opened the door to my house. "All clear, city girl." He leaned in and gave me a kiss. "Got to run now. We'll talk later about our trip, but if you can line up Logan and Adam to help Susan for a few days, it'd be fun to get away."

After he left I spent the next fifteen minutes inspecting every wall in the store. The last thing I wanted was another bat surprise.

* * *

Tracie, Charlee, and I biked the paved trails around Blue Bay a few nights later. I told them about my upcoming trip to the State Fair with Jackson. "Wow, someone sounds serious."

"Me?" I asked Tracie.

"No, Jackson. I've worked for him for years and don't remember him taking a trip to a place sure to make him gnaw his fingers off. Jackson willing to put up with the State Fair crowd for you…that tells me something." She adjusted a pink baseball cap over her short blonde hair.

"Not even for Wendy." Charlee agreed as she pedaled a few paces ahead of us. "She loves to go to concerts and even after she'd lassoed him, I remember Jackson saying no way in hell would he go to one of those mob-fests." She glanced back at me and smiled.

A mile later we stopped for ice cream cones. Something didn't sit right with me about Charlee's choice of words. They sounded a lot like Nancy's nasty comments about Wendy.

The three of us sat at a picnic table outside the ice cream shop, each with our double scoop of our favorite flavors. I'd chosen peppermint bonbon and peanut butter fudge. "What exactly do you mean by Wendy lassoing Jackson? You make it sound like she cornered him into the relationship."

"Well, she certainly cornered him into getting engaged," Charlee stated before taking a bite of her butter-brickle ice cream. Tracie elbowed her, her mouth pressed shut.

"What's going on? What aren't you telling me?" My eyes volleyed back and forth between their should-have-kept-our-mouth-shut looks.

Charlee averted her eyes to concentrate on her sugar cone and Tracie coughed out an "Oh, shit." Charlee had spilled the beans about something. I just wasn't sure what.

We experienced a few moments of silence as if we were paying our respects at a memorial. It was rare with these two. In the month's I'd come to know Charlee and Tracie, we were nearly at the same comfort level I had with Ella. That said a lot.

Tracie blew at her bangs. "What did Jackson tell you about their engagement?" Her words were slow.

This was a pivotal moment for me. I should tell them the truth. "Honestly? Nothing."

Tracie shook her head. "He was as serious about Wendy as he was about a piece of lint. Jackson likes life uncomplicated, and Wendy's middle name is complicated."

"So why did he date her?" I saw the physical attraction. Wendy is striking and smart. Just don't add alcohol to that mix.

"Other than for a good time? I'm not sure. I doubt it would have lasted more than a few dates if not for the phantom pregnancy."

My pulse throbbed in my neck, in sync with my drumming heart. *Phantom pregnancy?*

"Her shenanigans put Jackson off of women for at least a year…until you," Charlee said. "If you're a good person, Jackson does what he can to help you. He offered the kids and me his rental home for next to nothing years ago." Charlee shook her head. "He'd step up and do what was right whether you deserved it or not. Wendy telling him she was pregnant likely forced his sense of responsibility to make an 'honest woman' out of her."

Tracie laughed at the irony. "Of course, you can only pretend to be pregnant for so long before you have to produce a changing body shape. A few months into their engagement, Wendy pretended to miscarry, milking Jackson's sorrow to the max. By then he'd adjusted to the idea of impending parenthood and grieved the news of her losing the baby."

Charlee continued the story. "Until things didn't add up. Wendy hadn't kept track of her lies, how far along she was, and how the baby should have developed. After tripping over her deceit, Jackson figured it out. He took the ring back and swore off ever dating again. We know how that turned out." She grinned at me. "Now, Jackson's going to the State Fair."

My fingers became sticky from the melted ice cream I'd forgotten about. They'd assumed I knew of the engagement and pregnancy, figuring Jackson just didn't tell me details.

Hell, he hadn't told me *any* of it.

When I confessed my lack of knowledge to Tracie and Charlee they were mortified. "I'm so sorry for opening my big mouth! After Wendy's actions when we all went tubing down the river, I figured he'd have coughed up the truth." Charlee cringed.

It bothered me that Jackson had withheld this important part of his past.

To divert our conversation, Tracie asked how it was going for me with the motion detector lights. "They go on and off a lot at night with all the critters roaming around outside. I don't care. I think it may deter someone from sneaking around, but who knows?"

I poured water from my water bottle over my hands, rubbing them together to clean them up. I studied my stubby nails. "You two are going to think I'm nuts when I tell you this, but sometimes I feel like someone has been in my house moving things around or taking things."

They sat across from me on the picnic table. I raised my eyes to meet theirs. "Crazy, right? I've been locking my back door and all my windows 24/7 now, so nobody can get in. I think I'm just getting so distracted that I'm misplacing things." I needed a rational explanation of my lost bra, Pixie's cat food, my favorite coffee mug…I could make a long list of things lost.

"Oh my God, Molly! No, you probably aren't crazy." Tracie's eyes widened. "I mean, for sure you aren't crazy, and I doubt you're imagining things."

Charlee nodded. "She's right. There could be several people out there with copies of keys to Rosie's. She's had people working for her over the years, each of them having a set of keys. Rosie was so trusting. Who knows who all has access to your place?"

Tracie leaned forward on her elbows. "We should have thought of this before. You need to change the locks on the place. Did you talk to Jackson about it?"

"No, I didn't want him to think I was losing it." The irony wasn't lost on me.

I wasn't telling Jackson what was happening in my life now.

He wasn't telling me about his past.

It was time we both came clean.

"You need a break, Molly, a break from this town." Charlee drummed her fingers, the wheels in her brain turning as she pressed her lips together. Suddenly, she jumped up. "Hey, you could go to the upcoming 'Hell Club' event with me, as my guest!"

"The what club?" I squinted at her.

"I'm going to a book event next week and we've got an extra ticket since one of the women in this club I belong to had to cancel. It's a fun event called Wine & Words. You get a great meal, get to hear authors talk, and there's wine tasting and a silent auction. How 'bout it?"

"Are you going, Tracie?" I felt bad Charlee asked me in front of her.

"Nope, I don't think I qualify to be in her club." She winked at Charlee.

"What are the qualifications?" I couldn't imagine how I'd qualify for a club.

"It's called 'The To-Hell-And-Back Club', or 'Hell Club,' for short. The women who join have been through a variety of tough things. We have our own fun events or attend ones together and our motto is to lift each other up instead of allowing life to drag us down."

Charlee pointed at me. "You, girl, qualify. C'mon, it'll be fun. You could use some fun."

She was right. My life was being taken over by a psychotic person I couldn't identify.

And I was afraid what his next move would be.

* * *

Jackson was at a fireman's meeting that night, a night we usually didn't call each other. I was thankful for that. I had no idea what to ask about Wendy without sounding needy myself.

He stopped in the next morning on his way to the hardware store, as he did most mornings. As he helped himself to a cup of coffee, I rang up Old Lloyd's newspaper, half-and-half, and bananas. It was the fifth morning in a row Old Lloyd had stopped in, acting as if it was the most natural thing in the world.

After Old Lloyd left, Jackson leaned in and kissed me. "Morning, sweet cheeks. How was your biking with Tracie and Charlee? You didn't wear Tracie out so she's worthless today, did you?" He asked before taking a drink of his coffee.

"I think she'll be fine." I leaned against the counter. "Something came up last night that I'd like to talk to you about." I eyed a car pulling into the parking lot. "Maybe we can go for a walk tonight on the beach after I close the store?" It was one of my favorite things to do, and soon, those warm, balmy nights would be gone. I never imagined I'd be lucky enough to live right across the street from a lake. I needed to take advantage of it more often.

"Sure, I'll be here by seven." He kissed the tip of my nose before leaving for work.

Twelve hours later, we'd grabbed a bite to eat and walked over to the long stretch of beach. It was a breezy night, which kept the bugs away, and the setting sun gave off a kaleidoscope of oranges, reds, and yellows. I reached for Jackson's hand.

"You know we never really talked about Wendy's actions that day we all tubed down the river." I looked up at him and noticed Jackson clench his jaw.

"Not much to say. Wendy shouldn't drink."

I took a deep breath. "No, there's more to say. Why haven't you talked to me about being engaged to her? Why haven't you said anything about her pretending to be pregnant?"

Jackson squeezed my hand. "Because I'd rather forget it. It wasn't worth bringing up. She isn't worth talking about." His voice betrayed his nonchalance.

I stopped walking. "For you, maybe. But for me, it makes me feel like you're keeping secrets, or that you think so little of our relationship that being honest isn't important to you." I revealed my heart for him to flatten with a steamroller.

He pinched the bridge of his nose. I waited. Once we laid this conversation open, I'd tell him about my secret concern someone was breaking into my home.

"Wendy and I dated a few times, nothing serious, which is exactly how I wanted it. Watching my parents tolerate each other has made me in no hurry to settle down." He looked out at the lake. "Then Wendy tells me she's pregnant. We'd used protection the few times things happened, but I was aware it had a small percentage of failure. After showing me a positive pregnancy test she had me convinced."

He shrugged. "Initially, I thought we should do the right thing and get married. I barely got the words out of my mouth and Wendy was looking at engagement rings. She wanted to get married right away. It was last May—the beginning of our busy season—and just a few months after Rosie passed away. I had a lot to take care of and wanted to wait until September. Honestly, I was sick about the whole thing, already regretting my decision. I'm not proud to admit I'd likely have never gone through with the marriage.

"I may not know much about babies, but I knew enough that her stomach should've been getting bigger that summer. When I confronted her about it in August, she faked a miscarriage the next week. I'll spare you the lies and details, but when it was all said and done, I called off our engagement. That was last year. I was in no hurry for another relationship."

I raised an eyebrow but remained silent. Gently, Jackson reached over and tucked my hair behind my ear. "Until now." His whisper was husky.

It was what I believed in my heart, but I needed to hear it from him.

"If I didn't feel that way, I wouldn't be planning a trip to the god-awful State Fair with you, or the Twins game." He picked up my hand and kissed it. "Although I love baseball, I'm just not sure I'm looking forward to fighting my way through the crowd to see them play live."

I wanted to savor the knowledge he was willing to attend two crowded events just for me, but I needed to focus on my confession. I pulled him down on the sand next to me.

"I have something I should have told you, too. I think someone's been in my house off and on. Originally, I thought it was my overworked brain misplacing things. Now, I'm not so sure." I dumped my mental list of things I'd noticed missing off and on over the summer. Jackson's face turned so red I was afraid he was going to break a blood vessel.

"Molly! You need to tell me these things! After everything that's happened to you, you can't just assume it's you being absent-minded." His jaw was clenched.

"I know, I know. But I've checked. My locks aren't tampered with and none of my windows are broken." Looking back now, it was too much to ignore, yet I had. I told him Charlee and Tracie's theory of too many copies of my keys out to townspeople over the years.

"They're right. I'll order new locks for you tomorrow. A separate key for your store, and another for your house, like you have now." They were the only two doors in the whole building. Rosie had purchased an old house, and little by little had it remodeled over fifty years to add more and more room to the store.

Whoever had access to my house thankfully hadn't set foot in my store. They must not have a key for that door or I was certain my inventory would noticeably dwindle.

I'd feel better with new locks for my home. I was sure of it.

Chapter 23

Susan covered for me in the store the following Thursday afternoon. Charlee picked me up and we drove to a fancy resort on Gull Lake for the Wine & Words event. "We'll meet the other women there since most of them live in that area." We had a nearly one-hour drive.

"Tell me more about these women." I was curious about this "Hell Club."

"I joined several years ago after my husband left. We lived out in the middle of nowhere, no running water, no running anything, including my car. When my youngest was two he fell down our steps. His leg was broken, and possibly more." Her mouth was downturned. "I had no phone service to call anybody. I scooped him up and ran a mile to our nearest neighbor's house for help. I left Adam, who was six at the time, to watch his younger two sisters. It was awful."

I couldn't even imagine how horrible her struggles were back then. "Joining this club changed my life. I'd been too stubborn before to ask for help—the one thing I desperately needed. After meeting the amazing women in the 'Hell Club,' they helped me fill out paperwork to receive grant money and aid to go back to school and get my nursing degree. And because of Jackson, I was able to move closer to town and rent a house dirt cheap from him. I had nearby help for daycare and didn't feel so alone."

Charlee glanced my way. "The women from the club showed me I wasn't alone. With their support, I started a new life. It was a real game changer for me. Every woman joins for their own reason, but I can tell you, I've never heard a woman regret joining. I think you would benefit from this club. Not every event we have is fun. Some are educational, and the club has a pay-it-forward system to support each other and any new members."

"Do you know what your next event is?" My brain already told me Charlee was right.

"I'll check the calendar and let you know. Tonight, we are all about the fun. I want you to relax, kick back and have some wine, and I'll drive us home safely." Charlee smiled at me.

We arrived at the event center and stepped inside a crowded room filled with registration lines, wine tasting lines, and side rooms stuffed with silent auction baskets. After we received our table number and name tags with our bid numbers, we stood in the wine tasting line with the wine glasses we'd been handed. "I like this event already," I said as we chose which bottle of wine we wanted to taste. Charlee texted the other women and we met up with them in the silent auction room. Charlee made the introductions.

Michelle, tall and blonde, and Mary Beth, petite with sleek black hair, introduced their guest. "I'd like you to meet Lily. She's thinking of joining the 'Hell Club' too, and this is her first event." Michelle gestured to a petite blonde who gave me a slight smile.

I shook everyone's hand before we all dispersed to check out the silent auction baskets. We'd meet back at our assigned table for dinner.

I bid on one basket. It sang my name, full of various coffees and flavorings, rekindling my goal to eventually have a coffee bar in my store. At 6:00 p.m., we all sat at our assigned table and enjoyed a delicious meal in between laughter and information about past and future club events. My curiosity was piqued. These women seemed perfectly fine, but looks could be deceiving. I likely didn't come off as a woman who'd been threatened and was fighting mind games with a mysterious man who was determined to wreck my life.

Before I could dwell on it all, a spritely blonde woman with a smile as wide as her red glasses took the stage as our dinner plates were cleared away. "Lorna Landvik is a Minnesota author and emcees Wine & Words every year. She's a hoot," Charlee whispered to me.

Charlee was right. By the time she finished serenading us with her Norwegian accent and ukulele, we were all laughing so hard Charlee had to make a beeline for the bathroom so she wouldn't wet her pants.

The five authors who followed were the topping on an already delicious treat. As I listened to them talk about their books, plot lines, and their path to publishing, my resolve to not let anything stop me from attaining my dreams was energized.

And if they weren't inspiration enough, the table of "Hell Club" women around me was.

* * *

We picked up Ella and her fiancé, Rolf, on our way to the State Fair. Introductions were made between Jackson and Rolf while I moved to the backseat with Ella. She slipped in beside me and reached forward and ran her fingers through Jackson's wavy hair.

"Ahhh, one less fantasy to chase now." She joked while Rolf shook his head from the front seat, not surprised at all by his fiancé's action.

"I'd apologize for her behavior but I'm afraid if I did that, those are the only words you'd ever hear from me." Rolf winked at Ella before she swatted his shoulder.

"I've been keeping it longer, just for you, Ella." Jackson deadpanned as he pulled out of their driveway and drove to the State Fair.

We ate everything imaginable they served on a stick before heading to the Midway, where the rides and games were—a big mistake mixing fair food and fast rides.

Rolf and Jackson waited a couple hours before they allowed themselves to be strapped in the slingshot ride and then shot high into the air as they screamed like teenage girls. They'd tried to convince us to go on it with them. We had brains. We wanted to keep them.

The day flew by, and I never heard Jackson complain once about the crowd. Our night was topped off with the Carrie Underwood concert in the State Fair Grandstand and I beamed sandwiched between Ella and Jackson.

It was after midnight when we dropped off Ella and Rolf at their house. They'd invited us to stay there when we told them of our trip plans. We opted for a hotel with a hot tub.

The Minnesota Twins played at noon the next day. If the State Fair didn't seal my love for Jackson, hearing him again comfortably belt out the national anthem out of key at the Twins game cemented my feelings.

Unfortunately, I didn't know what in the hell to do about it.

* * *

It was the beginning of a hectic Labor Day weekend. Jackson and I would both be busy with our businesses. He stopped by Saturday morning on his way to work…right as I was drying my eyes while I waited on the phone.

"What now?" He mouthed, likely wondering what could make me cry so early in the morning.

"I forgot to lock my ice cooler last night. All of the ice outside was stolen. Every single block and bag." I wiped my eyes with the back of my hand and continued to wait on hold.

"Yes, I'm still here." I straightened in attention. "That would be wonderful. Thank you so much. I appreciate it." I hung up and pinched the bridge of my nose.

"I'm so stupid. I was so tired last night, we stayed open until after ten. When Logan and Adam were ready to leave, I talked to them out in the parking lot, came back inside, and spaced out about locking the ice cooler." I wiped my cheek with the bottom of my shirt.

"The ice truck is heading our way this morning anyway. Some other businesses are running low and won't make it through the weekend. I'm lucky, I won't get charged extra for them making this trip. But of course, I'm out over five hundred dollars with the cost of the ice."

Jackson paced. "I can't stand this. I want to strangle whoever is doing this to you."

"Maybe it was just some teenager, hoping to make money from selling the ice."

"Not when it's warm like this. If someone stumbled upon the open ice cooler, not planning ahead, they'd have had to come back with a pickup truck or something to haul a cooler full of ice. Unless they had a place to store something like that, they'd have nothing but water to sell today." He was talking logic. It was hard to think about this being one more thing someone purposely did to hurt me, both financially and emotionally.

He stopped in front of me, putting his hands on my shoulders. "I didn't want to tell you this, but I've asked my friends to help keep an eye on your place."

"I don't know if that makes me feel better or worse." Better, that people were looking out for me. Worse, that they needed to.

"I'd have heard if anyone saw something out of the ordinary last night. I have a friend who works the eleven-to-seven shift at the hospital. He drives by your place about ten-thirty at night." Jackson went back to pacing in front of me. "As you know, Scratch drives by early every morning to open the café, and Mike keeps a close eye from Ernie's Garage."

"Who else do you have watching out for me?"

He gave me a small grin as if I'd caught him caring about me too much. "Rick, since he swings shifts at the paper mill, Drake, being a realtor, drives through town all the time, and I've even asked Curt, even though he'd done his best to bad-mouth me to you. I figure he knows everyone in town from working at the bank. Basically, anyone who is out and about, I've asked."

Two cars pulled up in my parking lot. I needed to get to work, so did Jackson.

"Unfortunately, I've got a buying show coming up in Wisconsin for a few days. I'm not thrilled about having to leave town. Could you take some time off from the store and come with me?"

It was tempting. "I can't. Adam and Logan will be back in school. Susan can't work three days straight, she's too busy with her end-of-summer cleaning business." I gave him a quick kiss before customers walked in the door. "Thanks for asking though."

"Come over after work tonight. I'll make us a late dinner, foot rub included," he said.

"*That* I can do."

* * *

I was a puddle by the time he was done rubbing my feet and legs. We were lying on his bear rug in front of the fireplace. The nights were already cooling off and the fire helped take the chill out of the air.

He leaned over me. "I've got a little gift for you." His grin was mischievous.

"Something even better than the foot rub?"

He reached over to the fireplace hearth and handed me a small gift bag. "Made especially for you." He pulled me up to a sitting position.

I peered inside the bag and pulled out several neatly folded garments. I slowly unfolded seven pairs of boy briefs, each pair embroidered with tiny cursive writing that said: 'Sassy pants' followed by the day of the week.

"Where did you get these?" I chuckled. They were so cute, and so 'me.'

"Susan. We were talking about your underwear being taken from your house, among other things. Somewhere in our conversation, I may have said you wear sassy-pants every day, and she put the two together. She thought you could use some underwear that said 'Sassy Pants.' I told her you wear dental floss panties during the day but at night wear those boy-type briefs. She took it from there."

"I'm impressed at her talent." I knew Susan sewed but I hadn't seen any of her work. I ran my hand over the soft cotton material. "I love your sense of humor, and I love these undies." I leaned in and kissed him. What a sweet and clever gift.

He whispered back. "I love your sass. I love your spunk. And I love you."

As soon as the words escaped his lips, our eyes widened. Clearly, Jackson's admission surprised him as much as it did me. He leaned back against the hearth. "Well, *that* slipped out."

"Slipped out like you didn't mean it or slipped out because you weren't ready to say it?" I didn't want to ignore his words. My brain had been juggling those same words for weeks.

He took my hand and studied it as if it was something he'd never noticed before. "Oh, I definitely mean it. I don't think I've said it to another girl since I was thirteen and said whatever I needed to just so that Jennifer Carter would let me kiss her." He looked up at me and grinned.

I relaxed into his arms. "I've been thinking about saying it ever since the night a few weeks ago when we were out on your deck on that airbed." I cupped his chin in my hands. "I love you, Jackson Brennan. You may not be sassy, but you're sure bossy." I kissed him hard.

"Speaking of bossy, since you refuse to stay here, you need a security system." His mouth was set. It wasn't the first time he'd brought the subject up.

I pulled away. "I can't afford a security system. I'm barely carrying enough in my savings right now to get through the lean winter months."

"And I can't afford to have something happen to you. I'll lend you the money."

My gut flinched. It was a tempting offer but it reminded me too much of the financial road I'd taken with Nick. "I appreciate the offer, but I want to do things on my own. It's important to me."

Jackson rubbed his face with his hand. "I understand, Molly. What I don't understand is how you think nothing bad is going to happen to you. I'm afraid that whoever has it in for you is going to ramp up their threats."

I didn't want to think about what move the person might make next. So I leaned back on the bear rug and pulled Jackson on top of me. For now, it was easier to focus on the man I loved, than on the man who haunted my nightmares.

Chapter 24

In the weeks after Labor Day, I had plenty of time to focus on the nagging feeling someone was *still* in my home at times when I wasn't there, even though the locks had been changed on my store and home. There were no signs of a break in, so I worked hard at convincing myself it was my on-guard paranoid imagination. Surely nobody would take my winter boots. I must've stored them away last spring in an extra safe location.

Business died like a light switched off. Kids were back in school which meant no more families up during the week. Retired cabin owners hung around, but they weren't the daily customers who'd purchased sunscreen, T-shirts, snacks, and toys over the past few months.

Downsizing my orders after a summer of gluttony wasn't easy. If I ordered too much my savings would sit on the shelf instead of in the bank. The fact that it took two thousand dollars in sales to make up for the cost of the stolen ice robbed the joy out of my gang-buster weekend.

I almost looked forward to Drive-by-Daisy's nosy visits to the store. Almost. That woman was persistent.

With the days getting shorter, I treasured a walk on the beach after closing up at night. One night I stayed until dusk, tossing around ideas for the coming months—months that petrified me—something I was too embarrassed to admit out loud to anyone. When I unlocked my door a bat flew through my kitchen. I grabbed an ice cream pail and my tennis racket, and calmly turned every light on in my house, knowing the bat would stop flying.

I found it hanging on the wall above my sofa. I carefully trapped it between the wall and racket, sliding it down into the pail and covering the pail with the racket. I released it outdoors to fly away to freedom, much as I'd done a handful of times over the past month. Call me a former bat scaredy-cat. I called myself brave.

Hell, for all I knew, I was catching and releasing the same bats every time.

They were the least of my problems.

The bats scared me less than the uneasy feeling I had of being watched. My personal stuff was no longer personal inside my home. My locks had been changed, I kept my windows locked if I was gone or sleeping, so nobody was sneaking in. I blamed my secret stress. What in the hell was I going to do to keep financially afloat until next spring?

* * *

I'd cut my hours after Labor Day by a total of ten hours per week, which helped with my energy level, if not my financial future. I went Rollerblading or biking every night after work, getting to know the outskirts of town. The home with nine children and three clotheslines almost always weighed down with clothing, the elderly gentleman who sat on his porch every night, rocking in his rocking chair and smoking a pipe—a scent I came to enjoy as I went by. The heady aroma of pine trees and campfires…I took it all in, thankful to be outdoors.

I also spent many nights at Charlee's home, helping them can everything from salsa, green beans, and pickles, to homemade raspberry and blueberry jams.

Her talents were endless. "I want to live with you if Armageddon happens," I said as I washed canning jars at her sink.

"Yep, most of us out here are pretty self-sufficient. And what one of us doesn't make the other does. We trade and barter our homemade goods so that we have most of what we need." Charlee's smile held pride. "I'm thankful to have the opportunity to live here off the land again, and to have the neighbors that I do."

"I know Old Lloyd lives nearby. Who else are your neighbors?" The term "neighbor" was used loosely as most people lived on several acres.

"Paulina lives past me, over a mile away. She's the one who I ran to that day when my youngest had fallen down our steps. She had an old Chevy truck and drove all of us into town. She raises sheep and goats." After Charlee became a nurse, she'd come back to the land they'd struggled on and built a new home.

"Old Lloyd harvests wild rice, right?" Mr. Grumpy was a hard worker.

"Old Lloyd also taps maple trees, and makes some kick-ass wine," Charlee said.

I set sterilized canning jars on trays for her to fill with salsa. "What does everyone trade?" Charlee was surrounded by self-sufficient people.

"I mostly trade canned items from my garden. I get the raspberries and blueberries from Old Lloyd's patch. He lets the kids and me pick for canning. Lloyd provides wild rice he picks once he's had it processed, Paulina makes goat milk soap, and hats and mittens from the sheep wool, and of course her goats produce milk."

I helped Charlee put the lids and rings on the filled salsa jars. "Lloyd, as I mentioned, makes maple syrup and wine, and we all raise chickens. Most of us fish and hunt." Once we loaded the jars inside the canning processor, we carried it to the outdoor gas stove.

"So, yes, theoretically we could live off the land if it came down to it. We all heat with wood, although I have electric backup for those times we're away from home. But I feel self-sufficient, and that's very important to me." Charlee and I walked back in the kitchen to fill glasses of iced tea. We took the iced tea to her back steps and sat down.

"I think that's the big thing for me now," I said. "After relying on Nick for financial support, I don't want to rely on anyone else again." We sat next to each other, enjoying the lush green woods' scenery behind her home with our bare feet comfy in the soft, thick grass.

"Jackson wants to help, but I'm so afraid of going down that dependent road again."

"I felt the same after my ex-husband left us. Never again. I like being responsible for myself and my kids. Nobody to disappoint me." She raised her glass as a toast to independence.

That was it. If I only relied on me, the only person who could disappoint me would be me. I could live with that.

* * *

Rosie had installed a door buzzer when the store door opened to alert her in the kitchen if someone came in while she was back in her house. I'd disconnected it over the summer. It would've been going off non-stop, and I rarely had time to go back in the house for anything besides preparing a quick bite to eat.

But now? Mid-September had brought a quiet I hadn't experienced since I opened last April. It was nice to have time to throw in a load of laundry, clean my bathroom, or put an easy meal together. It gave me plenty of time to think.

On a quiet Wednesday, I stood in the store, trying to think outside the box to come up with a solution to the upcoming winter months. As I surveyed the store it hit me. It was more than no-customers-quiet. Other than the water in minnow tanks running, the grocery section was eerily quiet. The milk cooler wasn't humming.

I walked over to it, didn't hear the compressor running, slid open one of the glass doors, and felt the warmth. The thermometer I kept on the middle shelf inside read forty-eight degrees. Eight degrees higher than it should be. How freaking lovely.

Chapter 25

I'd been nursing the milk cooler since opening the store last April. I'd add Freon to the compressor and things would be good for a few weeks. I needed to replace the cooler. To go without it wasn't feasible. The four-door cooler held milk, eggs, butter, cheeses, meats, and 3.2% beer. Without those in the summer, I may as well lock the door. I called the refrigeration guy who'd helped me months ago by nursing the cooler along.

"It's been running on borrowed time."

It seemed to be the story of my life for the past year.

He showed up an hour later and studied it like it was a patient. "I'm afraid it's time to put this thing out of its misery."

Was it worth replacing right now, or was this another indication for me to close up shop for the winter? After he left, I pulled up a nearby supplier's website for a used grocery equipment business an hour south of town. I spent the remainder of the morning searching their website, and others located in Minnesota. The best deal I found was over two grand.

Susan came in and covered for me for half a day on Friday as I made a trip to the distributor to check out the three-door glass cooler.

"I'm coming with you," Jackson said when I spoke with him last night.

"Thanks, but you don't need to. I pretty much know I'll end up buying it. I don't have a whole lot of choice. There's no point in me staying open now if I can't even carry milk, butter, and eggs. Once I make the decision, they'll deliver it and connect everything, and then take my old one out. Piece of cake." Other than writing the check. Ouch.

"You doing okay for money? I feel bad that everything Rosie had was on its last legs."

"You mean your great-aunt who *gave* me a business and home to live in? Seriously, Jackson, the last thing I can do is complain about replacing some equipment. I'm more than thankful for her generosity." I sat down at the kitchen table to count the paltry money in my cash drawer. I appreciated what I'd been given. Okay, what my mom had been given. Things could be so much worse.

"It bugs the hell out of me that mom has every new appliance under the sun at her cabin here, and it sits empty nine months a year." In his spare time, he'd been winterizing Nancy's cabin since she'd left the end of August. Draining her water pipes, making sure everything was cleaned up, shut off, and ready to sit vacant until she showed up again next June.

"Pretty sure your mother doesn't have a large commercial-sized refrigerator." I didn't want to think about it anymore so I changed the subject. "What time are you picking me up Saturday? I'm closing at six." I'd been flexible with my hours, depending on the weekend traffic. Saturday was the town's annual harvest bonfire, and I didn't want to miss it.

"I'm taking the afternoon off to help set up for the bonfire," Jackson said. "What are you making for the potluck? I'm making grilled teriyaki grouse. You'll probably see a lot of wild game dishes there."

"I'm bringing double-fudge brownies." Every year, at a recently logged field somewhere outside of town, the townspeople gathered for a huge bonfire, hay rides, dancing, and plenty of food. Anyone who played an instrument was encouraged to bring it along and contribute to the "band." Travis said he'd be there with his maracas. Susan, his aunt, was bringing him. She'd told me he always looked forward to the harvest bonfire.

Many of the elderly people, who had owned their acreage for decades, remembered my grandpa. Over the months I'd lived in Love, I'd heard grumbles about my grandpa leaving town owing many families money. I now had a better idea of what my mom's upbringing was like after her mother passed away. Little money, a lot of work, and even more responsibility placed on her shoulders by my grandpa, who struggled to raise his daughters, run a fledgling sawmill business, and make ends meet without his wife.

* * *

When Jackson and I arrived at the bonfire, it appeared over half the town was there already…families with toddlers, the elders of the town, and every age in between. Hay bales were placed around the clearing for people to sit on. Tables made with particle board sheets placed on top of sawhorses groaned with food. Two hay wagons wove their way through the acreage, pulled by horses, and overflowing with kids and adults perched atop each wagon.

A band of sorts played off to the side, where brush had been leveled by bed box-springs to form a dance floor. There was Travis, actually smiling as he shook his maracas. Mike surprised me by playing a fast tune on a fiddle, Old Lloyd was harmonizing on a harmonica, and Scratch had a galvanized tub flipped over, banging on it with rubber hammers. A handful of people I didn't know rounded out the band with various instruments—real or homemade. And Tracie was front and center, playing guitar and singing her heart out.

"This is awesome!" I exclaimed to Jackson as I took it all in.

"I know." He teased in a pompous voice. "C'mon, let's put this food down." He led the way to the food tables where we added our contributions to the spread.

Over the next few hours, we ate, went on a hayride, and visited with everyone. Jackson introduced me to people I'd never seen enter my store. Some welcomed me and others made sure I remembered that my family left a bad taste in locals' mouths decades ago.

"It's their problem, not yours." Both Jackson and Tracie reminded me. "If they can't let go of something from fifty years ago, that's their crutch."

Jackson went to talk to the band as Charlee and an elderly woman approached me. "Paulina, this is Molly who I've told you about. Molly, meet the talented Paulina." Paulina had a sweet, weathered face, a welcoming smile, and the hands of a farmer.

"Ah, so this is Molly." She pumped my hand, squeezing it firmly. "I don't get to town much. Old Lloyd does most of my shopping for me. I'll have to make a point of stopping in your store the next time I'm in town."

Paulina, like most of Charlee's neighbors living miles from town, was a recluse of sorts. They were happy to work their land, content to be one with nature and not people. Paulina filled me in on more of the town's history until Jackson came and nudged my side.

"I'm sorry to interrupt, but Mike told me they're going to play "Red Neck Girl" in a few minutes." He turned to Charlee and Paulina. "I'm going to borrow Molly, ladies. Hope that's okay." Jackson did a quick bow and pulled me by the hand over to the dance floor.

"Do you know how to two-step?" He hollered over the band. I didn't, but I had a feeling I'd learn real quick.

"Follow my lead. Just think 'quick-quick-slow-slow.' I'll guide you." He looked down at my tennis shoes. "Those shouldn't hurt me too much." He took me firmly in his arms, his left arm around my waist, his left hand gripping my right.

Curt and Drake had taken center stage, each with a microphone. A full moon hung in the clear sky as the band revved up. The two took turns singing the classic tune, drawing a wide age range out to dance. I stumbled. Jackson sang off-key. We grinned like lovesick teens.

"I figured I'd fall in love with a redneck girl. Instead, look at me—a city slicker has me wrapped around her cute little finger." He shouted in my ear as we danced.

"This city girl's cute little finger has forgotten what a manicure looks like," I shouted back with a smile. As he guided me around the makeshift dance floor, I took in the local talent. Most everyone I'd met had a talent of some sort.

I was still trying to discover mine. It wasn't doing the two-step.

When Jackson left to help some of the other men disassemble tables, I made my way to the portable bathrooms at the edge of the field. A hand touched my shoulder. I turned around.

It was Curt. "Hey, Molly, I've been meaning to talk to you. I wanted to apologize for being such a jerk a few months ago."

"What?" My mind backpedaled to the last time I spoke with Curt.

"You know when I said Jackson wouldn't stay with you for long, I didn't mean it. I was jealous. He's a decent guy, and you two seem to get along well." He smiled politely.

"Apology accepted. And thanks for saying that. You're a nice guy, Curt, with a lot to offer. I hope you find someone who makes you happy." Curt was beach boy handsome, and well-mannered. He just wasn't the right guy for me.

"You've got a great singing voice. I enjoyed listening to you and Drake tonight." I smiled before turning to wait my turn in line.

Many of the families with young children had already left, and most of the older folks had gone home to sleep. It was nearing midnight and I had a store to open in the morning.

We said our goodbyes to everyone and drove several miles back to town. "You sure you don't want to stay at my place tonight?" Jackson asked as he pulled into my driveway. The dependable motion detector lights went on.

"I won't get six hours of sleep as it is. If I stay at your house, it'll be even less." We'd talked of him staying overnight at my place, but Trigger had been home inside since Jackson had left at noon to set up the party. He'd never make it until tomorrow without an accident.

It was one of the many things I liked about Pixie. I could leave her a day or more with no concerns. Not that I would if I could help it. She'd become the pet I didn't know I wanted.

Stifling a yawn, I unlocked my door.

I stepped inside, flipped on my living room light.

And let out a bloodcurdling scream.

Chapter 26

Instinct drove me to run to my bathroom and lock the door. With shaking hands, I called Jackson's cell phone from mine. The word written in blood on my living room wall screamed in my brain as I ran past my personal things strewn all over my home in a mad dash for safety.

Jackson couldn't be far away. He barely answered before I relayed the terror gripping me.

"Where are you now?" His words were rushed.

"I locked myself in the bathroom." I stammered, my jaw shivering with each word. "I think the person is gone." I prayed the person was gone.

"I'm staying on the phone with you. I'll be there in just a minute. Did you call 911?"

"No. I knew you'd be close by so I've only called you. Should I?"

"Stay where you are. I'll let myself in your back door and we can call when I get there."

Thank goodness I'd given him a copy of my new key. While I listened for him I mentally checked off every guy I saw at the Harvest party, trying to think of anyone I knew who wasn't there. Someone could have snuck away from the party. It didn't narrow down the list at all.

Jackson interrupted my mental list-making. "Okay, I'm at your back door." I heard him unlock my door in stereo, both through the phone and from the other side of the bathroom door.

"I'm coming out." I wanted to get a better look at everything. I walked into the living room and watched his reaction to what I knew was on the wall behind me. He moved closer to me. On the living room wall, facing my back door, one word was written in blood.

LEAVE...written roughly a foot tall. With light-colored cat hair stuck to it.

I gasped. I hadn't noticed the tan and white cat hair before, but I hadn't taken the time to study it. My hand muffled the sobs forming from my heart. I didn't need to look around to know Pixie was likely gone. She hadn't greeted me when I'd walked in.

Jackson's arms wrapped around me, a cold draft from the nearby open window adding to my shivering nerves. "Oh, Molly, I am so sorry!" He kissed the top of my head as his words muffled against my hair. "I don't have to tell you this is dangerous."

"I know." Oh, how I knew. We walked around the living room holding hands. All the lights were on. We took in the paperwork destruction around my desk, the mess in my bedroom through the open door, and the open living room window, its screen lying haphazardly on the floor. The emotional pain in my throat felt like I'd swallowed a medieval flail.

"Thank God you're okay." He looked around. "You check the door to the store yet?"

"No. It's closed though." I assumed the intruder wouldn't have gone out there and shut the door behind him, but at this point, I shouldn't assume anything would make sense.

He walked over and jiggled the door. It was still locked. "Let's call 911. You didn't hear anything while you were in the bathroom, did you?"

"No, nothing." I couldn't stop my body from shaking or my teeth from chattering. I grabbed a blanket from the living room before I picked up the landline and dialed 911.

The dispatch operator answered and I rattled off information as her fingers tapped away on keys. "There's a deputy in your area. He should be there soon." I thanked her and hung up.

Restless energy emanated from Jackson. I followed him into the bedroom where clothes were scattered about. "I don't get it. What would they be looking for?" I bent down and double-checked the small safe inside the bedroom closet. It was still locked. "They clearly weren't breaking in to steal from me. My safe is locked, the store is locked."

"Hell if I know, Molly. I hate to have you do this, but I think you should go back in the bathroom with your cell phone and lock the door again. I want to take a look through your store."

"Do you think he somehow got in there?" He would have had to unlock the door to the store and then lock it again before leaving, which, again, made no sense. "Can you stay with me until a deputy shows up? Will Trigger be okay?"

"Of course I'm staying. Trigger can wait another hour." He held my clammy face in his hands. "You're coming home with me, at least for tonight." It was the most reasonable solution. I wasn't going to argue with him.

"Do you think Pixie is…out there?" I didn't want to think about Pixie's condition.

He shrugged as he escorted me to the bathroom. "I don't know, but I'm going to look around. Stay here." A few minutes later he rapped on the bathroom door and I opened it. "No sign of anything out there, including Pixie."

It was small comfort. I couldn't bear to find her dead. We sat at the kitchen table and waited impatiently. I yawned even while fear and adrenaline amped my body. We jumped out of our chairs when we saw the headlights from the Sheriff SUV pull into the driveway.

Two Sheriff Deputies were walking to my deck when Jackson opened the door. One of the deputies, Deputy Patrick, was becoming a regular at my place. The other one introduced himself. "We'll take photos and select items to bring back to the Sheriff's Office to fume for fingerprints," he explained as Deputy Patrick looked around.

"There are some good surfaces here for Cyanoacrylate fuming, as long as the person didn't wear gloves." Deputy Patrick studied the window screen lying on the living room carpet.

"Do you think that's cat blood?" I all but begged them to say "no."

"Hard to say. I'm sure whoever did it was too smart to use their own blood." Deputy Patrick touched it with his gloved finger. "It's dry. We'll collect a sample with sterile fluid."

The other deputy took photos, collected my window screen, some papers, and other items the person would have touched. I'd get it all back after they fumed them for fingerprints.

We sat at my kitchen table with Deputy Patrick to give him my statement. "I've been very careful about locking up everything." My weepy eyes stared at the wide open window. I was sure I hadn't opened my windows in weeks. I dabbed under my eyes. "I'm so sorry."

"No need to apologize. You shouldn't have to lock everything all the time." The deputy's mouth made a stern line. "I suggest a security system." His eyes traveled to Jackson for reinforcement. Jackson was diplomatic in his choice of words when he told the deputy he'd already presented that wise suggestion to me.

It was after two a.m. before we pulled into Jackson's driveway and fell into bed. "I can't sleep." I stared at the ceiling. We were too wound up.

"Any chance you can get someone to work for you for a while today so you can take a nap?" Jackson asked. I'd have to open the store in less than five hours. He'd taken the day off.

"I'll see." I snuggled closer to him.

It was hopeless to try and sleep. Our minds spewed out too many suspects, too many possibilities, and too few answers.

For the first time in my life, I felt truly scared.

Chapter 27

I set my cell phone alarm for six and called Ernie, knowing he'd be awake. "He'll be there before seven." I sighed in relief and plopped down next to Jackson again, anxious to fall back asleep. The last time I'd looked at my cell phone it read 4:17 a.m.

I was happy I'd given Ernie keys for my new door locks. "I love that old man," Jackson mumbled into his pillow before we both fell asleep.

Hours later, over a breakfast of eggs and toast, we dissected the latest threat.

"Okay, you don't have the money for security cameras and you won't let me help you out financially. I think we should install game cameras around the outside of your house and store. I've got a couple extra ones I don't need this fall, and we can get a couple more from some of my friends. It's not the perfect answer, but we need to do *something.*"

I liked his solution. "I feel like I'm being watched all the time now—and not just by Travis who still stands across the street." My admission caused Jackson to shake his head. My stubbornness frustrated him. "How do the cameras work?"

Jackson pulled up some images and information on his cell phone. "They have a decent range, but there's no way to catch every move. Many of us use them in the woods to scope out areas to hunt before the season opens."

He leaned back in his chair, arms folded across his chest. "I wish you'd just stay here for a while, at least until they figure out who's after you."

Colorful leaves dotted the lawn outside his kitchen window. I'd always loved fall but now I worried about the decline in business that came with it. "I'm not moving, Jackson. I'm not running away. It's exactly what this person wants me to do." I took the last sip of coffee and pushed back my chair. "Plus, it makes sense for me to live at my house so I can get things done there when the store isn't busy." Which was pretty much every weekday.

He leaned over the table. "Please stay here—for me." His hand reached out for mine.

I looked at our hands, his strong and warm, holding mine. It would be so easy to *let* him take care of me. Which is why I couldn't. "It's hard for me to explain to you, a guy, who has always been self-sufficient." I rubbed my thumb over his rough hand. "If I move in with you, I'm right back where I started when I lived in Minneapolis…relying on a man to take care of me."

He stood up, gathered our empty plates, and took them to the kitchen sink. "I'm trying to keep you safe. That's not the same thing." His body was tense, as if ready for a verbal attack.

I softened my defense. "I know it isn't. But remember what the deputy said after he looked over all my notes from the past six months? If someone really wanted to harm me, they'd have done it by now." It was a conclusion I'd come to around four a.m. "They're just trying to get me out of town, to give up, for whatever reason. If I move from my home, it means I give up and they win. I'm not giving up."

Images of Pixie, and what likely happened to her, choked my words. I blinked back the tears, but not before he noticed.

"You're thinking of your cat, aren't you? You say he won't hurt you. Well, I didn't think he would hurt an animal either." I watched Jackson's Adam's apple go up and down. He was fighting with his own visions. "People who torture animals have no problem harming people."

Standing next to him, I needed him to understand. "I know. I can only remind myself that he's never come in while I'm there, which he would do if he wanted to physically harm me." I looked into his eyes. "I think his way of getting rid of me involves my savings being depleted every time something happens. Between things being replaced in the store, and the personal financial damage, if I end up leaving town it's going to be because I can't financially make it here." The headache that had formed last night found its way back as I fought off tears.

"I want to make it on my own. Please." I pried open his defensively-crossed arms and stepped inside his embrace. There was no good answer to appease both of us.

* * *

The report from the sheriff's department wasn't promising. Not a single fingerprint. Just as we feared, the man had worn gloves. And the blood? Not human.

I stayed at Jackson's the next four nights until he and Scratch installed their game cameras, hopefully giving me another layer of protection.

My days in the store were spent surfing the internet, trying to devise different ways to make money. I needed a way to make use of the store—year round.

I had my marketing degree, years of experience in marketing, and a vivid imagination. If only I could dump all this worry out of my head, maybe I'd think creatively again.

I no longer had to run to the post office between customers. It was so quiet I could have breakfast at the post office and not miss a sale. The house was even quieter and so much emptier without Pixie. How did a cat I'd had only a few months make such an impact in my life?

Sitting behind the counter, I shuffled through the invoices, worried about how I'd pay for extra inventory. When I came to an envelope from TCF bank, I paused. Nick and I had financed our new vehicles through Twin City Federal a few years ago. I'd paid the loan off on my Lexus when I sold it and bought my old Ford Focus.

Foolishly, my heart skipped a beat. Maybe I'd overpaid my loan balance and this was a refund check? Of course not. I'd paid off the loan nine months earlier.

Whatever my brain concocted in those few seconds before I sliced the envelope open and slid out the paperwork, it sure wasn't that they'd be coming after me for money.

Nick had defaulted on his pickup loan payments.

And I'd cosigned. I was holding a slip of past-due payments to the tune of over $1,500.

I wanted to throw up. What had I been thinking when I'd agreed to cosign for a man who made three times as much money as I did but somehow spent five times as much?

My head fell into my lap and I choked back silent sobs. Hell, I could bellow out loud. Nobody would be coming in the store anytime soon if the past month was any indication. I swore under my breath and slammed my fist on the counter. Ouch!

Once my hand quit throbbing, I stomped to the store door and turned the door buzzer on. It would notify me if, by some bizarre miracle, a customer came in. I grabbed the stack of mail, my coffee, and my dignity, and brought it all back to the kitchen where I could curse out loud, and throw things, if need be.

I missed Pixie. She should be purring and curling around my leg, understanding my anger. I should be picking her up and wallowing in her furry cuddle.

I should've known, shouldn't have listened to Nick's sales pitch on how we were committed to each other already with our mortgage loan, what was the big deal about cosigning his pickup loan? This, this default on his loan was the *big deal.* Nick had a high income but a low credit score. I may not have been thinking clearly back then. But I was now.

It was time to find Nick. I called Ella. She had her finger on the pulse of our friends, any gossip, and pretty much life in general in the metro area.

"I won't waste my breath saying what a selfish jerk he is." Ella hissed into the phone. "Instead, I'll use my energy to hunt him down. Geez, Molly, how long before you have to pay it? Are they really going after you for the balance?"

I reread the letter from the finance department. "It says they have the right to call in the balance, which is twenty-seven-thousand plus some change. Or, I can bring his loan current to the tune of roughly fifteen hundred. It's due in a week." I downed the rest of my coffee. "Don't kill him if you find him. Let me at him first."

"I wouldn't rob you of that pleasure. I'll be in touch as soon as I know something."

* * *

With the buzzer on for the store door, I could now sit and watch TV in my living room. If a customer stopped in, I could be out there in five seconds.

By the time Kathy Lee and Hoda started their show, my few early-bird customers were long gone. I could easily start drinking with them and be sober by my next customer.

Drew Carey and I became friends. I could watch *The Price Is Right* without an interruption as I shouted to nobody from my easy chair a price estimate on every game item.

My exercise was reduced to dancing every afternoon with *Ellen* as she began her show.

I told no one about how bad things had become—even Jackson. His words from last winter still ate away at my pride. His flippant prediction was becoming my reality. If I confessed it to my girlfriends I'd look like a loser. I fought daily to not feel that way on my own.

I'd done the math. My electric bill was sky-high. Maybe not quite as high as summer, but the coolers still had to run, same with the freezer in the grocery section. It was my highest monthly payment. I shouldn't complain. I had no mortgage.

Still, thanks to Nick, I now had a juicy truck payment instead. One I couldn't pay.

My mind compared what I didn't have with what Rosie did. She'd had social security, but it likely wasn't much. She'd built a loyal customer base over the years, some who would never enter my store now. She had the winter bait and tackle business, along with the fall hunting sales. After she passed away, Jackson toyed with adding her bait and hunting section to his store.

"I didn't have the room, and I didn't want to have to stay open all day on Sundays in the slow season." Jackson had explained when I'd asked why they'd sold the inventory to Drake.

"Like most guys around here, Drake's into hunting and fishing. He bought the inventory and had his building next to his real estate office up in a few months so that he was able to take over the fall hunting business. The town needed someone to keep that business going."

Hunting and fishing weren't my expertise anyway. What was?

Common sense told me to close the store until spring. Why keep wasting my days sitting here while paying a huge electric bill? Pride. I'd built mine up over the summer—something I hadn't had in a job before—and in less than two months, I'd lost it.

After too many phone calls to TCF bank with paperwork faxed back and forth, I made a payment of over fifteen hundred dollars to cover Nick's ass, until I could find it.

Less than three grand sat in my savings. It wouldn't last if I stayed open.

Seasonal jobs were scarce in our area. I needed to think of something for winter until I could reap the spring and summer store crop again. The upcoming months were looking bleak.

Until a game on *The Price is Right* featured a basket filled with items for a romantic weekend getaway.

That's when everything changed for me.

* * *

I wasn't exactly busy. When Charlee told me about the next "Hell Club" event, a self-defense training class, I signed up. Four hours on a Sunday afternoon to hone my self-defense skills. Okay, not hone. That would imply I had some to begin with.

Charlee went strictly for my benefit. Nobody was going to try kicking her ass. She'd have swatted them into the middle of next week. She may be sweet, but Charlee was all muscle. The class was capped at thirty people and the gym was full when we arrived. Most were club members, but some had brought newbies like me.

I wouldn't be an outsider for long. After everything that had happened, the "Hell Club" sounded like a good fit for me. I signed up as soon as we entered the gym.

The women I'd met at the Wine & Words event were there, and the ages of women in the group varied. Self-defense was important no matter if you were twenty or eighty.

Our male instructor stood in front of the six rows we'd been instructed to make.

"Today's focus is going to be on not only simple self-defense measures but also awareness and prevention," he explained.

"If you are aware at all times, many attacks can be prevented." He went on to explain how good decisions can turn a dangerous situation into a safe situation. Some I'd heard before, such as: if you think you're being followed, turn and look the person directly in the eyes. The problem with my "attacks"? All but the first one hadn't so much as touched a hair on me.

After our instructor described several common situations, he asked for people to volunteer personal examples from their life. *What the hell, Molly. Find out what you did wrong.*

I raised my hand. Standing in the hall at a friend's crowded house, waiting to use the bathroom…where had I gone wrong in preventing being attacked?

I relayed the scene to him. "Okay, let's break this down. As you waited in the hall, you should have faced the living room so you could see anyone coming down the hall. When he dragged you into the dark room with his hand over your mouth, you said you tried kicking him but didn't have heels on." He had me stand by him in the front of the class.

"I want you to play the guy, I'll play you." He was only a couple inches taller than me. I stood behind him, grabbed him around his waist and pinned his arms to his sides with one arm while my other arm clasped over his mouth. I felt empowered.

I shouldn't have. He softly banged his head back against my nose. Next, he gently grabbed the inside of my leg, and bent his knees to get enough leverage to carefully kick me in the kneecap. I let go and he explained his moves.

"A person's nose is sensitive. So what if you end up with a throbbing headache after you bang against his nose? In your case, he was close to your height so it would work. It doesn't always work if you're shorter.

"When I grabbed the inside of your leg, it's a move you could've done if your hands were pinned at your sides. You should have been able to pinch him in the groin." His eyebrows lifted. "And finally, if you can't stomp on his foot with high heels, a hard kick to the kneecap even if you are barefoot will hurt."

He excused me and I took my spot next to Charlee, Michelle, and Lily. We paired up with several others to practice the defensive moves, all with the constant reminder that if we are aware of our surroundings and people, we can usually prevent a bad situation.

Although the women in the "Hell Club" came in various shapes, sizes, and age, we all had one thing in common…something bad in our lives had led us to find each other. It was comforting. It was empowering. And I couldn't help but notice that tiny Lily and tall and lithe Michelle excelled at several of the moves—to the point where they'd surprise whoever thought they could overtake them.

It made me wonder about everyone's story. According to Charlee, I wouldn't find out for at least a year, something about preconceived ideas, and possibly judging each other.

It didn't dampen my curiosity. It convinced me to join.

Chapter 28

I had a swarm of ideas and thoughts buzzing in my head every day now. If I neglected to cough up my concerns and ideas to Jackson it was easy to believe it was only because I wanted to figure it all out on my own. If I forgot to describe how my financial world had become like a game of Jenga—one wrong move and it could all fall down—it was purely an oversight.

Jackson picked me up late Sunday afternoon after I closed the store. It was a brisk October day, but we took advantage of the sunshine and biked around Blue Bay's trails that hugged the lakes, until the sun set. Over bourbon-soaked chicken wings, homemade coleslaw, and sweet potato fries, our conversation was stilted. I kept reminding myself I wasn't stubborn, and I worried Jackson would never understand my need for independence.

We'd been talking about his brother Cody who'd called him earlier in the day, stating Jackson's father hadn't been feeling well. "I'm glad he lives near our parents. He's my eyes and ears, and is good about keeping me updated."

"I hope it isn't anything serious with your father," I said.

"I'm sure he's just overworked. He needs to retire, which I doubt will ever happen." He pushed his empty plate aside. "I know you've said before you always wished you had a sibling. Did your parents not want any more kids or were they just unable to have more?"

I dabbed my mouth with my napkin. "Mom told me they were unable to have more children, which is kind of ironic since she got pregnant with me right after they got married. You'd think if it was that easy the first time, it would've been easy again." I shrugged.

He put his elbows on the table, leaned his chin on his clasped hands, and stared at me. "When did your parents get married?"

I hesitated a second at his odd question. "October of 1976. Mom got pregnant within their first year of marriage and had me a few months after their first anniversary. She was only twenty-nine, but dad was already thirty-eight. It's weird to think that I'm already older than my mom was when she had me. I don't feel old, but I guess when it comes to that biologically fertile age, I'm no spring chicken." I tried to imagine myself with a child. I couldn't. Not yet.

He squinted at me, his mouth opening and then pressing shut. Finally, he pushed his chair back and folded his arms over his chest as he let out a big sigh.

"Is something wrong?" It was as if my answer to his random question had made him uncomfortable.

"Um, nope." He looked at my plate, not pushed aside. "Ready to go?" He'd already paid the waitress. We both stood and shrugged into our fall jackets before walking out into the night. The temperature probably dropped at least ten degrees while we were inside eating.

"Why were you asking me about my parents?" I stepped into his pickup.

Jackson inserted his keys in the ignition but didn't turn it on, instead, staring at the dashboard. The truck was quiet while I waited. Something was on his mind, and I had a feeling I wasn't going to like whatever it was.

"Honestly, this is going to sound stupid because you know how my mom is…" Jackson turned to me. "Apparently some woman she knows who used to live in Love decades ago, and who she still keeps in contact with by email, sent her an old picture of your mom pregnant, supposedly before she got married."

His arm rested on the back seat while he talked. "I think my mom was bitching to this lady about you getting the store, and I'm sure your mother's name was mentioned several times in the email. I don't give a shit if your parents ever got married, but man, it's my mom's new favorite topic." He shook his head.

I relaxed. Of course, Nancy would twist anything to try and make my family look bad. "That can't be right. Maybe my mom wasn't wearing her ring because her fingers were bloated if she was close to the end of her pregnancy."

Jackson chewed on his lip. "Yep, that was probably it. You know how my mom is. She can bend metal to form her version of the truth."

He started the truck and drove while I looked out the window into the darkness, trying to forget his mother's accusation. I couldn't. "You know what? I need to prove your mom wrong." I reached into my pocket and pulled out my cell phone.

Jackson glanced my way with a wary look. My dad's phone rang several times before he answered. "Hi, Dad, how are you doing?"

"I'm plugging along. Had a rough round of golf this morning." He coughed a few times.

"That's too bad. Are you playing again tomorrow morning with Fred? I bet you were just having an off day on the course." I let him ramble on about Fred having the luck of the Irish lately on the golf course, even though he didn't have a lick of Irish in him.

When he took a breath, I got to the point. "So, Dad, a friend and I were talking about mom and her old friends from town here. This is probably going to sound like a crazy question, but was mom pregnant with me when you two got married?" My words raised an octave before I held my breath.

"Why would you ask such a question?"

"Please, just tell me. Someone said they saw an old photo of Mom pregnant and not married. That's not true, right?" I chewed at a fingernail.

"You should know by now you can't trust everything you hear in a small town, Molly."

"I didn't hear it from someone here." That was technically true.

A long silence followed on his end, followed by a big huff. "Well, fine then."

"Fine, what?" It wasn't the answer I expected and I straightened my posture.

"Yes, she was. There, does that make you happy now?"

I blinked several times and looked at Jackson. He could hear my dad's side of the conversation too. He pulled over to the side of the road, put the truck in park, and reached for my hand. "Why did you and Mom lie to me? You both told me you got married in October of 1976. What's the real year?"

"A year later. The date is right, but it was 1977. Your mom was about five months or so pregnant. We didn't lie about eloping though." There was defensiveness in his voice. "We lied to you because your mom didn't want you to know the truth. You know how she protected you from any little thing. Sheltered you too much, if you ask me."

My heart and body went through a dozen emotions during the rest of our short conversation. He wasn't going to apologize, I wasn't going to ask him to. It was all in the past, and really, what difference did it make?

"Are you okay?" Jackson asked after I hung up. He reached for me.

I held up my hand. "I'm not ready to talk about it. I need some time to process this."

In the silence during our ride home, I chewed on this latest piece of family history—to be added to the possibility that my grandpa had stiffed several people and businesses in town before leaving. I couldn't help but feel a little down about our family secrets.

Had my dad felt forced to marry my mother? Was that another reason he struggled with his love for me?

In my driveway, Jackson turned off his truck. There was no "dropping me off" now. He climbed out, reminded me to stay put, and walked through the house and store checking everywhere he could before coming to get me.

We said little before he kissed me goodnight. I wished his mom would leave my family alone. I wanted one hour with my mom. *Please, God, just send her to me for an hour.* I had a lot of questions for her before this latest piece of history, and I couldn't stop thinking of how little I knew about her life before me…a life I'd never get the answers to.

I carried a hefty slice of anger that could easily be divided between my parents and Nancy. Nancy should've kept her gossip-nose out of my life, and at some point, my parents should have told me the truth. When I was in junior high and my mom had her "don't have sex" talk with me, couldn't she have used herself as a good example?

I may have taken offense at the idea she regretted getting pregnant with me. But still.

She likely figured I'd never find out. Even after Rosie left the store to mom in her will, I don't imagine my mother ever pictured me moving to Love and rubbing elbows with people who had no problem airing the ghosts in my mother's family closet.

As I attempted to shut off my brain and get some sleep, Jackson called. He'd just received a call from his mother. His dad had a massive stroke.

Chapter 29

While he relayed to me what little information his mom had given him, Jackson threw everything he figured he'd need for weeks, including Trigger, inside his pickup. We hung up as he started his truck to drive toward Wyoming in the blackness of the cold October night. He had a good ten-hour drive ahead of him.

I'd just stepped out of the shower the next morning when my cell phone rang. "Good morning. Thought I'd give you an update. I've got seven hours under my belt, and dad is stabilized right now." Jackson tried to sound cheery and optimistic. I knew him well enough to hear the worry and exhaustion in his words.

I'd not yet met his dad but heard enough about him through Jackson's stories. A workaholic with an unhappy marriage who kept his emotions buckled up…the pillar of the family had fallen. "I'm so glad you called. Do they think your dad will be in the hospital a while?"

"I think so. Mom isn't making much sense right now. She's completely useless in any situation like this, and Cody isn't a whole lot better right now. One of the reasons I called is I'd like to have you stay at my house while I'm gone. I hate having you stay at your place, even more so now without me close by. I wish I would have left Trigger there as a guard dog for you."

I studied myself in the bathroom mirror. The woman whose hair hadn't experienced TLC in months, the woman with what seemed to be permanent bags under her eyes, the woman with a dusting of freckles which always made her appear younger…that woman had changed.

A year ago that woman would have left her house, her store, and this town. Not now.

"Thanks for the offer, but your house is too isolated. I'd be more vulnerable there than I am here. I'll check in with Ernie, Charlee, and Tracie." I reaffirmed my conviction. "I want to do this on my own. Here."

"On your own? Really, Molly?" The stress of his dad's stroke and over twenty-four hours with no sleep had put a nasty edge to his words. "Who installed the motion lights, new locks on your doors, and game cameras?"

Ouch. "You did, and I appreciate all of it, Jackson. I do. But I just can't walk away from my home and hide. I'm sorry." I clamped my mouth shut so I wouldn't make things worse.

"And I'm sorry. I thought you needed me." Jackson's sarcasm pushed through the phone.

Our conversation had quickly spiraled. "I *want* you, Jackson. Isn't that more important?" But he wasn't listening. He'd hung up.

How could I get it through his pig-headed brain that I refused to go backward and need a man to run my life? Apparently loving and wanting him wasn't enough. He had enough going on right now. It wasn't a conversation we should have over the phone.

I'd wait until he came home.

* * *

That was a week ago. A week with no phone calls. His message was clear. If I didn't need him, he didn't need me. I'd left voice mail messages. They went unanswered.

Tracie kept me updated. His father had an ischemic stroke, typically less severe than a hemorrhagic stroke. He was getting out of the hospital today—eight days after his stroke. Jackson planned on staying in Wyoming while his dad stayed in transitional care.

A few days after he left, I told Charlee and Tracie of my plans to close. They didn't blink an eye when I dumped my failure at their feet. We were walking the paved trail south of town.

"I understand. The town can get desolate in the winter, even with ice fishing and snowmobiling," Tracie admitted. "We still manage to have fun, but business is slow."

"I can check at the hospital to see if they need part-time help." Charlee offered.

"I appreciate the offer, but I've got a few ideas I want to research first. I'm hoping to come up with a solution to generate more income year-round in the store."

Once I had my ducks in a row, I'd reveal my hopefully brilliant idea to them.

Ernie stopped by for coffee the next morning and I told him of my seasonal closing, stressing the word "seasonal." His rough thumbs were tucked behind his plaid suspenders as he nodded. "I believe this first year is the hardest. Over the winter you may find you have new ideas to bring to the store. Everything takes time. You are smart and I have faith it will all work out."

It was tempting to run my new idea past Ernie, but I needed to do more research first.

I hadn't planned to keep Jackson in the dark. His ignoring my calls made the decision.

I placed my CLOSING SOON FOR THE SEASON sign in the store window. By the end of October, reality would be staring me in the face.

Bait, tackle, and hunting supplies worked for Rosie—for me, not so much. It was coffee swimming around in my head instead of minnows. I'd done enough research over the past several months…before I ever even opened the store. The closest coffee bar was in Blue Bay—almost twenty minutes away. And that was off the beaten path. Going north and south? No coffee bar for at least an hour each way.

I couldn't be the only one who missed an iced mocha or pumpkin spice latte.

* * *

Once word got out that I was closing for the season, people were eager to help—something I loved about the town. Scratch offered a handful of hours if I was interested in a waitress job. Charlee thought they may be looking for a part-time receptionist at the clinic. Even Curt said they were short on tellers at the bank, thanks to a couple of women who'd recently had babies and decided to quit.

Drake stopped in late one afternoon. "Hello, Molly. I wanted to offer my services in case you're thinking of selling. The real estate economy is still down, but we're projecting an upswing in the next year or so."

My eyes widened. "Oh, I'm not going to sell. I'm just closing for the winter. Business is too slow, and it's costing me more to stay open than to shut things down." I stood tall. "I'll be back up and running next spring." I forced a cheery smile. "Plus, I enjoy working in the same place my mother worked some forty years ago."

He slid his hands inside his jacket pockets. "I bet that's comforting to have a connection with your mother like this." He glanced around the store. "My father died when I was ten. I wish I had something like this to connect my present with his past."

"Oh, Drake, I didn't know your father passed away so long ago!" Drake was older than me, which meant his dad had been gone a quarter century or so.

"He died when he was only thirty-three. I remember him well though. He had a tough upbringing and a hard go of things. But family is family and we need to keep that connection with them in any way we can." He nodded with his words and I wasn't sure if he was convincing himself or trying to convince me.

"Exactly, which is why I'm determined to keep this place going. I want to honor not only Rosie but my mom who apparently spent some happy years in this place."

As Drake turned to leave I remembered something. "I'm thinking of getting out of the minnow and bait business next spring. Since you bought Rosie's winter tackle and hunting supplies, I wondered if you'd be interested in the summer bait and tackle."

He stood legs apart, arms folded across his chest, and his forehead wrinkled in thought—the only thing wrinkled on him. "Maybe. I'll get back to you, okay?" He gave me a close-lipped smile and nodded goodbye.

Tracie stopped after work, shortly after Drake left. "Rick said they're always looking for workers at the paper mill. You may have to work swing shifts though." She stifled a yawn. "Sorry, with Jackson gone, my hours have multiplied."

"What would I do next spring? I don't want to train in on a job and quit in six months."

"You wouldn't be the first person to quit that soon. I know it's not ethical, but it's work."

Tracie was right. Hell, they were all right. Even Drake's offer to list the business was tempting. But the idea itching the inside of my brain refused to leave.

When Ernie stopped by a few days later, I decided who better to ask than Ernie? A confidant, a man who'd lived here for ages, a man who'd been shunned initially by this town for the color of his skin…a man who now was loved and known by everyone. Ernie was truly part of the town of Love. He'd know if my hair-brained idea would succeed.

We sat at my kitchen table, coffee and cookies for a late morning snack. The store was still open, but on a Wednesday in October, we'd likely not be interrupted by a customer.

"I think that is a clever and wonderful idea." Ernie pointed at me with his Lorna Doone cookie before taking a bite. "It would get the townspeople involved. Cement your friendship with some of them." His rheumy eyes fixed on mine. I loved this old man. He was another reason I couldn't just up and leave town. Ernie had become the grandpa I never knew.

I got up from my chair and walked over to hug him, breathing in his scent of wool, Aqua Velva, and soap. "I love you so much, Ernie. I don't know what I'd have done without you."

His rough hand patted mine. "You would have found your way. You are a stronger woman than you think, Molly. Rosie said the same of your mother. No matter what was heaped on her—her mother's death, raising her younger sisters, her father's struggles—your mother persevered. I see the same strength in you."

"You give me more credit than I deserve. That little voice in my head that says I'll never make it on my own gets the best of me at times." I took a few sips of coffee.

"Looking back, my mom made it so easy for me to do what I wanted to do, without any responsibility. I'd found the same characteristic in a boyfriend. Nick relished me relying on him." I studied my coffee cup, looking for answers in the vanilla-flavored liquid.

"I think that's why I don't want to take Jackson's offer to move in with him. That would be the easy way out. And I'm sick of doing the easy way."

"Did you explain that to Jackson?"

"I tried. I'm not sure he understands." I shrugged. By the time Ernie left with a kiss from me on his cheek, confidence in my idea had grown.

The next person I wanted to bounce my idea off of was Charlee. Ernie's niece was a chip off her uncle. They were two of the most supportive people in my life—and against the odds, had made a home for themselves in this town.

"What a great idea!" Charlee hugged me after I broke my idea to her. I'd driven out to her house after the store closed that night. She was making a Raggedy Ann wig out of red yarn for both her daughters for an upcoming Halloween dance at the high school.

"Don't forget to take pictures of them. I bet they'll be adorable."

Charlee looked up. "I don't think 'adorable' is what they're going for. If Logan had her way, she'd be a 'sexy-Ann' doll. I gave Susan strict instructions when sewing their outfits to make sure those knickers and dresses cover as much of their bodies as possible." She grinned. "They'll probably be the first biracial Raggedy Ann's."

It was hard to believe Halloween was two weeks away. My store would be closed by then. *Only for the season,* I reminded myself.

I drove home from Charlee's shivering in my car. It was that time of year where you needed the heat in your car, but not quite at the point where you had to let it warm up a bit before driving. Gone was my remote car starter for my Lexus. I was back to the old-fashioned way, starting it and running back inside while it warmed up.

My motion lights turned on, and as I walked toward the back door, fully alert with my key ready in hand as instructed in my self-defense classes, I waved to the game camera. I'd left all of my lights on in the kitchen and living room, never wanting to walk into a dark room again. After entering, I breathed a small sigh of relief. Everything was in place.

As I got ready for bed, I made another decision. I'd been thinking about Curt a lot over the past couple of weeks.

It was time to pay him a visit.

Chapter 30

I sat in Curt's corner office at the bank on Monday afternoon as Susan covered the store for me. Mid-October sunshine graced us through the large window overlooking Main Street.

As Curt and I went over the figures I'd calculated and recalculated over the past week, I studied his face. I heard he had a new girlfriend. I hoped it worked out for them. For me, I'd sensed a neediness in him that Jackson lacked. I'd hiked that rocky trail with Nick. I didn't want to be an ego-booster again.

Curt's words cut in on my wandering mind. "If we start the paperwork now, you should hear something within a few weeks whether the numbers work out or not. It is usually sixty to ninety days for the payout, so you're probably looking at some time in January for the loan closing." His well-groomed hands folded under his chiseled chin as he looked at me, waiting.

"That works for me. Meanwhile, I'll run my idea past some of the people I'll need to be involved. The sooner I know if I've got enough product, the better. After I close in a couple of weeks I'm going to the Twin Cities to meet with possible vendors and sign up for barista class."

After we'd finished with the paperwork, I shrugged into my fall jacket and he followed me from his office to stand outside the bank. "This is for sure what you want?" Curt asked. He gestured to Main Street in front of us, encompassing the slow fall weekday business.

"Yes, it is. I don't have anything drawing me back to the cities. This has become my home."

He leaned against the brick building. "You have something or someone pulling you to stay here?" His eyes searched mine for the obvious answer on both of our minds.

"Yes, I do have something here…a business that I want to build and good friends." I pasted a polite smile on my face, purposely neglecting to mention Jackson on my list.

His green eyes studied me, likely wondering why I hadn't included Jackson. "I hope it's enough for you, Molly." He walked back inside the bank while I soaked in the sunshine and high 40s temperature. I tipped my face upward and closed my eyes, digesting Curt's last words.

I hoped it was enough for me too.

* * *

With my loan application underway, I'd picked Ella's brain so much the past couple of weeks until she all but screamed into the phone, "Just do it!"

Now, if only I could run it by Jackson. *He can't stay away forever, Molly. You'll work it out. You'll see.* And if we didn't, I still wasn't leaving town.

I'd invited Tracie, Charlee, and Ernie over for dinner Wednesday night. I made a chicken and wild rice bake, and pumpkin pie for dessert. Our October weather had bounced back and forth from the high sixties to the high thirties. I couldn't avoid firing up my wood stove for much longer. I hoped to hold off until I came back from my trip to the Twin Cities so I wouldn't need anyone to feed it while I was gone. I warned guests to dress for low sixties in my house.

At precisely five, I welcomed Ernie into my living room and helped him shrug out of his parka. He reached up and removed his red plaid Stormy Kromer hat with the ear flaps down. I leaned in and kissed his cold cheek.

I hung up his coat and hat on my coat rack and led the way to the kitchen where I had a pot of decaf brewing. By habit, I pulled out a thick mug and added a dollop of half-and-half before filling it with coffee and handing it to Ernie, who had settled at my kitchen table.

Tracie was next and I greeted the overworked woman at the door with a large glass of wine. "Thank you. Where's the rest of the bottle?" Tracie stepped out of her tennis shoes and took the glass from me.

"That good of a week, huh?" As much as I wanted Jackson home, I imagined Tracie was missing him even more.

"Yup. I don't know if we will see Jackson before deer season. Sounds like it's a slow recovery for his dad." I mentally counted the days until rifle deer season started—sixteen.

Tracie was aware of my lack of conversation with Jackson so I was glad she kept me informed. We visited until Charlee showed up, letting in a gust of bitterly cold air. She stomped a few ice crystals off her shoes before removing them. It had been spitting bits of snow on and off all day, not a welcome sight in mid-October.

I poured a cup of decaf for Charlee, turned the oven off and slid the chicken wild rice bake out of the oven to cool a bit before joining them at the table.

Tracie leaned forward on the table. "Okay, Molly, I'm dying to hear the details."

I'd given them all a rough idea of my plans before, but nothing too specific. I had their full attention. "I want to open the store again next spring, keeping some of it the same. The snacks, pop, summer items, T-shirts all did well. As you know, my problem has been what to do for business the other seven or eight months."

My laptop sat at the other end of the table and I reached for it. I pulled up a photo of a mockup I'd put together on my computer, turned the screen to face them, and swung my chair around closer to Ernie. It was a photo of a large wicker basket filled with heart-patterned boxer shorts, candles, a bag of wild rice, jams, maple syrup, candies, salsa, goat's milk soaps, red knit wool mittens…and everything was labeled "Made by ***Love****mn.*" The tiny 'mn' was shaped in a way that the bottom of the 'm' and 'n' lines connected to make an entwined heart hanging from the word 'Love.' It was a trademark design I created but had yet to file.

"These are the 'Love baskets' I told you about before. They'll feature homemade or homegrown items from this area. Most marketing would be online—the main events would be Valentine's Day, anniversary, wedding, and birthday gift ideas. I'll also sell them in the store." My heart hopped in my chest. I reminded myself I was pitching my idea to friends, not a Board of Directors.

I focused on Ernie. "I may need your help sweet-talking Old Lloyd into selling me some of his maple syrup and wild rice."

Turning to Charlee, I continued. "All the salsa, jams, jellies, even the spiced green beans you can…I'd love to sell anything like them." My hands flailed in excitement. "And the wool mittens and socks Paulina makes from her sheep wool. Same with her goats milk soap."

I scrolled down to more photos. "Susan's daughter is moving in for the winter while her husband works on the oil rigs in North Dakota. Her daughter loves to sew as much as Susan does. Susan's got a serger for her sewing machine and has shown me knit tops, boxers, pajama bottoms…various items she's made for her daughter and grandkids." I held up a pair of the "Sassy Pants" boxers she'd made for me. "Items like this. I think she'll be on board for it."

I zoomed in on various pieces I'd cropped and placed in the basket. "Even Travis could help. He makes amazing candles from his dad's honeybees. It would get townspeople involved, give them an income on their talent, and give me plenty of 'homemade' items for the baskets. I think it could not only be a big boost for me and the store, but for the town itself."

I leaned back in my chair as if I had no worries. I was dying to hear their opinion.

Because if these people thought my idea wouldn't work, it wouldn't. I needed their emotional support along with their network of connections.

Hell, I just plain old needed them. I braced myself for their feedback.

Charlee's body danced around in her chair as if she had to go to the bathroom. "This is even better than I imagined!" She high-fived me.

Ernie beamed with pride. It brought tears to my eyes.

Tracie was quiet. "What do you think?" I valued her opinion, not only as my friend but as someone who'd worked at a business in this town for a decade.

"I think it's a perfect idea, Molly. Can I ask you something though? Will you do this even if you and Jackson don't get your shit together?" She turned to Ernie. "Excuse my French, but you know that's what they need to do."

"No offense taken, Tracie. I do believe Molly and Jackson will work things out. Shit or no shit." He winked at me.

We all chuckled and I went on with more of my plan. "I'm going to talk to Scratch about renting out his kitchen in the café after hours. Everything has to be made in a 'certified kitchen,' but since he closes by seven, I hope to rent it for whoever needs it to make their products."

Ernie reached over and took my hand in his, giving it a gentle squeeze.

"Don't you have anything to say?" I asked.

"Yes. Lloyd also makes some kick-ass wine."

Charlee busted out laughing. "Those were my exact words to Molly."

"Well then, I am only confirming your information." Ernie chuckled.

I added Lloyd's wine to my wish list, wondering if it would require a special license for alcohol sales. "So for this year, I know I can't offer the canned items or maple syrup until they're made next season." I looked at Ernie. "Same with Lloyd's wine."

"I'm going to talk to Jimmy about his beef jerky that is out of this world. I can ship that without worrying about spoilage. Also, I need to find out from Old Lloyd about the wild rice since I know that's processed for him in a plant. This first winter will be a trial run."

I sat back, emotionally exhausted as if I'd just purged a major confession. I had, in a way. "I talked to Curt on Monday about getting a small business loan."

"It is a splendid idea. You will be wise in your investment." Ernie's hand patted mine.

"The light bulb came on a couple weeks ago while watching *The Price is Right*. They had 'romantic gift baskets' as one of the bid items, and it stuck with me. Then, during the showcase showdown, the first contestant said she'd pass that showcase and wait for the bigger one. When she repeated the slogan 'Go big or go home' it reinforced my idea. Yes, I'll have to take out a loan, but hopefully, my increase in business will more than make up for it."

I relayed my recent conversation with Ella about *home*. "I'd told her how easy it would be for me to give up, to turn tail for home. It was when I said *home* that I realized my home was right here. Home was no longer the Twin Cities." I choked up.

"That's when I decided I needed to figure out a way to make this work. I kept thinking about the sarcastic remark Jackson had made last winter about me replacing my bait section with a sushi bar."

I leaned forward. "I've done research on a coffee bar. I've asked Drake if he wants to buy my summer tackle. I'll gut that section and replace it with a coffee bar." I set my computer aside. "I can take out a loan for the start-up expenses for the Love baskets, and get the small coffee bar installed where the minnow tanks are. Eventually, I hope to also package "Love beans" through a coffee bean distributor. And I'm purchasing an ice cream dipping case so I can serve ice cream cones again like Rosie did."

"Great ideas, Molly. I'm so impressed with all of your research!" Charlee beamed.

"I'm glad, because I'm going to need you all to help pave the way for me with everyone. I plan to stress that not only will it be a good business for me, but also a financial boost for the rest of them if this takes off. Not that people like Old Lloyd or Paulina care about money. But they like to work and keep busy, and hopefully this will keep them busy."

It was late before they all left for home, their heads filled with the ideas I'd shared. I sat in my recliner, a cup of hot tea on the coffee table, my laptop on my lap, yearning for Pixie to be curled up next to me…and for an honest conversation with Jackson.

Our lack of connection made me physically sick. My heart actually ached. Some of it was stress related due to my uncertain future with the store, but most of it was due to Jackson not returning any of my voicemails over the last several days.

Then there was Nancy's discovery about my parents and my 'premature birth.' I hadn't talked to my dad since I'd confronted him that night by phone. I was adult enough to see it was their way of protecting me. And in the end, what difference did a year make?

Chapter 31

My inventory was dwindling along with the weekday business. I began closing early afternoon the last week of October—my final week of business until next spring.

After closing the store, I walked to Jimmy's Meat Market downtown. Tall and slender like his Slim Jim's beef sticks, he led the way behind the meat counter. Herky Jerky Love was on my basket list. Jerky had a shelf life; his beef sticks didn't.

"My bestsellers are the jalapeno, teriyaki, and cheese flavors," said Jimmy. "We can make them any size you'd like. If you're offering a variety of sizes and items in your baskets, maybe you'd like smaller packs of the six-inch size for some baskets, and the ten-inch length for your bigger orders." He slipped on plastic gloves to show me a few samples.

Customers wandered in to buy meat for their evening meals. You could have eaten off the floor behind Jimmy's meat counter. His shop was as meticulous as he was: neatly cropped silver hair, clean clothes, hands, and white apron.

"I'll be in touch, Jimmy. Thanks again for the tour, and the samples."

"My pleasure." Jimmy tipped his white cap to me as I walked out the door, his old-fashioned bell above the door, announcing my exit. Nearly every vehicle parked downtown was a pickup weighted down with wood in the back. Townspeople were preparing for snow and frigid temperatures. They could appear any day now.

* * *

I stopped at Flap Jack Fever the following afternoon to speak with Scratch. After giving him details about my idea, I asked about using his kitchen after hours. "People like Charlee and Old Lloyd might use it. Charlee for her jams, jellies, and salsa and Lloyd for bottling his maple syrup. And I'd pay you." I handed him a flyer I'd typed up with information.

"I know you'll need time to think it over, and I haven't even asked Lloyd or some of the others yet." I had the pep of a salesman hoping to seal the deal.

Scratch, his red bandana tied around his bald head, leaned in and put his hand on my shoulder. "You can use my kitchen any night after I close. I'll gladly do what I can to help you." He reached behind him and untied his large white apron. "I think it's a great idea and it will help promote all our area has to offer."

"Thank you. I'll let you know once I talk to everyone. If Lloyd agrees, maple syrup season is usually in March, so that would be the first thing we'd need the kitchen for."

"What does Jackson think? I bet he's happy you've figured out a way to make the store work for you." Scratch folded his beefy arms over his chest. He reminded me of Mr. Clean.

"I haven't told him yet. He's been so busy with his dad." I flinched at my fib.

He squeezed my shoulder. "I think your ideas are great." He showed me around his large stainless-steel kitchen which was meticulously clean between his lunch and dinner crowds.

A few minutes later I walked the two blocks back to my house hunkered down in my sensible winter parka. My body was cold, and my heart ached at the emotional distance I was feeling from Jackson. It wasn't how I wanted things left between us.

I hung up my coat, took my cell phone out of my coat pocket, and saw I'd missed two texts from Jackson. I forgot I'd silenced my cell phone before walking up town so it wouldn't interrupt me. Finally, communication from him!

The first text message read: *I'm sorry I haven't returned your phone calls or texts. There's too much I want to say, so much I need to talk to you about. Let's wait until I come home.* It was quickly followed by the second message: *We need to talk in person, not over the phone. I love you. J.*

I sat down on the edge of the couch, rereading his messages several times. I let out a calming sigh, so relieved things weren't over between us. I typed out my response: *That's fine. I've got news to tell you too. I hope your dad's recovery is going well. Miss you.* There was so much more I wanted to type, but it could wait.

His reassurance would help me focus on my business future instead of my personal one. Saturday morning I dragged myself and the bags under my eyes to the bathroom, ready to splash cool water on my face to diffuse their puffiness. One more morning to go before I could sleep in again. One more day of employment.

I turned on the bathroom sink. No water came out of the cold-water side. Same with the warm water. I turned the nob on the bathtub faucet. Thankfully, the water poured out. I knelt down, splashed ice cold water on my face, and toweled it off before inspecting the sink pipes.

I opened the cabinet under the sink and cold air circulated up from the dirt basement. The end of October and my pipes had frozen already? What was the rest of the winter going to be like for me? How did Rosie make it through the winter?

I did some research online. Heat tape looked like the solution for me. A temporary fix was to keep the faucet on, leave the cabinet doors open, and thaw the pipe with the hairdryer. Hopefully, after I fired up the wood stove I wouldn't have this problem.

By the time the hardware opened I had my water running again and left the faucet open at a slow drip. Ernie came over to watch the store for me while I walked to the hardware store to buy heat tape. My tennis shoes crunched on the frost-covered sidewalk. The town was quiet, with just a few cars parked outside the hardware store.

"Too bad this happened while Jackson is gone." Tracie sympathized as she charged the tape to my account.

"Even if he was home, I wouldn't ask him to wrap it for me. I need to learn these things on my own." I signed the receipt.

"I'm impressed at everything you've done and learned since the first day you walked in this store."

"Thanks to you and Charlee. If disaster strikes, I'm moving in with you two. Between your fixit knowledge and Charlee's ability to live off the land, I think you've got it covered. Don't ask me what I'll contribute."

"Humor, Molly. You'll provide the humor."

I jogged back home, eager to get my project going since Ernie was willing to stay and work the store.

I went to work on my bathroom pipes, meticulously wrapping the heat tape around the water pipes with a half inch space between the wraps. I fished it through the hole under the sink into the icky-avoid-at-all-costs basement. There was no avoiding it for this job. I ran down with a flashlight in hand, fearing the lone lightbulb in the basement would burn out. I focused on the pipes, cringing at the possibility of dead mice nearby, and ignored the creepiness around me.

Dashing back upstairs, I plugged the heat tape into the same outlet as my electric toothbrush. I gazed at my handiwork and put another imaginary gold star next to my imaginary column of "things Molly can do for herself." After cleaning up, I went out to relieve Ernie in the store, my chest puffed out with internal pride.

* * *

Late that afternoon, I added the finishing touches to my "Love basket vendor list," waiting for Susan to come in. I'd called her a few days earlier and gave her my sales pitch about sewing projects for her and her daughter. "Yes, yes, yes. I'd love to help! You know how lonely my nights and weekends have been since my husband passed away. My daughter is probably a better seamstress than I am, but I'll never admit that to her," Susan joked. "I can put together some samples of work I've done and bring them in if you'd like."

I closed at four, right after Susan showed up. I had my laptop set up on the kitchen table.

"I'm very impressed with the boxer briefs you made for me." I showed Susan photos on the computer of tank top designs I hoped to feature along with boxer shorts for men and women.

"Pajamas and tank tops won't be a problem at all." Susan's glasses perched on her nose as she studied the items I'd loaded on my "Love basket ideas" page. Her blue eyes sparkled with interest. She'd told me she turned sixty around the time of her husband's death last year. If I'd have seen her walk by on the street, I'd have never imagined she was that old.

When I'd told her that, she laughed. "Sixty is the new forty, isn't it?" She nudged me.

I'd made us some hot cocoa and we huddled together over the screenshots of ideas I had saved. "Eventually we could branch out into other areas, but for now having his and her PJs, along with the boxers, would be a good start. I've also done research for putting this logo on the material." I showed her the photo of the various ***LOVEmn*** logos I'd been toying with.

"I've never used any of the design fabric websites. I'll ask my quilting club to see if others have," Susan offered.

When I walked Susan out to her car an hour later, gray clouds billowed overhead. "This day reminds me of late last fall when my friend Ella and I drove here from the Twin Cities for my first trip to Love. In fact, it was the day of the fish house parade," I reflected.

"Isn't it hard to believe you haven't even lived here a year yet?"

"Yes." I took in the peacefulness surrounding me. "Now I can't imagine not living here." Shrugging, I smiled at her. "Crazy, right?"

"Not at all, Molly. You belong here, just as I do. I grew up in Fargo, North Dakota, but my husband was from this area. Within months of moving here after we married I knew this was where I was meant to be." She opened her car door. "Are you going to see Travis now?"

"Yes, his mother said he's been working all week on a candle display for me."

"He's so excited. And my sister is so happy you've given him a new project to focus on."

"I'm thankful there are so many talented people in this town."

Shortly after Susan pulled out of the parking lot, heading to visit a friend, I loaded my laptop in the car and drove the few miles south of town to see the candle samples Travis had ready for me.

"Someone's excited." Travis' mother welcomed me at their front door, nodding to Travis, who gave me a wave from the kitchen table where several candle samples were lined up.

We all sat at the kitchen table as his mother explained the process. "The beeswax is unfiltered, so we go through that process first. We use canning jars since they're thicker, which is what you need for beeswax since it burns hotter than regular candles, especially if it's one hundred percent beeswax."

Travis handed me a sample. "Smell this one, Molly O'Brien. We used Mom's coconut oil. You can add that to the beeswax to cool it down."

His face was serious, his voice monotone and low, as if we were negotiating a shady deal. Social skills were not Travis' strong suit, yet this was as important to him as it was to me. I'd get nothing but the best product from him. "It smells nice and fresh too—reminds me of suntan lotion, as if I was relaxing on a beach."

"They're a cleaner burning candle than what you'd buy in a store, and we use thicker wicks for them since beeswax is a slower burning candle," his mother explained.

"Do you think your supply would be enough for us? Of course, I have no idea how many candles I'll need over the coming months, but I don't want to start a product that I won't be able to keep supplying."

"I spoke with my husband and he said there won't be a problem. He's supplied various businesses for years. There's a company in St. Cloud he supplies, they use the beeswax for lip balm and hand creams."

It amazed me all that nature provided in our area. I made a mental note to check on that company for a possible future Love Basket supplier.

My excitement grew with every possible supplier I spoke with.

I drove back home and did a quick scan of everything since I'd been gone. Daylight savings time would end next weekend. My goal was to get home before dark every night. Everything looked just as I left it. Maybe my nemesis left town for the winter? I could only hope.

I heated up soup for supper and was back at my never-ending research on the computer when Charlee pulled in the backyard, her van lights shining into my living room. I waved her in, my deck well illuminated by what I now called my "searchlights." They were so bright I sometimes felt like my store and home must look like a spaceship from above at night.

She'd called in advance so I wouldn't be caught off guard. As I opened the door for her she shrugged out of her long coat and I busted out laughing.

"What in the world are you wearing, girl?" Charlee's pants were hot pink and black checked stretch pants.

"Jealous? You want a pair of these?" She wiggled her hips as she paraded alongside me into the kitchen.

"Are you joining the circus or something?"

"Nope. I'm on my way to curling. Remember? I told you it started last week." She rubbed her hands together to take the chill off them. "We've got an upcoming 'Hell Club' event there in early December. Now that you're a member, you'll be notified by email. Come with me to the open curling event. You might like it."

"I just might. Do I get to dress like I'm from the sixties?"

"If you want. Sometimes we dress from the seventies." Charlee winked. "The women on the team we're playing against tonight will be wearing pink pants with flamingos on them. We may clash." She glanced at her watch. "I can only stay a few minutes."

I updated Charlee on the people I'd spoken to about Love basket items. "It's all coming together. I'm so happy for you!" She rubbed her hands together. "Did you still want to go to Paulina's tomorrow after you close the store?"

"Yes, if it works for you. I'll probably close by one. All the perishables have been sold, so anything I sell tomorrow is a bonus." If I could wrap it up with Paulina tomorrow, I could leave for Ella's. I had a lot to do in the Twin Cities.

Charlee left for curling and I stayed up to continue my research. The house was cold as I slipped on my pajamas after I'd thrown them in the dryer to warm them and pulled up my fuzzy slipper socks. When I got back from my trip to the Twin Cities and fired up the wood stove, my home would be cozy and warm. I looked forward to the coming winter months where I could curl up inside with my research work, knowing that next spring I'd open with a refurbished, more "Molly-like" store.

* * *

My last morning in the store was so quiet I closed at noon. After a quick lunch, I picked up Charlee and we drove to her neighbor Paulina's. She met us outside where her goats were grazing. We walked her fenced in field among the goats as she pointed them out. "The lazy one, lounging under the trees, makes the most milk, and the thin one over by the shed is finicky. One day she'll do three quarts, the next day, barely a quart." Paulina shook her violet-scarfed head.

I was clueless as to how much milk we'd need for the goat's milk soap I hoped to sell, via Paulina. In the shed, she pointed out her display of yarn from the sheep wool. "I dry it here, color it…all that messy stuff before I spin it."

We followed Paulina across the yard to her small home where she explained how she spun the goat's hair into yarn with her spinning wheel. "I took out a few of the socks and mittens I've made with the yarn. I don't have a lot of extra supply right now. Not sure how much I want to mess with all this." Paulina's eyes sized me up, deciding whether I was worth it.

I didn't blame her. She was no spring chicken. This looked like a lot of work. "I understand. Let's see how this goes. If the demand is more than you can keep up with, we will worry about it then." I had no way of knowing what the demand would be. All I could do is put the options out there. If we were unable to keep up a supply of something, I'd deal with it then.

The goat milk soap was a different matter. "I've got help with the soap, and we've got plenty of milk." Paulina displayed various soaps she'd recently made. "My friend comes here and we make soaps for a few gift shops in the area." The soaps gave off a clean, earthy scent. I visualized them in the baskets, wrapped in the designer fabric I'd work on.

"I'll keep in touch, Paulina, once I get a better feel for a quantity of everything and a timeline. Everything looks wonderful. You do beautiful work."

Her red and black buffalo plaid mittens were my favorite, so I bought a pair. It was a great feeling, knowing I was wearing something I'd hopefully sell all over the world within the next year.

I dropped Charlee off two hours later, went home and packed, and then called Ella as I walked around my house and store and triple-checked all my locks. I hadn't noticed anything amiss the past couple of weeks and it was easy to convince myself whoever was out to banish me had given up. I'd budgeted for a complete security system in my loan application with Curt. I just had to stay safe until the loan was approved. I'd sleep better after that.

"I'm leaving shortly, Ella. I'll be there for a late supper. Oh, and a drink."

She laughed. "Just one drink? I'll make enchiladas and we can have margaritas." She reminded me to drive safe and I said goodbye to her as I plugged my cell phone into my car charger and backed out of the driveway. I'd told Ernie I was going to Ella's. He had her phone number and knew about my trip plans. It was far more than a social visit with Ella. I had meetings lined up for various requirements needed for my store changes, and especially important to me was some unfinished personal business.

It was time to hunt down Nick.

Chapter 32

I tried every search imaginable to locate Nick since the day I'd received the overdue payment from his bank. I'd failed. Mutual friends conveniently dodged my phone calls. Ella, the bloodhound that she was, had been unsuccessful in her investigation as well.

But I knew where Nick's parents lived. At thirty-five, Nick should've been responsible for his own bills. If Nick had no qualms about letting me pay for a truck he was driving, I was pretty sure he'd have no problem letting his parents pick up the tab.

I liked and respected Mr. and Mrs. Zimmerman, but not enough to keep paying their son's bills. They lived in a high-buck area just north of St. Paul. I called them Monday morning after I'd agonized about it over breakfast with Ella.

Could I stop by to visit? "Of course," his mother said, too polite to ask why.

I entered their development; previously gated for several years to keep us "regular folks" out, and gawked at the meticulously groomed lawns and ginormous homes. I compared them to my bat-friendly, minnow-scooping store. We lived in two different worlds.

His parents were kind when I arrived, even after I laid out their son's unpaid vehicle loan that had fallen on my flat-broke shoulders. Mrs. Zimmerman poured us all espresso while Mr. Zimmerman examined the late fees, the harsh letters from the bank, and my copies of the check I'd written to cover Nick's irresponsible ass.

"This is distressing, but not surprising," Mr. Zimmerman said. His neatly trimmed silver hair shone as he shook his head in disappointment at his youngest child.

"I'm afraid we let Nick get away with too much as the youngest of our children. We did him no favors." He looked at me apologetically. "Excuse me one moment."

He walked out of the total ivory-colored kitchen and living room, and down the hallway toward what I remembered to be their master suite. He was back a moment later.

Mrs. Zimmerman made an attempt at pleasantries, asking where I was living now, and not doing a very good job at masking her surprise of finding out her could've-been-daughter-in-law was running an old-fashioned general store in Central Minnesota. It should have been obvious to her when I showed up in jeans, Asics tennis shoes, and a "Hook, line, and sinker" pullover. I tucked my chewed-down-nails under my legs.

Mr. Zimmerman wrote out a check, carefully tore it from the checkbook with his well-groomed fingers, and handed it to me. "I apologize on behalf of Nick, and I hope this makes up for the inconveniences he brought your way. I'll take over from here."

I looked down at the check for five thousand dollars—three times what I'd shelled out for his delinquency debt. "This is too much!" My eyes widened in surprise.

Mrs. Zimmerman reached over and folded my hand over the check. "No, it isn't. Nick left you in a financial mess last year, and we are sorry for how everything worked out." She eyed her husband. These two regal-looking people could have easily modeled for a retirement magazine. "It's high time Nick take responsibility for his spending, and his actions. You take the check. We will take care of Nick." Her smile was as kind as I'd remembered she could be.

I could have floated high enough to touch their vaulted ceiling. Money—or lack of it—had been one of the many elephants standing on my chest these past months. Did I feel guilty for accepting extra money from Nick's parents? Not enough to hand it back.

He'd driven away with furniture we'd paid for, left me making mortgage payments on a home by myself, and was, in general, a spineless weasel for leaving the way he did.

I'd deposit the check when I got back home and decided the money would be spent on a security system. I wouldn't have to wait for my mortgage loan to go through!

Ella had insisted on inviting some friends over for our Monday night dinner, women I hadn't seen since I'd moved to Love eight months ago. Although the beef stroganoff, wine, and belly laughs were an uplifting balm, they reminded me of how little there was to pull me back to the Twin Cities. Ella's wedding was half a year away and a major focus for her. Several of the other women were busy with their marriages and young children. I had no family ties here.

But I had family back in Love. An elderly man who probably knew more about my mom's childhood than I did, friends whom I could call in a heartbeat to come help me out. And Jackson. I hoped we'd find our way back to each other.

And I had a career I *chose* for myself, one I was building for myself. One I confidently believed I could make work. Moving to Love, managing the changes, trials, and successes over the past year had given me exactly what I'd needed…the confidence that I was smart enough to take care of myself.

Tuesday I met with basket designers and suppliers. Late afternoon, I checked out coffee bar options. Wednesday I toured two barista classes and signed up for one starting in January. On Thursday I texted Charlee to see if I could meet with her after she was done with work. I'd originally planned on staying in the cities a couple more days but was happy to be done ahead of time. I was more than ready to get home early.

Charlee was going to invite Old Lloyd over and play moderator as I negotiated with the cranky old man about wild rice and maple syrup for my Love baskets.

I heard back from her at noon. They were both free that night. I stopped by Ella's real estate office, the one I'd left less than a year ago, and hugged her goodbye. I'd be back several times over the coming winter and planned to stay with her. I had no store tying me down these next months. As long as I found someone to feed my wood stove, I was free as a bird. I still had a lot of business to take care of before spring.

Over the past few weeks, I'd started the paperwork for food licenses for both internet sales and sales through the store. I'd already met with the county for my food licensing.

I parked in the front of the store and dropped off my suitcase in my living room before carefully checking out my home, backyard, and store. I grabbed a few packages of old-people cookies. Yes, I knew what kind of cookies senior citizens liked. Lorna Doone or oatmeal raisin cookies were shoo-ins. By dusk, Charlee and I were at her kitchen table eating dinner.

Charlee's kids were gone for the night so we had her home to ourselves. Old Lloyd showed up an hour later. I had copies of my Love basket ideas and every piece of knowledge typed up for him. Yes, he'd warmed up to me and shopped at my store now, but I wasn't sure he was itching to help me with my idea.

He showed up with his typical Walter Matthau grumpy face, faded overalls, and an ancient "Reagan for President" cap.

I opened two packages of cookies and slid them his way before cutting to the deal.

"You told me in the store that you give a lot of your maple syrup away, or trade with friends for other items." I looked directly at him and received a slow nod. He reminded me of a man you'd have found in the woods a hundred years ago, living off the land. His wife had died in her forties and he'd never remarried.

"Yes, I do. And I'm fine with that arrangement. No need to make more syrup. I've got everything I need." He folded his clean but stained hands over his ample chest.

"How about your wild rice? I've heard you and your sons have done quite well."

"Ricing years have their ups and downs." He mumbled through his oatmeal raisin cookie.

"I understand. Just like maple syrup, goat's milk, beeswax, gardens…which is why I want to have a wide variety of options for the baskets." You'd think I was asking for gold.

He studied the papers with figures and photos in front of him. I was exhausted. I wanted to go home, shower, and slide into comfy jammies. I brought out my trump card, knowing Lloyd had a bit of an ego. "You know that anything you sell me will have a label on it? I thought 'Old Lloyd's Wild Rice' and 'Old Lloyd's Maple Syrup' would look nice with the ***LOVEmn*** logo."

Charlee had more important things to do than listen to us play tug of war. She booted up her laptop. "I've been revising my garden layout so we have plenty of room for berries for the jams if you don't want us to use your berries, Lloyd. Also, we'll need more room for additional tomatoes, jalapeno peppers, and onions planted for the salsa." She peered over her glasses. "The kids are fired up about something they'll make being sold all over the world."

I mouthed a silent thank-you behind Lloyd's broad shoulders. He snatched what I guessed to be his tenth cookie and settled back in his chair as my cell phone rang. Ernie's number showed up on the screen. "Hi, Ernie, what's up?"

"Where, where, where are you, you?" He stammered.

"I got home from the cities this afternoon. I'm at Charlee's."

Panic amplified his voice. "Come home right now! Your house and store are on fire!"

Chapter 33

He'd filled the five-gallon gas cans a week ago so nobody would tie his actions to tonight. He regretted filling them at Ernie's gas station though, instead of going out of town. That weird maraca-shaking-bike-riding guy with a crush on Molly had watched him fill the two gas cans. He watched Molly's place too much. But he never talked. That was the important thing.

It didn't matter now. He was done messing around. He'd tried a number of ways to get her to leave what was rightfully *his*. Burning the whole damn place down would not only give her no reason to stay, it would also get rid of the shitty old building he didn't want anyway.

It no longer resembled the humble home his grandparents had been booted from right after his father was born, a home his father had shown him black and white photos of…it was the last home they ever owned. The bank should've let them make things right before selling it to Rosie. No, he didn't care about the building. But the land? Oh yes, the land was valuable…and it should have been handed down from his grandparents, to his father, and then to him.

He'd own it soon, once she left.

Molly's family had done enough damage to his. His poor father was never the same after her grandpa came at him and broke his back. His dad was only eighteen.

She didn't deserve the property. *He* did.

Rosie had talked of selling it to him years ago. She all but promised it.

But he knew what promises were—nothing but an illusion to pacify someone.

This would take care of things. He'd heard she'd be in Minneapolis until the weekend—thanks to small-town gossip—and the game cameras didn't cover his secret entrance area outside the store. Ernie's gas station was closed, it was a quiet weeknight after dinner, and it was time.

He crawled through the damp grass, grunting. He should have used smaller gas cans. The large plastic containers were cumbersome to manipulate. He poured a thick stream of gas along the west wall where he'd rolled up old rags, now soaked with gas, emptying his first gas can.

He emptied the other gas can along the west side of Molly's home. He rolled up more gas-soaked rags. The rows of trees between her place and Ernie's Garage and Ernie's home would shelter anyone from seeing the flames, until it was too late.

He made a short stream of gas away from the rags, struck the match and lit the gas stream, watching the tiny fire work its way toward the rags, exploding in a fire against the store walls. The instant flash of heat warmed his body and he backed away.

He'd timed himself. Less than ten minutes. He scurried back to his vehicle parked a block away in the alley, empty gas cans in tow. Before he climbed into his truck, he turned toward the store and smiled.

"I did this for you, Dad and Grandpa." He raised his fist in salute to heaven before climbing in behind the wheel.

Chapter 34

Charlee offered to drive me to my home, but I wasn't sure what the night would hold. She followed me in her car, and I focused on not driving like a maniac. Seconds ticked like hours before I finally pulled into the gravel road leading to my home. Fire trucks surrounded the burning building. Firemen were everywhere…big yellow ants in their gear scurrying around with powerful hoses spraying waterfalls onto the sky-high flames.

Understandably, they were focused on the side nearest Ernie's gas station.

Floodlights from the fire trucks lit up the darkness. The scent of burned wood and waste permeated the calm night. My yard and driveway were already full of several fire-gawkers. I bolted from my car, Charlee hot on my heels, and spotted Ernie, pacing my driveway, a safe distance from the disaster unfolding before my eyes.

And jogging toward me? Jackson, in his firemen's gear, carrying his fire helmet.

Seeing him unsettled me almost as much as the fire. *Jackson was back from Wyoming?*

Part of me wanted to run into the comfort of his arms. The other part wanted to smack him for cutting any contact for three weeks. Three damn weeks! A couple of measly texts telling me he'd talk to me when he got home, and that was it. Well, I had no time to talk now.

And, if I could be honest with myself, I questioned how convenient it was that Jackson was suddenly back home—and my store was on fire. Like a snowball down a mountain, the horrible thought picked up speed.

From Tracie's party through every single threat since then, my mind tried to pinpoint each instance and whether Jackson could've been behind everything. I hadn't had any problems while he was gone. I shook the irrational thoughts away.

The idea he'd do any damage to his beloved aunt Rosie's house and store made no sense. But my life had quit making sense over the past year. *No, Molly. This man has said he loves you. This man has shown he loves you.*

My brain cells galloped to catch up with the last fifteen minutes of my life. Wasn't I just sitting at Charlee's kitchen table playing mind games with Old Lloyd?

Jackson, barely recognizable with all the soot on his face, was a handful of feet from me when two other firemen clad in their gear grabbed his arm. They pointed to the roof over my grocery section, caving beneath the hoses spraying to extinguish the flames. Before he had a chance to touch me or utter a word, Jackson turned away and followed them back to the fire.

It was just as well. We each had immediate problems to deal with that were far more important than our lover's quarrel, or whatever it was that had built a barricade between us.

"Travis called the fire in." Ernie stood next to me and shouted in my ear, bringing me back to reality. He pointed to Travis who was speaking with Scratch. And crying.

"Why was he hanging around my store again? It's been closed for a week!" I sounded gruff but I was at the point where every man was a suspect. Except for Ernie.

Charlee left my side to talk with a few firemen. I spotted Tracie, parked nearby, sitting in her car with her sleepy son wrapped in a blanket on her lap. Rick was also a fireman.

"Give it time, Molly. I am sure it will all make sense soon." Ernie held my cold hand in his gloved one and rubbed it.

Travis walked toward me, shoulders slumped in a, of all things, striped coat. His damp, round, face scrunched up. "I'm sorry, Molly O'Brien, I'm so sorry!"

My body stiffened. What was he sorry for? Did *Travis* set this fire before calling it in?

I stepped away from him, as if Travis had slapped me. Ernie took my arm. "No. You are misunderstanding Travis." He pulled me closer so the surrounding chaos wouldn't drown us out.

"Travis was walking down the sidewalk by the lake. Yes, he may have been watching your store, but that is what Travis likes to do, is that correct, Travis?" Ernie got a nod out of him. "He heard your smoke detectors go off inside and called 911." He wasn't exaggerating. I was so afraid of a fire in the big old store and house, I had smoke detectors everywhere.

I looked behind Travis at the corner of my store and home where the roof was caving in from the fire. Another fire truck from a nearby town pulled up. While they continued to fight the monster fire, Ernie shouted, "Let us continue this discussion at my home. We can warm up and Travis will tell you his story."

"Good idea. I'll let them know where I'll be. I imagine the cops will be here soon." I spotted Rick and ran over to tell him where they could find me.

Charlee met up with me as Ernie led the way to his home. We settled around Ernie's kitchen table, Charlee put on a pot of coffee, and I leaned toward Travis, encouraging him to tell me the real reason he happened to be across the street from my house at just the right time.

Poor Travis stuttered out his story—with gentle prodding on my part—a story I could scarcely believe. "W—w—when I saw his empty truck parked in the alley for no reason I knew he was up to no good." Travis stuttered out half of his words, something I'd never heard before. But I'd never seen him so upset. There was no way this young man had done anything wrong.

"It's okay, Travis. Calm down and take deep breaths." I reached for his hand and looked him in the eye, breathing with him as if one of us was in labor. Ernie and Charlee were silent. I'm guessing Ernie already heard the story.

"I didn't know what he'd done until I watched him walk back to his truck with two big gas jugs. He drove away and then I heard the smoke alarms." We did more deep breathing to slow his continued stammering. "Then I saw fire. I called the 911 people."

I steeled my heart for what I was afraid to hear. "Travis, who is this man you're talking about? Have you seen him before?" Please, please don't tell me it was Jackson.

"Yes. He's the guy who wears fancy pants and sells bait in the winter."

"Drake?" I sucked in enough air to pop the button on my jeans. Milquetoast Drake? "Are you sure?"

"I am sure, Molly O'Brien. I saw him fill gas cans last week. My dad only fills up his gas cans like that when he mows our yard or drives our boat. He had no need to mow now. Also, November is too cold for boating." Travis was so serious in his reasoning I'd have laughed if I wasn't so shocked.

Charlee and I exchanged surprised looks right as my cell phone rang in the suddenly-quiet kitchen. Jackson's name scrolled on my screen. It was tempting to ignore the call like he'd done to me for weeks. But him calling as a fireman was a call I couldn't disregard.

"You need to come back here. Daisy and a deputy are here. They want to talk to you."

"Daisy?" What did drive-by Daisy have to say?

"Yup." Jackson hung up, likely a little busy with the fire.

"I need to go back to the fire. A deputy is there, and I guess Daisy has something to say, too." I explained to the group at Ernie's table.

"Do you want us to come with?" Charlee offered.

"Thanks, but I'll be fine. Is it okay if I bring the deputy here, Ernie?" My body was shaking from nerves. I didn't want to stand out in the cold and make it worse.

"Of course you may. We will keep the coffee flowing." Ernie nodded.

I shrugged back into my coat and hurried toward the fire.

Jackson met me half-way on the path between Ernie's place and mine, his pale blue eyes rimmed in red.

"I've been waiting for you to come back from the cities." He looked exhausted.

We took in the loud chaos surrounding us. "I don't have time to explain right now, but when this is all done, I've got something important to talk to you about." He leaned in close to me. "And, I'm sorry. I wanted you to need me. It took me missing you to realize I *like* your independence. I *like* that you won't use me. I love you…and your stubborn Irish streak."

My emotions and thinking process were so jumbled from everything it was more than I could process. It was easier to turn to him and pound on his chest covered in his yellow firemen's turnout gear. He allowed me to vent via my fists, expending the frustration and shock of everything. "Your timing is damn impeccable, Jackson. You could've told me that over the phone!" I shouted into his chest before I collapsed into his arms.

My damp cheek pressed against his blackened firemen's coat. He needed to get back to fighting the fire. I needed to meet with the deputy, and apparently, drive-by-Daisy.

Chapter 35

Deputy Patrick led the way to Ernie's, with an electrified Daisy and me following close behind. Ernie greeted us at the door as Charlee set out a plate of cookies on the table. I had barely settled my butt in the kitchen chair when Daisy uncorked her information.

In her rapid-fire way, drive-by-sometimes-annoying-and-nosy Daisy rattled off the events in the past hour of her life while Deputy Patrick updated his notes.

"Ever since that bloated deer was left on your deck, I've been keeping my eye on Drake, keeping notes." Daisy licked her thin lips, likely thrilled to have her super-sleuth reporting pay off.

"Why that day?" She had my interest.

"I'd observed Drake out east of town loading a dead deer in the back of his pickup the day before. When I heard about the deer left at your house the next night, in that godawful heat, well, I made copious notes of it." Daisy wrapped her green and purple plaid coat closer to her frail body.

"That nutcracker is odd. Felt it down to my bones even before this." She nodded in agreement with her own wisdom. "The night of the harvest festival, I watched him leave. He was back in about an hour, and I wrote it down in case I heard something else happened to you. Sure enough, Charlee told Old Lloyd, who told me about someone messing with stuff in your house that night while you were at the harvest festival."

I leaned toward her, hanging on every juicy detail. The deputy walked away to take a call on his cell phone. I'd never been so thankful in my life for this nosy woman.

"So tonight when I spotted his truck parked in a dark alley nearby, I turned off my car lights, parked on the other side of Ernie's Garage, and hunkered down. Sure enough, I spotted him sneaking back across the road from your place to his truck. I deduced he was up to no good. So I followed him. When we were a few miles out of town, heading toward his house, I heard about your fire on my police scanner." She took a swallow of her coffee as if she needed more caffeine.

"I called in the caper to the 911 dispatchers, alerting them of the crime in process. Seems someone had beat me to the punch." She reached over and slugged an overstimulated Travis in the arm. "Good thing I know the way to Drake's house. He left me in the dust, flooring that old pickup like someone strapped a rocket to it. He lives out of town 'bout eight miles, in the middle of the woods…in case you're wondering." Her bug eyes focused on me.

"I parked along his road to make sure he didn't leave until the Sheriff arrived." Their response time could vary a lot. Luckily, there were often deputies in nearby towns. I'd met Deputy Patrick on more than one occasion from my previous reports. I hoped our relationship would finally end after tonight.

And I hoped at some point I'd find out what Drake had against me.

"So where is Drake now?" I asked Daisy, who turned and looked at the deputy still on the phone in Ernie's kitchen. She turned back to me and shrugged her bony shoulders. We wouldn't get an answer until the deputy got off his phone.

I looked around the table at this mismatch of people who'd been there for me. An elderly man I now loved like a favorite grandpa. A hard-working, wonderful mother, amazing friend, a woman who could live off the land, and who had my back. A young man of few words, a man I was wary of initially, who liked order, and apparently, liked me. This young man had been watching and protecting me in the only way he knew how and had become my knight in shining armor. And finally, a wiry, nosy, over-energized, elderly, retired gossip columnist who risked her life by tracking down my nemesis.

Like coffee spilled on a tablecloth, inch by inch the shock of it all overtook my body, coupled with an enormous gratitude for these people, and all the crazy, caring, people of Love. It broke me open and my tears poured out like a tsunami.

Runny-nosed ugly sobs erupted from my very core. "I…I can't thank you enough, Daisy and Travis!" I huffed out between tears. "He almost got away with it!"

Charlee stood and came around to stand behind me, rubbing my shoulders. "It's okay, Molly. Let it out. This is a lot to digest. Even *I* can't figure out what is behind Drake's vendetta."

Ernie discreetly placed a box of tissues in front of me while Deputy Patrick stepped back into the dining room. "Did they nab him?" Daisy piped up.

The deputy shook his head. "Apparently he has a trail through the woods in the back of his house and escaped that way. You did a good job of blocking him from leaving on the road though, Daisy. We appreciate you staying there until our deputies arrived." His dark eyes studied my face while he addressed her.

"We'll find him, Ms. O'Brien. I have some questions for you that may help us out. I'd like you to come to the Sheriff's office and we will file a report."

I glanced at the round clock on Ernie's wall. Barely 8:00 p.m. It seemed closer to midnight. "Sure. I'd like to get some answers myself." Mustering all my energy, I pushed myself up out of the chair. I'd lost my home and my business. All I had left was my will.

"I'll come with you." Charlee stated, and I mouthed a "thank you" to her.

"Travis and I will stay here. His mother should be here shortly," Ernie said.

"I've got some scoop to write. I best get heading home!" Daisy jumped out of her chair, yanked up her polyester pants, and downed the last of her coffee.

"Don't even think about it, Daisy." Deputy Patrick took a step toward her and softened his words by putting his large hand on her back. "We sure do appreciate your help in this, but if you leak information out now, it may keep us from finding Drake. You don't want to undo all of your hard work, do you?"

She stammered and fidgeted, puffed up about her contribution to the case, yet likely slighted she couldn't break the news. "Fine, I'll wait. I get the exclusive on this though, right?"

"Of course, Daisy. Once he is in custody, someone will meet with you for your story."

It was good enough to settle her down before making her way back to the crowd in my backyard. I hugged her as hard as I dare, I didn't want to be responsible for breaking a bone. I did the same to Travis and Ernie before Charlee and I followed Deputy Patrick out the door.

Charlee called Tracie as we walked to Charlee's car. Tracie had left to put her son to bed, and the crowd in my backyard had somewhat thinned. Several fire trucks still surrounded my place, the air thick with an acrid, sooty, smoky scent.

I stopped and stood to face the desolation. Less than two hours ago, the place was standing. Now it wasn't. And everything I owned was inside there.

Yet I was so thankful the fire hadn't reached Ernie's Garage and gas tanks.

We followed the deputy in his squad SUV for the roughly thirty miles to the county sheriff's department. During the ride, I was mostly quiet, still trying to absorb the reality of it all.

"I texted Jackson when we were at Uncle Ernie's to let him know you're staying at my house tonight." She glanced at me. "My clothes will be too big for you, but Logan's should fit."

"Thank you…for everything." I leaned my head back and closed my eyes until we arrived. The inside of my eyes burned, my head throbbed, and my brain was scrambled.

Over the next hour, I was asked questions that Charlee was able to answer far better than I could. "What do you know about Drake Wilson?" Too little.

"What can you tell us about your relationship that may have given him reason to threaten you these past months?" I haven't a clue about his past. And there was no "relationship."

It went on and on, and I'm afraid they thought I was hiding something. It helped to have Charlee fill in what blanks she could. Drake had moved to Love over ten years ago, opened his real estate business, was never married that Charlee knew of, and had no ties to the area.

"I think most of the people you should be talking to are fighting the fire right now. Drake was quiet, but he did have friends," Charlee offered. "I'd say his girlfriend Wendy might be of help, but they haven't dated very long. Or maybe some of the realtors at his business?"

The deputy continued taking notes, and I sighed for about the hundredth time.

"Okay, we're good for now. We'll keep you informed. I don't think Drake will have gone too far. Eventually, he's got to come back to his house and business. And his cat, if he cares for it at all." He shook his head as if that may not be the case.

As we all stood, something connected in my brain enough to put two and two together. "Drake has a cat? What does it look like?" I held my breath.

Deputy Patrick scratched his head. "I can ask the deputy who searched his house." He scrolled through his phone and typed out a quick text. In a matter of seconds, he received his response. "Looks kind of tan and white."

Charlee and I exchanged looks. "Is there any way I can get in his house? I think that might be my cat." Recognition registered on his face as he remembered the bits of cat hair stuck to the blood on my living room wall.

"I'll let the deputy who is watching Drake's home know you'll stop by."

I covered my mouth and blinked back tears of joy. Something to finally be happy about! I'd thought Pixie died a horrible death. I tried not to get my hopes up. "If it's Pixie, this humanizes Drake a bit," I said as we walked to Charlee's car.

"It does," Charlee agreed. "Which helps. I mean, everything he did was awful, but that's the one physically harmful thing he's supposedly done that I just couldn't fathom."

I nodded. "I think that's the thing for me. Yes, he physically threatened me at Tracie's party but never did anything, and he could have." We rode for a while in silence.

"Hey, Molly?"

"Yes?"

"Think you're qualified enough now for the 'Hell Club'?" Charlee teased.

I chuckled. "Yes, I'd say so. What did you say the next get-together is?"

"Curling, in early December. Maybe, if you're lucky, I'll lend you some of my cool and colorful curling pants to wear."

Leave it to Charlee to take my mind off things.

Chapter 36

If I slept at all it was only a few hours with a thinner Pixie curled up next to me. The bags under my eyes resembled blue saucers as I shuffled into Charlee's kitchen. She was already busy making a pot of coffee. The sun hadn't risen yet if it even would on this cold November day.

"It's not fair," I said. "You people of color don't show the lovely shade of blue under your eyes like us pasty white people." I nudged her shoulder in jest.

She touched my hand. "Don't I know it. I feel sorry for you poor white folks. Every. Single. Day." Charlee winked, looking as refreshed as if she'd slept ten hours. I wrapped her roomy bathrobe around me.

We sat with our coffee in Charlee's kitchen where I'd negotiated with Old Lloyd just twelve hours earlier. Now his maple syrup and wild rice were low on my list of concerns.

"You hear from Jackson at all?"

I took my cell phone out of the bathrobe pocket. "Yes. Six texts last night. I'll call him in a while. His last text came in after midnight and said the fire was finally out." I stared into my coffee mug. "I don't get it. Nobody does. When Tracie called last night she said Rick and the guys were shocked Drake was behind all of it."

Charlee leaned her elbows on the table. "I thought all night about Drake. I think he moved from somewhere in North Dakota. He was already a realtor when he came to town. He didn't ask you out on a date or anything, did he?" Her nose scrunched up with her question.

"No. I've been thinking about when I first met him. He acted normal…I think. I barely knew him when I was attacked at Tracie's party last May. One thing I remember is how a couple months ago he'd stopped in, saying he'd be more than happy to help me list the place, figuring I'd want out since the business had died after the summer."

Now I had to wonder, if I'd have listed it, would things have turned out differently? Was it just that he wanted the place? I couldn't imagine him running Rosie's old business. I also remembered him mentioning his father died when Drake was ten. Had that damaged his outlook on life? "I also wonder how he got inside my place. Yes, initially he could have had an extra set of keys, but after Jackson changed the locks, I don't get how Drake made it inside without breaking in."

"We can speculate all day. Once they find him, you'll get your answers."

I hoped so. I showered after a light breakfast and threw on a pair of pants and a shirt of Logan's that Charlee loaned me. They'd be back from their grandparents later today.

Jackson called after I dressed. "Drake's been arrested. A deputy will call you soon."

"How did you find out so fast?"

"Easy. I found him. Too much adrenaline from fighting the fire to get to sleep. He made the mistake of hiding in woods that I know like I know my dog. Two deputies trusted me and my gut. I found him hiding out in a shack no bigger than an old fish house."

"Wow. That was his backup plan?" Drake seemed way more organized than that.

"I don't think he had a backup plan, Molly. He never thought he'd get caught, by Travis and Daisy, no less." I heard the smile in his voice. The voice I'd missed. The voice that used to whisper to me late at night.

"Oh, and I've got your suitcase with your clothes in it, and your safe. I want you to come home with me, Molly. Please. Not because you need me, but because I want to be with you every day. We've wasted enough time already."

"You have my clothes?" And my safe? Did he run inside a burning building?

"Yes. I was at Ernie's when my pager went off." He broke off for a few seconds. Was he sniffling? "I didn't know if you were inside or not! Your lights were on but you hadn't been home every time I checked during the day. I ran in quick and dragged your safe out. When I was crawling out, I saw your suitcase so I grabbed that too."

My suitcase I'd packed for my trip to Minneapolis would help a lot. Not only for my clothes and toiletries, but my laptop and paperwork for the Love baskets was inside.

"Thank you for doing that. Rescuing those things helps." My mom's wedding ring was inside my safe, along with my emergency cash. Jackson had given me a hard time about my small safe the first time he saw it, saying anyone could take it and run. I agreed, but it was one I could afford, and figured I'd eventually replace it. Now I was glad it was moveable.

"Can I meet you at Ernie's in about half an hour?" Jackson asked.

"Ernie's?"

"Yes. I have something I need to show you, and I'd like to have Ernie there too."

I didn't have time to question what it was since I had another call coming in—from the Sheriff's department. "I have to go, Jackson. I've got a call from the Sheriff's department. I'll meet you at Ernie's."

The deputy's call was short. Drake was in custody. I said I'd be there in an hour or so.

I thanked Charlee for her hospitality before I drove to meet Jackson and called him on the way. "The deputy said Travis and his mom will meet us there." I realized I assumed Jackson would be with me. "That is, if you want to come with me."

"Yes, and I talked to Ernie earlier this morning. He's coming with us too. In fact, I just pulled into your driveway. I want to talk with you first, though, before we pick up Ernie."

A few minutes later I drove down my gravel road and saw Jackson's pickup parked in the driveway. I turned off my car as he stepped out of his pickup. He greeted me with a hug, lifting me off the ground, before kissing me like I was water and he was dying of thirst.

When we pulled back, our eyes met and we laughed. "I have so much to tell you," we both said at once.

I touched his unshaven cheek. "You go first. I could talk about my situation for an hour. What was it you wanted to show me?"

"Let's sit inside the truck." The temperature hovered around freezing and it felt good to climb into his warm vehicle. We stared for a minute at the charred mess of what used to be part of my home and store, fifty feet away. Yellow tape encompassed the building. I wasn't allowed inside yet. The idea that my home was now a "crime scene" tasted as acrid as the air from the smoldering ashes.

I forced my attention to Jackson, and what was on his mind. He started by going back to the night he'd received his mother's frantic call about his dad's stroke. He explained the hurried state of his packing before leaving for Wyoming. "She wanted me to bring the deeds they have to their cabin and another lake lot. The papers in my safe are a mess, so I grabbed everything and threw it in a box." He let out a long sigh. "When I had time at my parent's house, I went through a folder of Rosie's papers I'd tossed in my safe after she passed away."

He reached into the breast pocket of his shirt. "I've got a letter here from Aunt Rosie's son Tom, written to her. Remember I said he died in Vietnam? This was obviously written before you or I were born. The letter talks about your mom." He fished it from his pocket and handed me the one-page letter. "I was going to wait and have you read it later, but I think it's better for you to read it now before we pick up Ernie. He'll be able to answer some of your questions." His face was grim when he handed me the well-worn letter. What could be so horrible in a letter from Rosie's son? And what did it have to do with my mom and me?

I unfolded the paper, so soft and thin I was surprised it hadn't fallen apart over the years.

Dear Mother,

I'm sorry for bringing this up again, but you are the only one who knows, the only one who can possibly understand the torture I'm going through.

Not a day goes by that I don't think about her. I never even got to hold her! Never got to look at her tiny face, see her first smile, or cradle her soft little body.

Celia has insisted I stop any contact with her. She won't let me be a part of her life, worried that the few who knew of her pregnancy will realize I was the father.

She wants me to just forget. I can't. And I struggle to forgive Celia.

I'm so sorry for the troubles I've caused you. And there you are, with a granddaughter out there somewhere. It is all so unfair. What do I do, mother, what do I do?

Love,

Tom

I dropped the letter onto my lap before my hands covered my mouth hanging open in shock. *What in holy hell? I had a half- sister somewhere?*

Chapter 37

My mouth struggled to form two syllables to ask the thousand questions whipping through my mind.

Jackson squeezed my hand. "Now you see why I didn't want to talk on the phone. I was afraid I'd blurt this out. I was sure you'd never believe me until you read the letter for yourself."

I fished in my coat pocket for tissues. "I can't believe this! Do you know what this means?" The past twenty-four hours had taken my emotions on the craziest roller-coaster ride they'd ever experienced.

He grinned and thumbed away tears from my cheek. "Yes. You've got an older sister."

I smiled back at him, this newfound happiness helping to overshadow the fire.

He put the truck in gear. "We better get going. We can interrogate Ernie on the way to the Sheriff's department. I stopped at his place last night after I got back from Wyoming yesterday and found out you weren't home. I had the letter and hoped he could shed some light on it. I had just shown him the letter when my fire pager went off." He drove the hundred yards to Ernie's home, pulled up near the front door, and got out.

I slid over to the middle as Jackson helped Ernie into the passenger side of his truck.

"Ah, my dear Molly. What a time you have had lately." Ernie patted my knee as he settled in next to me.

"That's for sure. I'm so happy and sad at the same time, it feels like a tornado of extreme emotions inside me." I handed him the letter. "Did you get a chance to read this last night?"

"Just a smidgeon." Ernie held the letter as his watery brown eyes studied every word on the well-worn page. Jackson and I watched intently. Ernie was too calm as he read it. If he hadn't known this information ahead of time, his eyes would have been wide with shock.

"You knew about her, didn't you?" Jackson spoke calmly even though I sensed his curiosity. Tom's daughter would be related to him too. He kept the truck in park.

"Why didn't you tell me?" I was crushed that this secret was kept from me.

"It was not my story to tell. Where did you get this letter?" Ernie's hand caressed the paper as thin as his aged skin.

Jackson told Ernie of how he'd all but emptied his safe, taking all the paperwork with him to Wyoming. He nodded toward the letter still held by Ernie. "This was in there. I'd been reading some of Rosie's papers and the name Celia caught my eye."

Ernie removed his glasses and pinched the bridge of his nose. "I do believe Rosie hoped her granddaughter would find her way to this town at some point. Perhaps she thought you would do some digging and research." He looked at me. "Your mother also wanted to find her daughter. I do not know why it did not happen."

"I see there is no year on it." Ernie rubbed his smooth jaw for a minute. "From what I recall, Rosie's Tom enlisted in the service shortly after he graduated from high school. He died in 1970, I believe. You may need to ask Nancy about that date."

"So my half-sister was probably born in 1969." I did the easy math. That meant she was roughly nine years older than me. A half-sister who was Jackson's first cousin, once removed.

Jackson glanced at the clock on his dashboard and backed out of Ernie's driveway. We didn't want to keep the Sheriff's department waiting. "Clearly my mom doesn't know of this or she'd have said something about it long ago," he said. "I thought Tom and Celia were more like a brother and sister to each other. That's the way Aunt Rosie made it sound when she told me about leaving her store to Celia."

Ernie nodded. "I believe they started out that way when Celia went to work for Rosie. But things happen. Young love many times blossoms from a friendship. Rosie said that is the real reason Molly's grandfather up and moved away with his daughters…after Celia confessed her pregnancy to him shortly after she graduated from high school."

Things were different back then. A girl, whether eighteen or not, unmarried and pregnant, was usually whisked away for a long visit to some unknown fictitious aunt or grandma's place until she mysteriously appeared months later—without the baby everyone pretended to forget ever existed. Or, she found herself in a quickly-planned marriage with an unusually short pregnancy. *My poor mother!*

"I was told my mom had a boyfriend in high school and that grandpa had gotten into a fight with him, injuring the guy right before mom's family left town. So that wasn't true?" Had I misunderstood? I didn't know what to believe anymore.

"I am just relaying what Rosie told me years ago. I do believe Celia had a boyfriend in high school while secretly seeing Tom. I do not think anyone had knowledge of them other than Rosie. The townspeople saw them together so much in Rosie's store that they likely assumed Celia and Tom were merely friends. Tom left for Vietnam when Celia was a senior in high school. According to Rosie, for some reason, Celia thought she was not good enough for him and had tried breaking it off."

"Sounds like that didn't work out so well," Jackson mumbled as he concentrated on driving. The freezing temps and light mist were perfect for slippery road conditions.

"Rosie said she knew something was troubling Celia, who still worked at her store the summer after she graduated. I was told Celia hiccupped a lot if she was under duress. She had the hiccups so much, Rosie said she insisted Celia tell her what was wrong."

"Yes, she did." I smiled at the memory of my mother's hiccup outbursts.

Ernie continued. "After confessing to Rosie, your mother told your grandpa, who was quite livid about her family way. He never asked who the father was and deduced it was her high school boyfriend." Ernie reached for my hand.

"How did Rosie know it was Tom's baby?" It felt like someone had plopped me in the middle of a soggy daytime drama. This was my own flesh and blood we were talking about.

"I recollect Rosie said when Celia found out her father had gone after her old boyfriend and caused him great physical damage, she came to visit Rosie at the store." Ernie continued to purge decades-old family secrets. "Rosie said she pleaded with Celia to stay and live with Rosie. Celia was afraid to tell her father, who had no knowledge of her relationship with Tom."

"How do we know the baby wasn't her boyfriend's?" I didn't want to think about my mom having sex in high school with even one guy, much less two. Yet my heart ached for what she must have gone through.

"She told Rosie she had never had relations with her boyfriend. There was no doubt in Celia's mind that it was Tom's child. He was the only man she had lain with."

Jackson and I looked at each other and grinned. Sometimes Ernie's old-fashioned words made us chuckle.

"So Tom died without ever seeing his baby girl?" How heartbreaking.

"That is correct. Your grandfather dropped your mother off at a home for unwed mothers in the Twin Cities. After that, he drove out east to New Hampshire with his younger daughters. When the little girl was born, your grandfather insisted Celia give the baby up for adoption. The nuns at the Catholic home for unwed mothers reinforced that decision. Celia had made Rosie promise to not tell Tom about the baby." Ernie shook his head, his drooping face etched in sadness for the story he relayed.

"How did he find out then?" If I'd ever have had any sort of relationship with my aunts, I could have asked them. This explained a lot as to why mom was always treated like an outcast. The minimal contact between her and her younger sisters over the decades made me wonder what they'd been told about my mother by their father. It saddened me to think my mom had cared for her sisters after their mother passed away, and a cold shoulder was the thanks she'd received from them.

"Rosie said Tom came home on leave the spring after the baby girl was born, after Celia's family left Love, with no word from Celia for him. On the day he shipped out again, Rosie broke her promise to Celia and told Tom. She was not happy with herself yet could not keep the secret from her only child." Ernie's watery eyes searched Jackson's face for a sliver of understanding at the painful choice his great-aunt Rosie had made.

"At that point, Rosie did not know where your mother was living; only that she had given the girl up for adoption. Rosie hoped it would help fuel his commitment for a safe return."

I dabbed at my eyes. These were real people with real losses we were talking about. Real families with real grief.

Jackson nudged me. "The photo my mom saw of your mother pregnant may have been from when she was pregnant with your sister." I nodded. It was another item with no year on it.

The three of us were silent for minutes, each lost in our own unveiling thoughts.

"I can't believe you've kept all this information to yourself," I said to Ernie. I could've never done it. I admired him honoring Rosie's secrets, yet I was upset about being left clueless.

"I was not positive you did not already know this information, Molly. Yes, you were surprised Rosie left your mother the store. Still, I was not sure if your mother had spoken of the child she gave up for adoption. I also did not feel it would be a good thing for you to know if your father was not aware of the child. Secrets can be haunting." Ernie's words were slow as he searched for the right way to let me know he had my best interests at heart.

"I didn't even think about if my dad knows!" It unsettled me either way. If he'd known all these years, after hearing me bemoan about being an only child time after time…well, that would be just cruel. And if he didn't know? I sure didn't want to be the bearer of that news now. Either way, it would be a tough subject to broach.

"Now you see my dilemma." Ernie nodded at me. What a weight to carry.

"It explains why Rosie left your mom the store, and the "or her descendants" part. Aunt Rosie probably held out hope that her granddaughter would find her way to Love," Jackson said.

I made a mental note to call my dad soon. The half-hour drive to the Sheriff's Department seemed short, thanks to the captivating topic we'd been dissecting.

We hadn't discussed the fire at all.

Chapter 38

The fire took center stage again when we arrived at the Sheriff's Department. Travis and his mother stood in the hallway, his unzipped winter coat revealed his trademark striped shirt. His face was puffy, and his eyes, red-rimmed.

"Look at all of us. Exhausted…all because of Drake." I apologized again to Ernie as if I had a hand in Drake's actions. At Ernie's age, he needed more than just a few hours of sleep.

Travis fidgeted. "Jackson said last night that you need to get the story from Drake. So if you are going to hear a story from Drake, do I have to be there too, Molly O'Brien?"

"No, you don't have to be there. This is between Drake and me."

"And Jackson. Right, Jackson? You said you want to hear his 'sorry excuse before you kick his ass into next Sunday.'" Travis' voice was monotone as he repeated Jackson's words.

Jackson fought to suppress a laugh. "You're right, Travis. I did say that." He winked at Travis. "But this is something Molly will take care of on her own."

During the past month, I'd thought about how important it was for me to take care of myself. This was another step I needed to do. I needed more information. I coaxed it from Travis. "You've been watching the store for quite some time, Travis. Is it just because we're friends?" I assumed once I closed my store that Travis had quit coming around.

He studied the gloomy November day outside the windows. "Yes, Molly O'Brien. I like making sure you're okay because you're my friend and you're nice to me. I have been watching that man with the fancy pants drive by your store very slow, like an old person drives." His eyes shifted to Ernie, in case he was offended.

"On the weekend where we honor people who work hard in America, I was riding my bike in town extra early, before the many cars and people arrived. I saw him loading something outside of your store into his pickup. It did not seem right to me."

I remembered Labor Day weekend. I'd had all of my ice stolen.

"On the TV shows, if people do something unusual, you are supposed to keep watching them. 'Suspicious activity,' it is called, Molly O'Brien. So I kept watching him. That's what they do on NCIS." His face was solemn.

"Did you see him hanging around my house again after that?" I didn't know if we'd have enough evidence to go on or if Drake would have an alibi and deny everything.

"Yes, I have seen him sneak behind Ernie's gas station where you have the pretty thick bushes that grow lilacs in the spring. Two times. I wondered why he would go back there where it would be dirty from brush and leaves. I don't think he likes getting dirty."

I tried to visualize what was over in that corner. It was an area thick with brush and trees between my store and the gas station. Jackson and Ernie wore puzzled looks on their faces as they contemplated this information. Suddenly Ernie's eyes lit up and he touched my shoulder.

"Molly, I do believe Travis may have solved another piece of the puzzle." His eyes sparkled as he beamed at Travis. The receptionist informed us Deputy Patrick would be ready for me shortly and gestured for us to take a seat in the waiting room.

I sat, literally on the edge of my seat, as Ernie described a part of the old basement I'd only been in twice. "There is an old root cellar in the corner of the dirt-floored basement. Those old wood steps lead to a small crawl space door going outside." He scratched his head. "I was sure that old thing was boarded up years ago," Ernie mumbled to himself.

I visualized the area Ernie described. "You mean he was entering through that creepy basement?" I cringed. I'd been down there recently to wrap the bathroom pipes with heat tape.

"Yes. I do believe when Travis spotted Drake in those bushes it was the route he used to gain access to your home without anyone noticing his path," Ernie explained.

I didn't have time to be stunned. Deputy Patrick was heading my way.

"We'll sit in what we call a 'recording room' with a TV in it." He led me down the hall to a room with a couch and a couple of comfortable chairs. The TV was mounted on the wall.

"Here's how it works. Drake is in an interrogation room where an investigator and two deputies are recording his interview. We will be watching it live here. We're hoping you can corroborate any information he mentions or come up with questions on anything we might miss. We will pass those questions on to the investigator in the room with Drake."

I settled in one of the cushy chairs, Deputy Patrick sat in the other. Within a few minutes Drake appeared on the TV screen, sitting in his orange jumpsuit. No gel in his hair, a five o'clock shadow on his normally clean-shaven face, and his eyes downcast.

Sitting across from him were two deputies and a woman I assumed to be the investigator.

He'd been read his rights. At any given moment Drake could change his mind and stop talking. I leaned forward in my chair as if that would hurry their questioning along.

I found myself talking out loud to the screen. "Why, Drake? Why?" Anger and disbelief wrestled in my stomach.

It didn't take long for them to ask Drake what he had against me.

"Her grandpa wrecked my dad's life. He pushed my dad down steps and broke his back. He was only eighteen. And it was all Molly's mother's fault! She lied about my dad, said he did something he didn't do!" Spit flew from his grim mouth.

"Dad never recovered from his back injury. Sure, he was eventually able to walk again. He married mom and had me and my two younger brothers, but he drank himself to death trying to ease his back pain." His dark eyes stared at the investigator while his body visibly vibrated, probably from trying to restrain his anger.

I turned to Deputy Patrick. "I thought he didn't have any family around here." I knew now though exactly who his father must have been. I listened as Drake's icy voice dripped a grim, ancient picture. His dad was my mother's high school boyfriend—the one she'd deserted for Tom—unbeknownst to anyone at the time. Drake didn't mention a pregnancy, I'm sure his father never knew why my grandpa came after him.

But I knew now. Grandpa had wrongly gone after Drake's father, getting into a fight with him at a dance hall, where they scuffled outside. Drake's father was either pushed or fell backward down cement steps, having no idea why my grandpa came after him.

According to Drake, his dad told him my mom had broken up with him right before their high school graduation. It coincided with what my mom had told me years ago when I'd asked if it was hard for her to leave her hometown. "I'd just broken up with my boyfriend. It wasn't too hard to move away and start over."

"After Father died, our mother worked two jobs, I raised my two brothers, and we barely got by." Drake tried to wipe his tears with his shoulder, his hands in cuffs.

"Lucky for us, my mom remarried a decent man. I took his last name and so did my brothers. He taught us to work hard. I've done that and was willing to pay a fair price to Rosie for a place that should have been mine to begin with—my grandparents owned that land—the only home they ever owned. The bank sold their home to Rosie and my dad's family struggled afterward with no permanent home, no money." Drake's cupped hands shook in his handcuffs as if he wanted to strangle someone.

"Rosie told me years ago I could buy it from her when she was ready to sell. Then she changed her mind. Gave it to Molly's family, of all people. The least deserving people! That place should've stayed in my dad's family. It was all they had!" His face was so flushed with anger I was afraid he was going to have a heart attack.

It wouldn't help to tell Drake what fueled my grandpa's actions. As hard as it was to admit, my mother should've come clean with her dad. She didn't. And look what happened.

I wondered if this all made sense to the investigator and deputies. Drake's twisted version of how life should've turned out, targeting me for things that happened long before I was born, reminded me of one thing: we were responsible for our own happiness. I couldn't help him, but I could help myself.

Chapter 39

My body and mind spun as if they'd been put through one of those old-fashioned wringer washing machines.

Our ride back was quiet. As we pulled into Ernie's driveway, I asked the question that had been burning my tongue. "Do you think I dare ask my dad about this?" I needed to have this conversation with my dad, but I had no clue whether he knew about the baby or not. Any insight from Ernie would be helpful before I called my dad.

Jackson and I stared at Ernie, waiting for his wisdom. "I think for your peace of mind, it is a conversation you should have. Remember to choose your words carefully." He squeezed my hand. "Back in those days, your mother could not keep a child and raise it on her own. If she indeed informed your father, it would likely have been a difficult thing for him to hear. I was not blessed with children but I do imagine if my wife would have sprung a surprise child on me, I believe it would have inspired some soul searching on my part." Ernie waited a minute for his words to sink in before he planted a soft kiss on my cheek and Jackson opened the truck door to help him out.

I hoped I'd have the restraint to tread lightly with my dad on this delicate subject. Judgement was such an easy thing to use and usually accompanied by its friend, ignorance. I hoped to understand my father's actions, no matter what, much as Ernie had to do all those years ago with the townspeople of Love when he first moved to town.

Jackson pulled out of Ernie's driveway and parked in my backyard. We stared at my building mess. "I know this has all been too much at once. Hell, it's been too much for you all year. Things will be better now, right?" His voice was hopeful.

I noticed the shadows under his eyes. Eyes that reflected his love for me. "Is there still an opening at the Jackson hotel?"

His eyebrows shot up. "Hell yes. You can take up permanent residency there…if you want. Wasn't that one of the stupid things we argued about before I left for Wyoming?" He reached for my hand and kissed it.

"Yes, and I'm sorry. I just never wanted to end up in the position I was with Nick."

"Your independence and determination are two of the many things I love about you, Molly. I'm not trying to take them away." He studied my home. "C'mon, let's go around in the front door of the store. There's tape around half of the building, but I asked one of the deputies if you could go in and retrieve some personal things from the area of your home that wasn't touched by the fire. He said it was fine. We sometimes do this if we know there are safe areas containing items the homeowner will want to retrieve."

"Yes, I'd like to see what's left."

He led the way as we carefully walked through the house and store parts that weren't affected. Enormous blue tarps had been placed around the openings left by the fire. Most of my living room was gone, along with the grocery section of the store. My bedroom had smoke damage but was structurally untouched.

I couldn't hold back the tears, and it wasn't from the acrid smoke. I wasn't embarrassed. Jackson's watery eyes matched mine. This had to be harder on him than me, walking through what was once his great-aunt's place—a place he'd spent so much time at it became a second home for him.

The kitchen had partial damage, and the bait and gift section, minimal. We talked about a possible timeline for repairs, once the insurance claim was filed. I thought about the changes I'd planned just a few weeks ago while meeting with Curt at the bank. It made me chuckle.

"What's so funny?" Jackson squinted at me as if I'd lost a marble or two.

"It's ironic. Yes, this is going to be a nightmare to rebuild, but the fire affected some of the areas in the store I'd planned to remodel anyway." I wiped at the tears in my eyes.

"You're going to remodel?"

Jackson's question reminded me we hadn't talked about my vision for the store's future. "Yes. I spoke with Curt at the bank a few weeks ago. I've applied for a small business loan."

His eyes widened. "That's why you were with him at the bank?"

"Yes. How did you know that? You were in Wyoming when I met with Curt."

He averted his eyes. "Scratch told me he saw you and Curt talking outside the bank a week after I left for Wyoming. I was afraid he'd swept in and wooed you off your feet."

My laughter turned into a cough as I inhaled the stench from the fire. "Let's get out of here. We can talk at your house."

It didn't take long for me to collect the few things I needed that were usable. "Can you get a cooler from my shed and bring it in? I might as well bring what I can from my freezer over to your house or it will spoil." My power was disconnected now.

We filled the cooler with the contents of my freezer, mostly leftover inventory items from my store freezer. I found a few more clothes that would need to be dry-cleaned, and we brought everything out to his truck.

"Yuck. Ten minutes in that soot and dampness makes my throat hurt. My respect for firemen has gone up tenfold." We climbed into his truck and he turned down Main Street instead of heading outside of town to his home. "Where are we going?"

"Scratch insisted on making you some sweet and sour chicken stir-fry." He veered his truck next to the curb. My tummy growled in anticipation. I jumped out of the truck and followed Jackson inside so I could thank Scratch personally.

He was busy in the kitchen. My arms barely fit around this big, beefy, man. "Oh boy, I owe you." My words were muffled against his chest. I leaned back to look at his cheery face.

"My kitchen is still open for you, Molly, whenever you feel ready," said Scratch.

"Thanks. That means a lot to me. I'm going ahead with my plans." I smiled confidently before Jackson and I left the café, yummy lunch in hand.

"What was that all about?"

"I'll tell you after we eat, I unpack, and you rub my feet."

"You must be wearing your bossy underwear."

I slugged him. "Charlee said she'd keep Pixie for as long as I needed. Think she can be given a second chance here with Trigger?" I didn't know how long it would be before I could move back to my home, but I didn't want to go weeks, or months, without Pixie.

Jackson sighed dramatically. "Fine. You can bring that bossy cat of yours back over here. Trigger will put her in her place though if she goes after him again," he teased.

We carried in the few things from his truck and sat down to eat by his fireplace. Afterwards, while he gave me a foot-rub on the rug by the crackling fire, I filled him in on my plan of Love baskets stocked with locally made items. "And no, I'm not replacing the minnow tanks with a sushi bar, but I *am* replacing the bait section with a coffee bar. Although Drake and I had spoken of him buying my summer tackle inventory, that won't happen now."

It was one more thing in a long list of worries. I'd think about them later. Right now, I wanted to hear about Jackson's trip and his father. "Let's play catch-up. You pretty much know what's happened with my life these past few weeks. Tell me how your dad is doing."

He leaned against the couch and stared at the fire. "My dad's a tough old bird. Actually, sixty-six isn't that old. But damn, he should've retired by now. It isn't for lack of money. The more he works, the less time he spends at home with mom."

Jackson shook his head. "Dad used to have hobbies. He used to take Cody and me fishing when we came to the cabin here each summer. I have great memories from our days at the family cabin…waterskiing, fishing off the dock, swimming with dad as he'd throw us into the air off of his shoulders so we'd land in the water with a big splash." He looked at me. "Dad even built us an enormous tree fort in the backyard at our old cabin."

"It sounds like you had a great time with him," I said softly.

"We did. It's hard to connect that guy with the workaholic he became over the years."

"How's your mom handling everything?" Not that I cared about her, but she was Jackson's mom, and I cared about him.

"You know, it was funny. Mom rarely left his side at the hospital. I don't know if it was guilt cementing her to him, or if deep down she loves him." Jackson ran his hand through his hair. "I do think they love each other still, in their own twisted ways. And mom kept telling me and Cody how important family is, and how we need to go home to visit more…which, of course, I'll do now. Seeing dad look so vulnerable in the hospital reminded me he won't be around forever."

I thought of my mom. "Take it from me, when your parents are gone, you'll think of a hundred things you wish you'd have told them or asked them. And, you'll wish you'd have let them know how much you loved and appreciated them. It's the number one thing I wish I could still tell my mom. I can only hope she knew it."

"I'm sure she did, Molly. It sounds like you two were always close."

I laughed at the irony. "But not enough for her to tell me about my older half-sister."

Jackson reached for my hand. "Imagine the can of worms that would've opened. History is so hard to digest. She was probably trying to protect you, and herself, from possible rejection by this now-grown woman. If your sister knows she's adopted, she may have no interest in ever finding her birth mom, and your mother likely thought about that possibility."

We sat in silence as I petted Trigger who'd shimmied his way over on the floor next to me. I thought of the family dynamics with his mother. She was related to my half-sister—a relation I didn't want to think about. "What do you think your mom will have to say about this newfound child of her cousin Tom's?"

"I've wondered the same since I found the letter. I almost showed it to her when I was home, but she had enough to worry about with dad's stroke. Plus, I hoped Ernie would be able to fill in some of the blanks before I told her." He brought my hand to his lips and kissed it. "I keep thinking about her reminding me and my brother how important family is. I'm hoping that this will soften her anger toward Rosie for not leaving her the store."

I hoped he was right. Right now, Nancy's feelings were the least of my concerns.

* * *

The next morning was opening of rifle season for deer hunting, which had fueled Jackson's return to town. He left before dawn to sit in his deer stand. I had no problem sleeping in until almost ten. The past few days had wiped me out emotionally.

After my late breakfast, I decided it was time for me to call my dad. He golfed early most mornings. I had a glass of water next to me in case my throat seized once I started talking.

The phone rang several times before he answered. "Hello, Dear. I didn't expect to hear from you today. I just got in from golfing." He cleared his throat. "Getting cold there yet? Have you fired up that beast of a wood stove you told me about? They seem like such a mess…"

He mumbled a bit as if he was talking to himself, which he probably did a lot now that he lived alone. I tried to make pleasantries and ask about his golf game. It was no use. I couldn't feign interest in his birdie on hole number twelve right now. We talked about me flying to New Mexico for Christmas. I couldn't wait another six weeks to talk to him in person about this.

I'd made sure to cushion enough of my savings over the winter to include a trip to see my dad. But that was before I'd lost most of my house, business, and found out about a half-sister. Before I could come face-to-face with my dad again, I'd need to air some ancient laundry.

"There's been a lot of things that have happened the past few days in my life, Dad," my voice cracked. "I need to talk to you about something."

I sunk back in Jackson's recliner, clutching my water in one hand and the phone in the other. As my words tumbled through the phone to describe the fire to my dad, and about Drake and his twisted anger toward my mother's family…it was a natural introduction to the million-dollar question.

"Dad, I need you to be honest with me." I worried about his past heart attack and hoped this wouldn't throw him into cardiac arrest again.

"Are you going to ask about our wedding date again? I told you, I wanted to be honest with you. It was your mom who insisted we lie about the year," he grumbled.

"Yes, I want you to be honest, again, but it's about a different baby. My half-sister." I waited…and heard nothing but silence. I'd decided if he didn't know about her before, he would now. She wasn't a secret I wanted to keep. She was a woman I wanted to find.

I didn't hear a thump so I assumed he hadn't fallen to the floor. "Dad? Are you okay?" I should've waited until I saw him in person in December.

"Yes, I'm fine. How did you find out?" I heard defeat in his voice, could envision the drooping of his shoulders as his aged hands rubbed his closed eyes.

"From someone in town here." I was careful with my information. Yes, it was unfair, me holding back information while expecting my dad to fork over the truth, but I still wasn't sure how much he knew, and I didn't want to make things worse.

"It's another thing I thought your mom should've told you about. But again, she wanted to protect you. She'd told me about the baby she had to give up a number of years before we started dating. Celia wanted me to know what I was getting up front. Hell, I was thirty-seven when we married, I wasn't sure I'd ever have kids of my own anyway, and figured a baby she'd given up years ago was in the past—where it should stay."

Everything my father was telling me sounded like a reasonable action on his end. "It wasn't until the girl was a young adult that Celia started bugging me about trying to find her daughter. I said no. It was pointless because the child was now an adult. Celia's reasoning was that once the girl turned eighteen, she may start looking for her birth mother. She wanted to put the information out there about her address in case the girl wanted to find her."

I heard dad open his fridge and crack a beer. I couldn't blame him. It was noon somewhere. "By then you were eight or nine, and I didn't think it was a good idea. She'd bring it up off and on. When her daughter was nearing the age of twenty-one we got into a heated argument." I heard him take a long drink. "Are you sure you want to hear this?"

I pressed my fingers to my forehead, pushing back the stress headache of the past sixteen hours. "Yes." Although my heart was screaming at my brain, "Say no!"

"We got into a huge fight one night. She pushed again to give the Minnesota Department of Health her name and address so the girl could find her. She assumed

I'd welcome this girl, who wasn't mine, with open arms and heart. I told her I'd never be able to love her daughter the way she wanted me to."

I sat up straight, shocked to hear my dad recite a fight which had played over many times in my mind. "You were talking about my older sister back then?" Those words I'd overheard after failing my science test in fifth grade…they weren't about me?

"Well, yes. You weren't there when your mother and I had the fight. We were in the kitchen and you were upstairs in bed." His voice was quiet, hesitant. "Weren't you?"

Tears overflowed as I sobbed, my chest and heart constricting in pain…the pain I'd felt for over twenty years at the thought my dad didn't love me enough. The dissatisfaction I had in myself as I struggled with science, among other subjects, in school. The disappointment I'd carried as the daughter of a microbiologist? Even worse.

"Noooo, Dad!" I held my fist to my mouth, hoping to stop the wailing cries. I got up to find tissues to mop my eyes and nose, emotion flowing like a waterfall on my face. It took me a minute to gain control. Dad patiently waited.

"I was standing at the top of the stairs because I heard you yelling and you and mom never yelled at each other." Every single detail was etched in my mind. The *Full House* pajamas I was wearing, the spaghetti we'd had for supper along with my dad's favorite chocolate cake for dessert…it was a typical night at our house until I heard their arguing. It was so rare, so unsettling, that I'd run down the hall to our upstairs bathroom to vomit from nerves. It was as if it had happened yesterday.

"I had brought home my science test that day from school with an 'F' on it. I remember mom saying she wouldn't show it to you and that she was sure I'd do better next time. When I heard you talking, I thought you saw my test and were disappointed at my poor grade." I huffed a few times, hoping to reel in my regurgitated pain.

"I was sure you were disappointed I wasn't as smart as you," I continued. "You always told me I needed to do better so I could get a good job and take care of myself." I pressed my fingers to the bridge of my nose. I was going to need a good stiff drink after this.

Surprise laced his voice. "I told you that because I wanted you to be a strong woman like your mom. She had a good teaching job and wasn't marrying me because she needed me to take care of her. I didn't want you marrying someone for their money."

Instead, I'd lived with Nick for years for that very reason.

Chapter 40

Thanksgiving brought our first snowstorm which was perfect for the town's "Snowtastic Saturday" event. It was hit or miss, depending on the weather but if the town got enough snow before it got too cold, they'd hold an impromptu party on the beach and lake.

The weather had to be the right temperature for making snowballs and snow forts. There was a snowball toss contest, judging for the best snow fort, a hot fudge sundae stand, an ice skating rink cleared off in the bay, and a bonfire on the beach.

The weather was perfect. The day was fun. And the town was my heart.

The week of Christmas, Jackson and I flew to New Mexico. We spent four days with my dad and they were the best for me since Mom had died. The majority of the change had been on my part. My perception of how he felt about me had changed a hundred percent.

We decorated his Christmas tree together, played a few rounds of golf, and I made a big pot of dad's favorite chili, freezing several meals for him. The handful of years since mom died had taken their toll on him. He hadn't taken good care of himself before his heart attack. I wasn't sure he was doing any better now.

He wouldn't move back to Minnesota. And I wasn't moving to New Mexico. Nor did he want me to.

We said our goodbyes at the airport with promises from Dad that he'd come visit in the summer. A golf buddy of his agreed to drive to Minnesota with him and spend a week or so golfing. It was a step in the right direction in our relationship.

Jackson and I walked through the Albuquerque airport. "Did you hear Dad this morning? Mom wanted to give the Department of Health her name and address for the birth certificate for my half-sister, but never did." I gave him a sideways glance. "But I can contact the Department of Health. *I* can put my name and address as a contact."

We landed in Minneapolis on December twenty-seventh and stayed overnight at Ella and Rolf's. The next day we drove to Robert Street in St. Paul and left my contact information in case my sister ever decided to look for me. I could only hope she was out there searching.

* * *

In March, I welcomed the final rebuilding of part of my store and home thanks to the insurance payout and my small business loan. My home kitchen was now a certified kitchen, which meant the canning and packaging for the Love basket food items could be done in my kitchen—a huge bonus.

The remodeled store now held a coffee bar where the minnow tanks once stood. Gone was the fishing tackle inventory, sold to a bait shop in Blue Bay. Sample Love baskets now lined those shelves, including flavored coffee beans packaged with the ***LOVEmn*** logo.

In January, I'd spent several weeks in the cities enrolled in barista classes. There was far more to learn than just grinding coffee. Spring brought extra planting for Charlee, Old Lloyd, and even Jackson, who determined it only made sense to turn some of his huge yard into a garden full of vegetables and fruit specifically geared to make salsa, pickles, and jam for the Love baskets.

January had been a good test of the baskets for Valentine's Day gifts. Within a handful of days advertising on my new website, we sold every concoction I'd been able to throw together in a Love basket. It fanned the fire inside me. Not only was I building a business for me, but I was helping others in the area earn a profit from their many talents.

By April 1, I had the store open again, sans bait and tackle. The wide planked old hardwood floor had been matched well for the burned section, and with the addition of a shiny, new coffee bar, hand-scooped ice cream area, and expanded snack section, the store looked cleaner, fresher. More of what I was proud selling, especially the area featuring Love baskets.

I kept the seasonal sundries area and had wide oak shelving placed where the pegboard that once held tackle had been. I'd added another cash register at the end of the coffee bar, and more than once I'd stand in the middle of the store, surveying it all with a silly grin on my face.

My perfect location—one that Drake had so coveted—almost guaranteed a great summer business. In winter I'd close the store and focus on my Love basket sales online.

Drake's trial was set for the fall. Over the months my anger had lessened, replaced by empathy for the way Drake's family life had turned out. I wholeheartedly prayed my grandpa hadn't pushed Drake's father down the steps, that instead, it was a terrible accident. But I'd never know. The few eyewitnesses of that event were long gone.

* * *

I moved back to my house in March before I reopened the store. Jackson and I talked in great length about me continuing to live at his home.

I wasn't ready yet. He wasn't pushing. We both liked our independence. And we loved each other. For now, it was enough.

I converted my extra bedroom into storage for the Love basket stock. When Ella came to visit, she'd have to bunk with me.

And Jackson? In early May we took a four-day weekend off from our businesses to whoop it up on the shores of Lake Minnetonka at Ella and Rolf's wedding. I had my hair done by Macie again, and she gave Jackson two thumbs-up after he left to go fish on a nearby lake. "Much more suited to you than Nick," Macie said as she finished trimming my ends.

"Yes, well he's not exactly the spa certificate kind of boyfriend that Nick was. You'll probably never see me here for French-tip nails again." My shoulders and back begged for a good massage though after all the unpacking of inventory I'd done in March and April.

"You weren't meant for manicures and highlights, girl," Macie nodded toward my short, bare, fingernails. "This is the real you, the person you used to be when I started doing your hair."

Our eyes met in the oversized mirror. She was right. And I liked this Molly much better.

A few weeks later, Dad and his golfing friend came to visit. It was the week after Memorial Day and the fishing was still good. They rented a cabin nearby on the lake. I beamed with pride when he told me how impressed he was with the store.

My life had turned out nothing as I'd thought it would, yet better in so many ways than I'd ever imagined. Yes, it had been difficult to make my place in a town that had roots of many generations running through it. I'd had to conquer Drake's threats, family ghosts, and my fears.

I felt as my mom must have all those years ago. The town of Love was my *home.*

* * *

It was a Monday morning in July and I'd just finished with a small coffee rush. A group of young women left with their iced cappuccinos to go sit out on the deck and enjoy the lake view when another woman walked in. I smiled at her and went about cleaning the coffee utensils. She walked right up to the coffee bar.

"Good morning. What can I get for you?" I played a game with myself trying to guess what people would order. This woman, possibly early forties, tall, athletic build, wavy dark hair… I guessed her for an iced Americano.

"Um, nothing at the moment. Thanks, though." She covered her mouth and hiccupped. "I'm looking for information. Do you know a Molly O'Brien?"

I studied her a little better. She had beautiful blue eyes, a small cleft in her chin, and a familiar smile. "I'm Molly O'Brien. Do I know you?" She was too old for me to have gone to school with her. I didn't think we'd worked together at Edina Realty. Yet she looked familiar.

Her eyes widened and she cupped her hand over mouth again as another hiccup escaped.

"Holy"—*hiccup*—"cow!" Her other hand clutched her stomach and for a second, I worried she was going to be sick all over my clean counter.

"Are you okay?" I didn't know if I should find a bucket or get her a chair.

She looked around at the now-empty store, before turning back to me. "My name is Claire Benson." Her hiccups were constant staccatos now. "And I think I'm your sister."

I'd have fainted if I hadn't been leaning on the counter.

Of course! Her mouth was so similar to pictures I'd seen of Rosie's. And those eyes? A mirror image of my mom's—and mine. I was so busy studying her for similarities I didn't realize she was talking.

"You probably want proof or something. If you have a few minutes, I'd love the chance to visit." Claire's eyes welled up, and I could feel the dampness of mine.

I couldn't round the counter fast enough. Proof? I didn't need proof.

I almost knocked the wind out of this woman who was even taller than me as I came at her for a hug. "Are you kidding? I don't need any proof from you. It's written all over your face!" I hugged her hard as she hiccupped in my ear.

I leaned back to study her face. "And if that wasn't proof enough, your hiccups are."

"It's so embarrassing. I get them every time…"

I interrupted. "I know. You get them every time you get nervous, right?"

"How did you know that?" She dabbed at her eyes, her mouth forming an *O* of surprise.

"Simple. Our mother always got them when she was nervous."

I held her hand, taking her with me to the counter as I picked up the phone. Pure joy danced through every cell in my body as if I'd just opened the best birthday present ever. I had.

I dialed Jackson's cell phone. "Can you come over to the store for a minute? There's someone here I think you'll want to meet."

The End

ACKNOWLEDGEMENTS

I owe a huge thanks to my husband, a/k/a Mr. Patience, who as a beta reader for me kindly pointed out my love for words like "grab" while also answering my "manly" plot questions. Many thanks to Sharon Beaman, beta reader, for her valuable writing and librarian experience. And my critique partners, Lynne Marino and Kerry Morgan. Their valuable feedback is priceless and was helpful in making this story better because of their knowledge.

To Zara Kramer and all of the Pandamoon Publishing staff. From the editors, graphic designers, and marketing department…this book would still be sitting on my computer without your help to bring it to life.

To Deputy Pat Pickar, for allowing me to pick his brain about the many situations in this story where I could only guess how things would play out with law enforcement. To Ben Rudrud, for his helpful self-defense input. To Kathy Ogden, for her insight on the many facets of autism.

People have asked me if any of my characters are based on real people. Normally, the answer is no…except in this story. My dear, sweet, kind-hearted Ernie is loosely based on Bill Flagg, who passed away two years ago at the age of ninety-six. I appreciate Bill, and his wife, Eva, for allowing me to interview him without knowing what I'd do with the information. I'd felt drawn to this elderly man in our small town, curious about his life, and just knew I'd find a place for it someday. When I began writing this book I realized he was Ernie, in a sense, and he became my favorite character. And no, Love isn't *my* small town (although we did own an old General Store for several years.) But maybe it will find a place in your heart and become *your* town!

To all the book clubs, libraries, and businesses who welcomed me and my first book over this past year. Meeting with other readers and talking books has truly been the best part of being an author. Your feedback of what you like and don't like in books was helpful in me writing Molly's story.

To fellow authors who have guided me along the way, and to all the book reviewers, librarians, and bookstore owners who spread the love of all books every single day. A special mention to some of the amazing book bloggers/reviewers out there (I could devote a whole page to all of them!): A Novel Bee (Kristy Barrett), Linda's Book Obsession (Linda Zagon), Baer Books (Barbara Khan), Sue's Booking Agency (Susan Peterson), Blue Point Press (Cindy Roesel), Suzy Approved Book Reviews (Suzanne Leopold), Women Writers, Women's Books (Barbara Bos) TarHeelReader (Jennifer Clayton) One Book at a Time (Bethany Clark), Kate Rock's LitChick, Heidi Lynn's Book Reviews, Bookworms Anonymous (Kayleigh Wilkes), Midwest Ladies Who Lit, and every single reader out there. If you've chosen one of my books to read, I hope you've found the time well spent.

ABOUT THE AUTHOR

Jill Hannah Anderson lives on a lake in Minnesota with her husband in their rarely-empty nest where they enjoy their six adult children and many grandchildren when they come to visit. Her first women's fiction novel, *The To-Hell-And-Back Club* debuted in May 2017. *Crazy Little Town Called Love* is her second novel and features a character from her first novel.

When she's not writing or reading, you'll find her running, curling, biking, and enjoying the great outdoors.

Jill loves to connect with book clubs. To connect with her, please visit her website, www.jillhannahanderson.com.

Thank you for purchasing this copy of ***Crazy Little Town Called Love***, Book Two of the ***The To-Hell-And-Back Club Series***. If you enjoyed this book, please let the author know by posting a review.

Growing good ideas into great reads…one book at a time.

Visit www.pandamoonpublishing.com to learn about other works by our talented authors.

Mystery/Thriller/Suspense

- *122 Rules* by Deek Rhew
- *A Flash of Red* by Sarah K. Stephens
- *Fate's Past* by Jason Huebinger
- *Graffiti Creek* by Matt Coleman
- *Juggling Kittens* by Matt Coleman
- *Killer Secrets* by Sherrie Orvik
- *Knights of the Shield* by Jeff Messick
- *Kricket* by Penni Jones
- *Looking into the Sun* by Todd Tavolazzi
- *On the Bricks Series Book 1: On the Bricks* by Penni Jones
- *Rogue Saga Series Book 1: Rogue Alliance* by Michelle Bellon
- *Southbound* by Jason Beem
- *The Juliet* by Laura Ellen Scott
- *The Last Detective* by Brian Cohn
- *The Moses Winter Mysteries Book 1: Made Safe* by Francis Sparks
- *The New Royal Mysteries Book 1: The Mean Bone in Her Body* by Laura Ellen Scott
- *The New Royal Mysteries Book 2: Crybaby Lane* by Laura Ellen Scott
- *The Ramadan Drummer* by Randolph Splitter
- *The Teratologist* by Ward Parker
- *The Unraveling of Brendan Meeks* by Brian Cohn
- *The Zeke Adams Series Book 1: Pariah* by Ward Parker
- *This Darkness Got to Give* by Dave Housley

Science Fiction/Fantasy

- *Becoming Thuperman* by Elgon Williams
- *Children of Colondona Book 1: The Wizard's Apprentice* by Alisse Lee Goldenberg
- *Children of Colondona Book 2: The Island of Mystics* by Alisse Lee Goldenberg
- *Chimera Catalyst* by Susan Kuchinskas
- *Dybbuk Scrolls Trilogy Book 1: The Song of Hadariah* by Alisse Lee Goldenberg
- *Dybbuk Scrolls Trilogy Book 2: The Song of Vengeance* by Alisse Lee Goldenberg
- *Dybbuk Scrolls Trilogy Book 3: The Song of War* by Alisse Lee Goldenberg
- *Everly Series Book 1: Everly* by Meg Bonney
- *.EXE Chronicles Book 1: Hello World* by Alexandra Tauber and Tiffany Rose
- *Fried Windows (In a Light White Sauce)* by Elgon Williams
- *Magehunter Series Book 1: Magehunter* by Jeff Messick
- *Revengers Series Book 1: Revengers* by David Valdes Greenwood
- *The Bath Salts Journals: Volume One* by Alisse Lee Goldenberg and An Tran
- *The Crimson Chronicles Book 1: Crimson Forest* by Christine Gabriel
- *The Crimson Chronicles Book 2: Crimson Moon* by Christine Gabriel
- *The Phaethon Series Book 1: Phaethon* by Rachel Sharp
- *The Sitnalta Series Book 1: Sitnalta* by Alisse Lee Goldenberg
- *The Sitnalta Series Book 2: The Kingdom Thief* by Alisse Lee Goldenberg
- *The Sitnalta Series Book 3: The City of Arches* by Alisse Lee Goldenberg
- *The Sitnalta Series Book 4: The Hedgewitch's Charm* by Alisse Lee Goldenberg
- *The Sitnalta Series Book 5: The False Princess* by Alisse Lee Goldenberg
- *The Wolfcat Chronicles Book 1: Wolfcat 1 by* Elgon Williams

Women's Fiction

- *Beautiful Secret* by Dana Faletti
- *The Long Way Home* by Regina West
- *The Mason Siblings Series Book 1: Love's Misadventure* by Cheri Champagne
- *The Mason Siblings Series Book 2: The Trouble with Love* by Cheri Champagne
- *The Mason Siblings Series Book 3: Love and Deceit* by Cheri Champagne
- *The Mason Siblings Series Book 4: Final Battle for Love* by Cheri Champagne
- *The Seductive Spies Series Book 1: The Thespian Spy* by Cheri Champagne
- *The Seductive Spy Series Book 2: The Seamstress and the Spy* by Cheri Champagne
- *The Shape of the Atmosphere* by Jessica Dainty
- *The To-Hell-And-Back Club Book 1: The To-Hell-And-Back Club* by Jill Hannah Anderson
- *The To-Hell-And-Back Club Book 2: Crazy Little Town Called Love* by Jill Hannah Anderson

Book Club Questions

1. If you were Molly, would you have made the move to Love or stayed in the Twin Cities? Why?
2. Do you think Molly handled her "threats" in the right way? What would you have done different?
3. Do you have a favorite character?
4. What would you have done with the store when business died in the fall?
5. What do you think about the town of Love?

Made in the USA
Columbia, SC
12 January 2020